SILENT WITNESS

The child glanced at Rose's hand but made no move to climb down. She shifted her head slightly so that she looked into the distance. Rose followed her gaze and realized the girl could see the plum tree from which Hugh Griffiths had been hanging.

She might easily have witnessed what happened...

"Deborah Woodworth's suspenseful exploration of the Shaker way of life—and death—will fascinate mystery readers. Sister Rose Callahan is a marvelous heroine with wisdom and charm to spare."
Carolyn Hart

Other Sister Rose Callahan Mysteries by
Deborah Woodworth

DEATH OF A WINTER SHAKER
A DEADLY SHAKER SPRING
SINS OF A SHAKER SUMMER

DEBORAH WOODWORTH

A Simple Shaker Murder

—— A ——

SISTER ROSE CALLAHAN

MYSTERY

AVON

TWILIGHT

AVON BOOKS, INC.
An Imprint of HarperCollins*Publishers*
10 East 53rd Street
New York, New York 10022-5299

*In memory of Dan Cooperman, mentor and friend,
and for Suzanne and Jen, with deep affection*

AUTHOR'S NOTE

The original Owenites, a short-lived utopian community led by Robert Owen, lived in New Harmony, Indiana, in the early nineteenth century and had a lasting impact on American education. In 1825, at the Pleasant Hill Shaker village, a group of young Believers, influenced by the ideas of Robert Owen, agitated for reform. The result was a crisis in leadership and the apostasy of many Shakers.

However, the New-Owenites—along with the North Homage Shaker village, the town and the county of Languor, Kentucky, and all their inhabitants—are figments of the author's imagination. The characters live only in this book and represent no one, living or dead. By the 1930s, the period in which this story is told, no Shaker villages remained in Kentucky or anywhere else outside the northeastern United States. Today one small Shaker community survives: Sabbathday Lake, near Poland Springs, Maine. The Pleasant Hill Shaker community (near Harrodsburg, Kentucky) and the Hancock Shaker Village in Massachusetts have both been restored and are open to visitors who wish to see how Believers lived during the nineteenth century.

Deborah Woodworth
May 14, 1999

ONE

A SHADOW LEAPT UP THE BARN WALL, FOLLOWED BY A SQUEAK of animal terror from a corner. The dirt floor softened the sounds of scuffling. A man swore, loudly at first, whispering by the end of the oath. He paused and straightened, resting a moment on the heavy crate he'd been dragging from a corner of the barn. He had no idea what might be in the crate—he had never been near a farm before, let alone a barn—but the thing was large and heavy and nailed shut. He'd need something tall and stable, just in case all this didn't work out and he had to take drastic steps.

The thought of what he might have to do sent a shiver through him and brought back the damp chill of the November morning. He shivered again. He was a slight man, unused to discomfort or physical labor. Fear drove him on. He leaned against the crate and pushed again. It scraped across the floor, leaving a trail of gouges in the dirt.

He positioned the crate under a low rafter, crawled on top, and reached upward. Should be just about right. He jumped to the floor and stood silent for a moment, conscious of the soft thump his shoes had made. He sucked in his breath and released it as a field mouse squeezed from under a hay bale and skittered away from the human presence.

After a brief search, the man located a neatly wound coil of heavy rope, worn but not too frayed. He unwound the rope along the floor, nodded when he'd estimated its length, then

1

carried it over to the crate. He glanced up at the beam, and for a split second his eyelids fluttered, the only outward sign of the terror that flashed through his body.

He had done all he could. If the meeting went as he hoped, he'd have no need of these preparations. There would just be time to move everything back in place, and the Shaker brethren would notice nothing amiss when they arrived to feed the animals. If the meeting didn't go well, the brethren would be in for a shock. But he couldn't concern himself with that. *This is the way it's got to be,* he thought; *it's the only way.* They couldn't go on like this.

The creak of the barn door told him the time had come. He brushed the dust off his coat and forced his lips into the curve of a smile. It wouldn't do to look desperate or frightened. Although he was both.

TWO

THE NORTHERN KENTUCKY SUN ROSE SLOWLY, ALMOST RELUC-
tantly, as if it would just as soon sleep till spring. Not that
autumn, or even winter, was brutal in this part of the country;
though damp, the temperature was rarely cold for more than
a short spell.

Sister Rose Callahan pulled her long wool cloak tight
around her thin body and sprinted the distance to the Center
Family Dwelling House. After the sultry summer, it was a
relief to be able to move quickly again. As eldress of the North
Homage Shaker village, Rose had decided to flout tradition
and take most of her meals away from the Ministry House,
where she lived. She told herself her decision kept her more
involved with the sisters, her spiritual charges. Still in her late
thirties, she was eager to grow as a leader and to help her
declining community endure a Depression that seemed endless. But she had tired of meal after meal in the Ministry dining room, sitting across the table from Elder Wilhelm Lundel,
who planned unceasingly how to return North Homage to its
days of greatest strength in the 1830s, a century earlier. Let
him plot alone.

The evening before, Rose had returned from a month away
visiting the Hancock Shaker village in Massachusetts, very
near the Lead Society of Mount Lebanon, in New York. Communication between the eastern and western Shakers had often
been poor, and the Lead Ministry worried that North Homage

3

had drifted astray recently, so Rose had been called to give a full report of doings in her village. The visit had been tense and exhilarating, and the train ride back exhausting. Rose wanted nothing more than to be home with her own Shaker family, enjoying the familiar routine of hard work and worship.

She was late, so she took a few running steps, already planning her morning tasks. Eight men and women from the world, members of a utopian society calling themselves New-Owenites, would be at breakfast—or at least, some of them would. According to Sister Josie Trent—the Society's Infirmary Nurse, who'd dropped by Rose's retiring room early, to catch her up on the village news—the visitors kept their own unpredictable schedules. Josie had said they'd been in North Homage for twelve days to "study" the Shakers, whatever that meant. Rose intended to find out. It was just like Wilhelm to take advantage of her absence to accept a group of strangers for an extended stay. Undoubtedly he had his own reasons for doing so.

The sisters would be inside, waiting for her in silent prayer. They would expect Rose, as eldress, to lead them single-file into the dining room for their silent meal. Since Wilhelm rarely dined with the community, their trustee, Brother Andrew Clark, would lead the brethren and the New-Owenite men to their table at the opposite end of the room.

Now just a few steps from the sisters' entrance to the dwelling house, Rose reached up to untie her heavy palm bonnet. The door flew open and several flustered women burst through. One of them knocked Rose's elbow, and her bonnet fell back on her shoulders, pulling her thin white indoor cap with it. Without thinking, Rose adjusted the cap to cover her unruly red curls. The sisters hadn't bothered to grab their cloaks. As the cool air hit them, they crossed their arms tightly against their bodies to pull their white kerchiefs closer.

Without turning her head, Rose knew the brethren's door had also opened, and several men were running across the grass toward the southeast end of the village. She nearly toppled over as a large, soft body careened into her.

"Rose, dear, so sorry. Must run." Sister Josie patted the air near Rose's shoulder and bounced past.

"Wait, Josie; what is happening?"

Josie twirled a half circle and kept moving, a remarkable feat for a plump eighty-year-old. "There's been an accident. I'm needed," she called, as she completed her turn and picked up speed.

"Where?"

"In the orchard," Sister Teresa said as she, too, rushed past. Rose picked up her long skirts and joined the race across the unpaved path through the village center, between the Meetinghouse and the Ministry House, and into the orchard.

At first, Rose saw nothing alarming, only rows of strictly pruned apple trees, now barren of fruit and most of their leaves. The group ran through the apple trees and into the more neglected east side of the orchard, where the remains of touchier fruit trees lived out their years with little human attention. The pounding feet ahead of her stopped, and panting bodies piled behind one another, still trying to keep some semblance of separation between the brethren and the sisters.

The now-silent onlookers stared at an aged plum tree. From a sturdy branch hung the limp figure of a man, his feet dangling above the ground. His eyes were closed and his head slumped forward, almost hiding the rope that gouged into his neck. The man wore loose clothes that were neither Shaker nor of the world, and Rose sensed he was gone even before Josie reached for his wrist and shook her head.

Two brethren moved forward to cut the man down.

"Nay, don't, not yet," Rose said, hurrying forward.

Josie's eyebrows shot up. "Surely you don't think this is anything but the tragedy of a man choosing to end his own life?" She nodded past the man's torso to a delicate chair lying on its side in the grass. It was a Shaker design, not meant for such rough treatment. Dirt scuffed the woven red-and-white tape of the seat. Scratches marred the smooth slats that formed its ladder back.

"What's going on here? Has Mother Ann appeared and declared today a holiday from labor?" The powerful voice snapped startled heads backwards, to where Elder Wilhelm emerged from the trees, stern jaw set for disapproval.

No one answered. Everyone watched Wilhelm's ruddy face blanch as he came in view of the dead man.

"Dear God," he whispered. "Is he . . . ?"

"Yea," said Josie.

"Then cut him down instantly," Wilhelm said. His voice had regained its authority, but he ran a shaking hand through his thick white hair.

Eyes turned to Rose. "I believe we should leave him for now, Wilhelm," she said. A flush spread across Wilhelm's cheeks, and Rose knew she was in for a public tongue lashing, so she explained quickly. "Though all the signs point to suicide, still it is a sudden and brutal death, and I believe we should alert the sheriff. He'll want things left just as we found them."

"Sheriff Brock . . ." Wilhelm said with a snort of derision. "He will relish the opportunity to find us culpable."

"Please, for the sake of pity, cut him down." A man stepped forward, hat in hand in the presence of death. His thinning blond hair lifted in the wind. His peculiar loose work clothes seemed too generous for his slight body. "I'm Gilbert Owen Griffiths," he said, nodding to Rose. "And this is my compatriot, Earl Weston," he added, indicating a broad-shouldered dark-haired young man. "I am privileged to be guiding a little group of folks who are hoping to rekindle the flame of the great social reformer Robert Owen. That poor unfortunate man," he said, with a glance at the dead man, "was Hugh— Hugh Griffiths—and he was one of us. We don't mind having the Sheriff come take a look, but we are all like a family, and it is far too painful for us to leave poor Hugh hanging."

"It's an outrage, leaving him there like that," Earl said. "What if Celia should come along?"

"Celia is poor Hugh's wife," Gilbert explained. "I'll have

to break the news to her soon. I beg of you, cut him down and cover him before she shows up."

Wilhelm assented with a curt nod. "I will inform the sheriff," he said, as several brethren cut the man down and lay him on the ground. The morbid fascination had worn off, and most of the crowd was backing away.

There was nothing to do but wait. Rose gathered up the sisters and New-Owenite women who had not already made their escape. Leaving Andrew to watch over the ghastly scene until the sheriff arrived, she sent the women on ahead to breakfast, for which she herself had no appetite. The men followed behind.

On impulse Rose glanced back to see Andrew's tall figure hunched against a tree near the body. He watched the crowd's departure with a forlorn expression. As she raised her arm to send him an encouraging wave, a move distracted her. She squinted through the tangle of unpruned branches behind Andrew to locate the source. *Probably just a squirrel,* she thought, but her eyes kept searching nonetheless. There it was again—a flash of brown almost indistinguishable from tree bark. Several rows of trees back from where Andrew stood, something was moving among the branches of an old pear tree—something much bigger than a squirrel.

❦

THREE

ROSE WALKED AT A CASUAL PACE BACK TOWARD ANDREW, PRE-tending nothing was amiss. She kept her head straight but watched the pear tree through her lashes. The movement stopped, then started again, slow and smooth. As she approached, Andrew straightened. His smile of pleasure turned to puzzlement as she passed him by, telling him with a slight hand gesture to stay where he was.

The movement stopped as Rose picked up her skirts and ran toward it. She was glad to be wearing her tough winter shoes. Her thin-soled summer shoes would never have protected her feet from the dead branches and sticks lying in wait under a camouflage of fallen leaves.

By the time she was a few yards from the pear tree, she knew what she was seeing. She just couldn't believe it. It was a person, a very small person, perhaps a child. Not a Shaker child; the clothes weren't right. A child of the world?

Rose stopped at the tree's trunk and stared up through the branches at the figure. Masses of pale brown hair fluffed around an impassive face, much as Rose's curly red hair would if she freed it from her white cap and cut it short. The girl's body appeared tiny, about the size of a six-year-old, but her face looked older. Her skin was a warm honey brown, a few shades lighter than her loose brown pantaloons. She looked as if she'd stepped in from another era or another land. Rose peered into eyes of a rich green flecked with copper. Those

8

eyes held no fear, but depths of vigilance. The girl neither moved nor cried out. She simply watched.

Rose slowly lifted her arm and extended her hand, palm up. "It is time for breakfast," she said, keeping her voice gentle and warm. "Come on down, and we'll get you something to eat."

The child glanced at Rose's hand but made no move to climb down. She shifted her head slightly so that she looked into the distance, toward Andrew. Rose followed her gaze, and her arm dropped as she realized the girl could see the plum tree from which Hugh Griffiths had been hanging. She might easily have witnessed what happened. Even if she did not see the act, she might be in shock after seeing its consequences.

Rose turned back to find the child watching her again. Still she exhibited no fear. Her eyes had dulled, as if the spirit behind them had fled. It occurred to Rose that the girl might not be quite right. She certainly appeared older than her size; perhaps her mind was stunted, as well.

"My name is Rose. What's yours?"

Rose held up her hand once more, but the girl only blinked at the invitation. Climbing the tree after her was out of the question, and sending Andrew up might have the girl scurrying in terror onto weaker branches.

"I know you're frightened," Rose continued softly, "but I promise I want to help you. Do you have family nearby? If you'll tell me where they are, I'll get them for you."

The girl's gaze shifted toward the Shaker village, and her small body seemed to shrink against the tree limb. Still she said nothing.

Perhaps she can't even speak, Rose thought. Well, she couldn't just leave the girl to fend for herself.

"All right, then, little one. You can stay right there, if you wish." Rose filled her voice with all the soothing cheerfulness she could muster, and hoped she did not sound like a bad actress. "I'm going to be gone for just a minute, and then I'll come back to chat with you."

She edged away as fast as possible without alarming the

girl. Andrew watched her approach with undisguised curiosity.

"Could you see who I was talking to?" Rose asked, as she came into earshot.

"Nay, but I'll admit I indulged the fantasy that an angel had come down to tell you what happened here." Andrew avoided looking at the dead man on the ground.

"That would make it so much easier," Rose said. "But I'm afraid it is a terrified child, who may have witnessed the incident but won't tell me so much as her first name. I need Charlotte's help with this. Would you run and get her from breakfast? I'll watch everything until you return." Rose described the child, then walked back toward her as Andrew took long, loping steps in the direction of the Center Family Dwelling House.

The girl had settled in the crook of two branches. She still said nothing, but she seemed to relax slightly as she watched Rose return. Perhaps even being with a stranger was more comfortable than being alone.

Rose decided to try once more. "I'd really like to know your name," she said. The beautiful eyes regarded her with mute distrust.

"It's just that I'm a little nervous around people when I don't know their names, and I'd feel so much more at ease if you'd tell me yours."

The girl's small chest expanded, as if she were inhaling to speak. But the silence dragged on until, ready to give up, Rose sighed and leaned against the tree trunk to keep an eye on the death scene in the distance.

"Mairin."

At first Rose thought it was a trick of the wind she'd heard, not a soft voice. She peered up into the serious light brown face.

"Did you say your name is Mary?" Rose asked.

"No." The girl's voice held a hint of irritation. "Mair-in," she pronounced.

"What a lovely name. It's Irish, isn't it? For 'Mary'? My full name is Rose Callahan; I'm part Irish, too." From the girl's coloring, Rose guessed she must be of mixed race. All the more reason to bring her back to the Shaker village; a mixed-race child could not have an easy life, especially in this part of the country and during such difficult times. It had been more than seventy-five years since North Homage had bought slaves in order to free them, so Rose, only in her late thirties, was too young to remember. But the Shakers had retained their firm belief in the basic humanity of all people.

The girl said nothing.

"My mother's family was part Irish, but she grew up around here," Rose continued brightly, as if chatting to someone in a tree, with a dead man in the distance, was the most natural thing to do before breakfast. "My father was from Ireland. I don't remember them, not really. My mother died when I was born, and my father died when I was three. That's when I came to live here. How old are you?"

Mairin opened her small mouth, closed it, then opened it again. "Eleven," she said.

For a moment, words failed Rose. The girl looked far too tiny to be eleven years old, yet she did have an air of self-sufficiency. "Eleven? Truly?"

Mairin nodded, without smiling. "Twelve come spring."

"Oh? When is your birthday?"

The girl shrugged one slight shoulder. "Don't know. Spring is all they told me."

"Mairin, do you think we could be friends now? Would you come down here and talk with me?" Rose once again raised her hand.

Mairin rolled on her stomach and lowered herself to the next branch, just above Rose. She slid to the ground so quickly that Rose barely had time to step aside. She moved with the agility and assurance of one who spent much of her time hiding in trees.

Brushing off her pantaloons, Mairin straightened and gazed up at Rose, who was taller than average and must have seemed a thin giant to the girl who didn't even come up to her waist. Rose lowered herself to the ground, smoothing her cloak over the blanket of dried leaves, so that her eyes and Mairin's would be equal.

Rose bubbled with curiosity about this strange child and what she might have seen, but before she could begin her questions, the sound of crackling leaves and branches told her the others were approaching. To her irritation, she saw not just Charlotte and Andrew, but a group of three women and three men tramping toward them. Leading the arrivals was a tall, slender woman. There was no mistaking the emotion in her forceful stride. She was furious.

FOUR

"YOU WICKED CHILD, YOU RAN AWAY AGAIN!" THE WOMAN'S pale cheeks flushed, which only served to emphasize her high cheekbones. Her loose-fitting mud-brown trousers and shirt barely disguised her long, well-shaped body as she trampled undergrowth. Though older than the woman by perhaps a decade, Rose couldn't help feeling a twinge of alarm, as if she were the wicked child.

Before Rose could push to her feet, Mairin lurched against her shoulder. Shivers ran through the girl's small body. Instinctively Rose circled an arm around her. Mairin stiffened slightly and pulled away.

The woman stood frowning down at Rose and Mairin, one hand on a slim hip. Her beauty disappeared as she waggled a finger at the child. Her blue eyes hardened, and grim lines appeared around the corners of her mouth.

Standing beside the woman were Gilbert Griffiths and Earl Weston. Gilbert came up behind her. "This is Celia," he explained to Rose. "Hugh's wife." He put a calming hand on her shoulder, which she shook off.

"No, Gil, not this time," she said. "This girl is impossible. I can't imagine why we took her in, and I think it's more than time I reconsidered, now that Hugh's gone." She crossed her arms over her chest and glared down.

By this time the rest of the group had straggled in, panting. They heard Celia's comment and responded with silence. Celia showed no apparent grief or shock over her husband's ugly death. Mairin watched Celia dispassionately, as if observing the behavior of a mildly interesting but common species of bird. Mairin was a small girl, yet somehow she managed to look haughty.

Sister Charlotte slipped in front of Celia and held out her hand to Mairin. "You remember me, don't you, Mairin? I'm Charlotte. I teach at our school, and I care for the Shaker children. We met when you first arrived, remember?"

Mairin did not respond, but her stance softened, making her look younger. "I hear you've been a little, uh, bored since you got here," Charlotte said, with a quick peek at Celia. "I have an idea. If your mama doesn't mind, perhaps you could come back with me to the Children's Dwelling House. We've canceled school for the morning, so we thought we'd all bundle up and go hunt for black walnuts after breakfast. Would you like to join us?"

"She's not my mama," Mairin said. She had a low, melodious voice with no more than a hint of childhood left in it.

Charlotte threw an unhappy glance at Rose, as Mairin thrust her arm straight out in front of her.

"As you can see," Mairin said, "we're different colors." In the silence that followed her matter-of-fact observation, the girl dropped her arm, stepped toward Charlotte, and said, "I'll come with you."

"I'll drop by to visit you a bit later," Rose said, "just to see how you're settling in."

Mairin turned her head and nodded once. Without looking at Celia, Earl, or Gilbert, she followed Charlotte out of the orchard. Josie walked along beside her. A squirrel skittered away from them into the dry undergrowth. The adults watched in silence as Mairin disappeared from view.

So far no one seemed to have tumbled to the notion that Mairin might have witnessed a suicide—hardly surprising, given the girl's unflappable manner. Andrew might not have mentioned that she had been hiding in the tree, in full view of the tragedy, but it still surprised Rose that Gilbert and Celia showed no concern for the child's emotional state. Perhaps they were too accustomed to not knowing what that was. Following an instinct she didn't stop to analyze, Rose kept quiet about what Mairin might have seen. She'd talk to the girl later, alone.

"That child is so ungrateful." Celia leaned a slender shoulder against a plum tree and crossed her arms and ankles, creating a tableau. Earl stood beside her like a hefty bodyguard.

"Now, Celia, she's had a hard life," Gilbert said, running his hand over his balding head.

"All the more reason she should be grateful. She had nothing, and we've given her everything she could possibly need—a warm home, food, clothing, education. And what does she do? Runs away, over and over."

"She just needs more time to learn how to conduct herself in society," Gilbert said.

"She's had two full years," Celia snapped. "How long does it take to become civilized?"

Observing the brief argument, Rose had a fair suspicion why Mairin was disinclined to stay home. Now she was eager to learn what she could about the girl's background.

"I gather Mairin is adopted?" she asked.

"Not adopted," Gilbert said. "You might say we took her in."

"That girl is certainly not ready for adoption," Celia said.

Rose cringed inwardly. "So she is an orphan? Where did she come from?"

"We found the poor thing wandering the streets of Indianapolis, dirty and starving," Gilbert said. "Or rather, Hugh found her while he was traveling about Indiana, looking for a suitable place for our new community. We wanted to be close to the original Owenite colony, New Harmony, you see, so that we might draw inspiration from—"

"Gil, she doesn't want to hear your speech," Celia said. "We don't know Mairin's background, except it's obvious she was never taught manners. Hugh felt sorry for her and brought her home; he's the soft-hearted one." Celia's tone conveyed clearly that "soft-hearted" translated as "irresponsible."

"*Was*, my dear. Hugh *was* the soft-hearted one," Gilbert said softly.

Celia had the grace to look chagrined at this reminder of the dead man lying just out of their sight.

"Hugh was far too gentle to die like this," Gilbert continued.

Celia rolled sapphire eyes. "On the contrary," she said, "it's just like him to leave his mess for everyone else to clean up."

"Celia!"

"Well, it's true, and you know it. You just don't want to admit it. Look at how he stuck us with Mairin. He brought her home and dumped her on us—on *me*—without so much as a warning. Now we'll never be rid of her." Celia rubbed her upper arms. "I'm freezing. Must we stay out here?" Earl Weston removed his jacket and slid it around her shoulders.

"I'm puzzled," Rose said. "Why did Hugh bring Mairin to you in the first place? We Shakers certainly took in many orphans at one time, but now that there are orphanages, we take only those who are left with us by a family member or friend. Yet Hugh brought Mairin from Indianapolis to live with you. Did he try to locate any of her people?"

Celia and Gilbert exchanged an unreadable glance. Gilbert cleared his throat. "I'm sure he just thought it would be best for the child," he said. "Remember how he took care of you when your stage career faltered, Celia?"

"Oh, Gil, stop it, for heaven's sakes." Celia shivered and pulled Earl's jacket tightly around her. "Let's be honest," she said. "Neither you nor Hugh has ever been genuinely soft-hearted. Hugh just had his head in the clouds. I think he actually felt sorry for her, but really he brought her home for the same reason you agreed to take her in—she's a project—to be saved, reformed, made happy and productive, so the world will admire your devotion to the betterment of mankind."

It was Gilbert's turn to flush. He sputtered inarticulately, but Celia ignored him and turned to Rose.

"Gilbert's middle name is Owen," she said. "He believes he

is directly descended from the original Robert Owen, who founded New Harmony over a century ago."

"I more than just believe it, I know it. I *am* a descendant of Robert Owen," Gilbert said.

"Have you even come close to proving it?"

"Well, not yet, but—"

"Just because he was born in southwest Indiana, and his parents gave him Owen as a middle name, he has convinced himself he was born to recreate Robert Owen's utopia—and to make it work this time." Celia's sleek black bob swung across her cheeks as she shook her head. "The original Owenites took in a homeless boy, who became successful and wealthy, so Gil and Hugh had to do the same. Unfortunately, they picked a girl with a disturbed mind and questionable parentage. And then they expected *me* to turn her into something. As for locating her family, Hugh didn't even bother. The shape she was in, she couldn't have had anyone looking out for her."

"I see," Rose said. She didn't know which disturbed her more, Gilbert's crass use of a child to further his reformist reputation, or Celia's heartless attitude toward the girl. With difficulty, she hid her distaste; if she wanted any more information, it was best not to criticize the New-Owenite leaders. Not yet, anyway.

"Are you certain her mind is disturbed?" Rose asked.

Again Celia and Gilbert exchanged a quick glance.

"Well . . ." Celia hesitated. "She has always been somewhat odd. Everyone has noticed it. She has no manners whatsoever; we have to keep her out of civilized company for the most part. Mostly she says nothing, just watches everyone as if we were all in a play and she was reviewing us. Then all at once she'll blurt out a more or less intelligent sentence."

"She looks quite young to have been wandering the streets by herself."

"She's eleven, or so she told us," Gilbert said. "I know she looks to be much younger, but I'm afraid that's a legacy of her sad past. She won't talk about it, so we may never know the details, but when we took her to our physician, we discovered she had rickets, and it was stunting her growth. If you look carefully, some of her bones are malformed."

"You may have noticed that she swings through trees more easily than she walks upright," Celia said, with a short laugh. "In fact, she—"

"She may never be able to bear children normally," Gilbert said. "Her body is certainly damaged, but her mind is capable." He tossed a reproving frown at Celia, who glared at the ground. "No matter what Celia may believe, the girl is redeemable."

As Celia opened her mouth to retort, the sound of voices distracted her. Rose almost preferred Celia's outrageous comments to the presence of Sheriff Harry Brock, who was approaching the death scene a few yards away from them. What sounded like a curse pierced the air, and Rose assumed he'd discovered that the body had been cut down. Deputy Grady O'Neal accompanied the sheriff, which lessened Rose's dread as she and the others approached them. Grady was a friend to the Shakers.

Sheriff Brock's wiry body stopped its agitated pacing as Rose came into view. He arched an eyebrow at her. She shot a hopeful look at Grady, who avoided her gaze, and she then knew no support would come from that quarter.

"I suppose you're responsible for this mess," Brock said.

For a startled second, Rose thought she was being accused of murder.

"You shouldn't have moved the deceased, and you know it. Don't matter if it was suicide, not that we can figure much out now you've let a herd of cattle trample the ground. Makes me wonder what was on your mind." Brock kicked aside a dead branch in frustration.

Anger flushed her cheeks, but Rose held her tongue and reminded herself to be cautious. She did not bother to blame the condition of the scene on Wilhelm. It would make no difference to Brock which Shaker was responsible; he would undoubtedly use the information to discredit all of them. As this Depression wore on, North Homage's Kentucky neighbors grew more restive in the face of the Shakers' relative prosperity. The fact that Believers willingly shared their food with the poor families living nearby did not always quiet the resentment of the world.

Brock watched her, his mouth hovering on the edge of a smile, which only heightened Rose's wariness. She beckoned toward Gilbert and Celia.

"Sheriff, you should be aware that our guests, Gilbert Griffiths and Celia Griffiths, are kin of the unfortunate man. They are very upset, as I'm sure you can imagine."

Brock's quick eyes snapped to the couple, who looked anything but upset.

"Wife?"

Celia nodded.

"Don't miss him much?" Brock asked.

"Sheriff, I can assure you that Celia is devastated," Earl said, stepping to Celia's side.

"True," said Gilbert. "Celia does not easily display her emotions."

"Uh-huh. You a brother of the deceased?" Brock asked. "I see you're about the same size."

"First cousin," Gilbert said.

"You were close, then?" Deputy Grady O'Neal asked. Rose knew the sympathy in his voice to be genuine. His own people were local tobacco growers and well-to-do, but they maintained the closeness of hill-country families. Grady had practically grown up with his first cousins.

"Hugh believed as we do in the principles of Robert Owen," Gilbert said. "You see, we are convinced that a civilized and happy human being emerges only from the right kind of education; that is, if all children were taught to be rational and truth-seeking in their thinking, they would inevitably—"

"Anybody hate your cousin enough to want him dead?" Sheriff Brock asked. He tilted his head as if to observe Gilbert from a more revealing angle.

Gilbert stared at him for several moments. "Hate? I . . ." His eyes slid over to Hugh's still form, now covered by a worn blanket. He cleared his throat. "I hardly think so. Hugh had a very kind heart. Are you . . . do you really suspect he might have been murdered?"

Brock's smirk suggested that where Shakers were concerned, any abomination was possible. Rose's jaw set in determination. She knew that from now on, when she put her hands to work, it must be in the search for truth. Sheriff Brock would stop searching as soon as he'd settled on the truth that pleased him.

FIVE

"WAS IT THINE INTENTION THAT I NOT BE TOLD OF THE SHER-
iff's arrival? Isn't it enough that I must dine alone in the Ministry House; is the village now run without me? Am I no
longer elder?"

"Wilhelm, there was no slight intended," Rose said, feeling
weary, though it was still morning. Wilhelm often drained her
energy, like a fire sucking oxygen from a burning building. It
didn't help that he insisted on using the archaic "thee" instead
of "you." Somehow it lent an almost scriptural significance to
anything he said.

"Sheriff Brock and Grady know the layout of the village,"
she said. "You told them the body was in the orchard, so they
simply went directly to the orchard. They believed there was
no time to waste. Would you have preferred that I leave them
there alone, while I came back to fetch you?"

Wilhelm glowered toward the Trustees' Office, at the west
end of the village, where the dust was still settling from the
recent departure of the sheriff's brown Buick. Rose stood near
him, but not too near, in front of the Ministry House. To be
truthful, she very much wanted to keep Wilhelm out of the
way. He had a habit of stirring up pots that were already boiling. She hoped to determine the truth of Hugh Griffiths' death
quickly and quietly.

"Well, what did the sheriff conclude? Are we to be blamed,
as usual?"

Rose paused to measure her words. "He certainly did not conclude that we Believers are responsible for Hugh's death," she said. "As you know, the sheriff is not a supporter of ours, but he is not an unreasonable man. And certainly not stupid."

Wilhelm snorted. "Thy faith would be better placed in Mother Ann."

"My faith *is* in Mother Ann, and in the Father and Holy Mother Wisdom, and I'm sure they will be with us, as they always have before."

"So it is thy belief we should put ourselves in the hands of the Sheriff?"

"For the time being," Rose said. "All evidence so far points to suicide, and the Sheriff did not deny that." She did not add that Brock seemed open to, even eager for, any evidence to the contrary.

"Was there a note? It is my experience that suicides compound the cowardice of their crime by requesting forgiveness beforehand, as if wanting God to give them permission to sin."

"Nay, there was no note found near the . . . near Hugh." Rose worried that Brock might pursue the murder notion out of spite that all apparent sources of evidence had been tampered with, but she kept that concern to herself.

"I haven't time to waste; there is work to be done," Wilhelm said. "We shall have a worship service following the evening meal. We must make sure our visitors attend."

"Wilhelm, you know the New-Owenites are not in tune with our faith. Why don't we just—"

Wilhelm's blue eyes hardened. "It seems the fire in thy heart is dying out. I fear what we have come to, with such a worldly eldress as thee. There is clearly a sickness of the soul among these visitors of ours. If we can turn even one of them from his carnal life, we will have served. See that the women attend this evening. I will see to the men." Wilhelm settled his flat-brimmed work hat on his head and strode toward the barn.

Rather than tackle the task of convincing the New-Owenites—who were opposed to any form of organized religion—to attend evening worship, Rose gave in to her curiosity and concern about the quiet waif, Mairin. It was nearly time for the noon meal; Charlotte and the children should be back from their hunt for black walnuts. Though it was Tuesday, the morning's lessons had been canceled due to Hugh's death. The children would not need to return to the Schoolhouse until the afternoon, so now they might be doing chores in the Children's Dwelling House.

Despite the tragedy she had so recently witnessed, Rose's spirits lifted as the sun edged away from its cloud covering and warmed her shoulders. She untied her long cloak to let the breeze billow the wool away from her skin. Avoiding the dusty, unpaved central road, she walked through the bluegrass, now brown and layered with fallen sour gum leaves, their intense reds fading to rust.

As she passed the open door of the Sisters' Shop, a strong, insistent voice reached her. It sounded familiar. She paused and listened. She couldn't make out the words, but the tone sounded persuasive. She walked closer until she recognized the harsh voice of Celia Griffiths. It surprised her that Celia would bother to visit the Sisters' Shop so soon after her husband's death, let alone talk earnestly with the sisters—who, presumably, were working hard at their dyeing, weaving, and sewing.

Rose began to feel self-conscious. She knew that Wilhelm had given Celia, and the other visitors, permission to roam the village freely and learn what they could from the Shakers, so their own utopian experiment might avert the chaotic demise of the original Owenite colony. But what she was hearing in the Sisters' Shop sounded more like teaching than learning. If Rose interceded now, Celia would probably stop immediately, but Rose was curious to know what was going on. She moved on quickly toward the Children's Dwelling House, promising herself that later she would chat with Sister Isabel, who should be weaving in the Sisters' Shop. She could count on Isabel to remember every detail of the episode.

Within moments, Rose heard children's laughter coming

from behind the Children's Dwelling House. She followed the sound to the garden in back, given over entirely to the care of the children. The plants—herbs and vegetables, with a few flowers, in defiance of the rule against ornamentation—were mostly dead now, with the exception of a few hardy perennials. The children were taking advantage of the warmth to dig up dead annuals and turn the soil in preparation for spring. Charlotte was hard at work along with them.

Mairin sat off to the side, cross-legged in a corner of the garden. With slow and careful movements, she was turning over spadesful of black loam and breaking up clumps. Rose approached the girl. Charlotte and several other girls smiled or waved at her, but Mairin concentrated on her task. She did not look up until she saw Rose's feet in front of her.

She gazed at Rose with wide coppery-green eyes and her mouth slightly open. She did not smile or even register recognition. From Rose's height, Mairin looked like a toddler. The urge to sweep her up and hold her was strong, but the girl's odd detachment kept Rose still.

"You remember me, don't you? I'm Rose; we met in the orchard."

Mairin gave a solemn nod.

"Would you like to go for a walk with me?"

A moment of hesitation, then another nod. Rose held out her hand. Mairin rolled up on her knees and stood with a hint of awkwardness, as if her joints weren't set quite right. But she did not reach for Rose's hand. Something told Rose to stay as she was. After what felt like interminable moments, Mairin slid her small hand into Rose's.

The lifting of her own heart startled Rose. She didn't know how or why, but this strange little girl touched her. Perhaps she sensed the wound lurking beneath the detached self-possession.

"I have an idea," Rose said. "Have you ever tasted candied angelica root? I think the Kitchen Sisters recently finished putting up a large batch. Most of it we sell to the world, but we do keep some aside for ourselves. Let's go see, shall we?"

"See you later, Mairin." Nine-year-old Nora glanced up from her digging and grinned. "I'll ask Charlotte if you can stay in my retiring room, okay? We could have a lot of fun— you, me, and Betsy."

"Okay." It was the first word Rose had heard Mairin speak since her departure from the orchard earlier. Rose was encouraged. If Nora could befriend her, Mairin might begin to blossom. Rose gave Nora an approving smile before leading Mairin toward the Center Family Dwelling House kitchen.

As they opened the outside door to the kitchen, they were enveloped with warm, fragrant air. Sister Gertrude, the Kitchen deaconess, was just removing a dozen or so pans of sweet potato bread from the bread oven. From a smaller oven came the fresh, crusty smell of vegetable potpies. There was plenty of good food this time of year, following the harvest, but the North Homage Shakers had elected to designate vegetarian days, both to stretch out the precious meat and in the belief that such a diet would be good for their health.

Rose had forgotten that the noon meal would be served within the hour. She should not be feeding candied angelica root to Mairin, who clearly had suffered from malnutrition. It might seem too tempting and spoil her appetite for more nourishing food. But when she saw the girl's face, she changed her plan. Mairin's eyes were wide and shiny as she gazed at the sweet potato bread, and her mouth stretched into a hopeful smile.

"Would you like to try some of the bread first?" Rose asked.

For an answer, Mairin reached out her free arm toward the nearest loaf. Her fingers arched in clutching desperation, the shape of her hand all the more clawlike because her knuckles were unusually large and knobby. She made a quick, impatient sound in her throat.

"Nay, child, the pan will burn your fingers," Gertrude said, but gently. It was clear Mairin was showing the effects of chronic starvation. Her desire for food was urgent. They would have to be careful she didn't gorge herself and become ill, Rose thought.

"Polly, cut the child a piece of bread," Gertrude said. "And put a bit of butter on it."

Mairin's eyes never left the loaf as Polly popped it upside-down out of the pan, righted it, and cut off a thick, steaming slice. The butter melted and sank into the orange-tinted bread. Polly slid the slice onto a white plate and put it on the large nicked work table in the middle of the kitchen. Mairin pulled toward it, leaning her weight away from Rose's restraining hand.

When Mairin reached the table, only the top of her head showed. Not to be daunted, she flung up her arm and grabbed at the plate. Sensing disaster, Rose held the girl around the waist with one arm and reached for a cushioned foot bench with the other. Some of the smaller girls were in the habit of using the foot bench to give themselves more leverage when working at the table. She plunked Mairin on top of it.

Instantly, the girl grabbed the bread and stuffed a corner in her mouth. She bit off nearly a quarter of the slice. Her cheeks puffed out, so filled with bread that she couldn't chew. With a cry of frustration, she spit the bread back on the plate. All the kitchen sisters watched, horrified and fascinated. None of them had ever truly been hungry, and they had never seen such sad greed. Rose was also surprised that in the week and a half or so that the New-Owenites had been in North Homage, none of the sisters had seen Mairin eat before.

Tears streamed down the child's face. It was the first show of genuine emotion Rose had seen in her.

"It's all right, Mairin," she said, stroking the girl's fuzzy hair. "Just take it a bit more slowly, and you'll do fine. I promise you can have all the food you need. That's it, just a small bite."

Mairin adjusted her mouth on another corner of the slice, until the bite was a reasonable size. Her tears dried and her eyes closed in ecstasy as she chewed and swallowed.

"Nay, slower now," Rose said, as Mairin tried to stuff more into her next bite. "That's right. See how delicious it is when you take it slowly? Now, just put the bread down and take a break, so your stomach can enjoy it, too."

Mairin paused a few seconds but could not let go of the bread, nor could she shift her gaze anywhere else.

"Time to put your hands to work, now, Sisters," Gertrude said, breaking the spell. "The bell will be ringing any minute, and we aren't nearly ready." The kitchen sisters scattered.

Rose talked Mairin through the remainder of her slice of bread. By the time the struggle had ended, it was clear that the girl would need firm coaching to learn to eat properly. She still ate as if she'd just been brought in off the streets. How could she possibly have been with the New-Owenites for two full years and still be so controlled by the memory of starvation? Had Celia spent any time with her at all? Or had she quickly written the girl off as incorrigible? Celia had mentioned keeping her "out of civilized company." Did she ever eat meals with other people? Rose felt the stirrings of a fierce protectiveness that before now had been reserved for Gennie Malone, a girl she had befriended at about this same age. But Gennie was grown up and planning to marry soon, and the mothering corner of Rose's heart had gone dormant. Until now.

"I'll tell you what, Mairin. There's someone I want you to meet. She's a very good friend of mine, but she is too frail to come to the dining room, so why don't the two of us join her for lunch in her retiring room?"

Mairin's face went blank again.

"I know you'll like her," Rose said. "Her name is Agatha, Agatha Vandenberg, and she was very kind to me when I was your age. We'll go find some candied angelica root and bring it along to share with her, shall we?"

Mairin gave her single solemn nod, and Rose led her to the pantry. Intent as she was on food, Mairin also seemed fascinated with the kitchen. She paused to stare at the row of shiny copper-bottomed pots hanging from pegs spaced along a narrow strip of wood that encircled the kitchen wall at just above head level. Rose was glad to see her show some curiosity in her surroundings.

Rose cut a healthy slice from one of the sugar-coated boiled angelica roots laid out to dry on cookie sheets. She wrapped it in a kitchen cloth and decided to carry it herself after seeing Mairin's avid gaze follow every movement. After telling Gertrude where they would be for the noon meal, Rose led Mairin out through the empty dining room and into the hallway. A few retiring rooms were located on the ground floor and reserved for the aged and infirm. Agatha now lived in one of them.

"Rose, what a double treat you've brought me," Agatha said when Rose introduced Mairin and showed Agatha the angelica root. "Candy and a new friend, both." She reached out a thin, trembling hand and touched Mairin's arm. To Rose's surprise, Mairin did not pull away. She studied Agatha's fine-boned face with as much interest as she had given the copper-bottomed pans.

Mairin sucked on her lower lip for a moment, then smiled a slow, soft smile. "You are a pretty lady," she said, in her low, lyrical voice.

Rose was stunned. She had never known anyone so full of surprises.

Agatha laughed with delight, a sound Rose had not heard since before her last stroke. "Thank you, child. You see with your heart. My own eyes have grown dim with age, but I can tell that you have quite lovely and unusual eyes. Did you get them from your mama or your papa?"

"Both," Mairin said. "Mama had brown eyes, and papa's were green. They're both dead."

Rose had to sit down. Agatha had always been able to speak directly to the soul, but lately Rose had to wonder if she was beginning her final angelic journey. Her powers seemed to intensify as her body weakened.

"It is very sad when your mama and papa die so young," Agatha said. "Mine died when I was three, and poor Rose really doesn't remember hers, either. How old were you, Mairin?"

"Five. But I remember them both."

"Tell me about them."

Mairin pulled a small rocking chair over near Agatha and climbed into it. Her feet dangled above the ground, so she tucked them underneath her. Agatha handed her a soft, brown blanket from the arm of her own rocker. Mairin wrapped herself into it up to her neck. For the first time, she looked almost like a normal child.

"My mama was beautiful," she said. "Her skin was darker than mine, and she sang a lot, especially when she was drinking. Papa was from Ireland. He drank a lot, too, and sometimes he and Mama beat on each other, and then Papa would beat on me. He always said he didn't mean to hurt us." Mairin's tone was nonchalant.

Agatha's smile had disappeared. "How did your mama die?"

Mairin's face once again went blank. "One day they were beating on each other, and Papa threw Mama against the stove. She fell down and didn't get up."

"You were there?"

Mairin nodded. "I was hiding behind the door, and I could see through the crack."

"What happened then?"

"Papa got his gun and shot himself through his mouth." Mairin's voice was lightly conversational. Nothing in her manner invited expressions of understanding or sympathy. It was as if she were recounting a bucolic scene she'd witnessed on a recent train ride. She snuggled down in her blanket, seemingly unaware of the silence that followed her revelation.

"Child, who took care of you after you lost your parents?" Agatha asked.

Mairin shrugged one thin shoulder. "Oh, I went here and there," she said, "An aunt for a while, but then I had to leave. Other folks after that." Her eyes wandered over to Agatha's lamp table, where the candied angelica root lay wrapped in its cloth.

At that moment, a knock on the partly opened door announced the arrival of a kitchen sister with lunch. Rose set the tray on a small, pine desk. She cut portions from a vegetable potpie and delivered them to Agatha and Mairin before settling at the desk with the last portion for herself. The steam warmed her face, and she paused to breathe in the rich scent of herbs and pie crust before saying a silent grace.

As she munched her first bite, she glanced at Mairin to find her leaning close to her plate and shoveling the last bits of potpie into her already full mouth. Agatha watched, too, her own food untouched. She turned to Rose, sadness and understanding in her cloudy blue eyes.

"You know," Agatha said, "I find I'm not terribly hungry just now. Would you care to help me eat my portion, Mairin?"

The girl slid off her chair, holding her blanket over her shoulders, and sat on her knees in front of Agatha's rocker.

"Why don't you bring over your spoon?" Agatha said. "I'll keep the plate on my lap so it won't spill, and we'll share the food. How does that sound? I'll take a bite, and then I'll hold the plate so you can have a bite." Agatha was weakened, especially on her right side, from a series of strokes. She had learned to eat with her left hand because her right was unreliable. Now, however, she picked up her spoon with her shaky right hand. Slowly she scooped up a small bite of pie and tried to lift it to her mouth. Halfway up, her hand began to tremble and dropped back to the plate.

Mairin's eyes flashed with feral impatience. Her shoulders tightened and her hands clenched and unclenched as if she could barely keep from grabbing the plate from Agatha and pouring the food in her own mouth. Rose held her breath.

Agatha smiled gently. "I'm so sorry, child. You see, I've been very sick, and sometimes it is hard for me to manage to eat. I get very hungry, as you can imagine. I wonder if you would help me?"

With amazement, Rose watched Mairin's face as Agatha spoke. Greed turned to confusion, and in an instant, when Agatha said how hungry she got, Mairin's expression dissolved into pain. She rose up on her knees and took the spoon from Agatha's shaking hand. Aiming carefully, she placed the spoon at Agatha's lips and waited for her to chew and swallow. Agatha nodded to encourage the child to take her own portion, but instead of picking up her own spoon, Mairin scooped up another bite and brought it to Agatha's mouth. Agatha was so surprised that she took several moments to accept the food.

"You are very kind, my dear," Agatha said, when she had swallowed. "But do be sure to take some for yourself. Go ahead, have a bite."

Mairin took her own spoon and ate a small bite, chewing carefully. Rose couldn't help grinning. With persistent effort, perhaps they could do more than pry information out of Mairin. Perhaps they could nurture her soul.

SIX

AFTER THE NOON MEAL, ROSE DROPPED MAIRIN OFF WITH Charlotte to spend the afternoon at school, then made her way to the Sisters' Shop, just next door. Isabel was expecting her. From the sparkle in her hazel eyes when Rose had asked to chat about Celia's visit to the Sisters' Shop, Isabel had a lot to tell.

Bright sunlight warmed the fall afternoon. Rose longed for some outdoor work and would have assigned herself to help mulch the tender perennial herbs for the winter but for the nagging thought that Hugh Griffiths' death might not have been by his own hand and that little Mairin was a witness. The child was gradually warming to her, and especially to Agatha, but it could take too long for her to trust enough to confide in them. Until then, she was alone with her secrets, and she might be in danger.

The door to the Sisters' Shop was ajar to allow air to circulate. Rose slipped inside and went directly to the room where the sisters dyed and spun their fine wools. In the days when more than two hundred Believers had lived and worked in North Homage, wool dying had been done outdoors in the spring, so that a full crew of sisters could weave all winter. But now their numbers were so depleted—a few dozen, at best, and many grown aged and weak. Other Shaker communities had given up making their own wool and purchased cloth from the world. Elder Wilhelm wanted the North Homage Shakers to retain as much self-sufficiency as possible, to strengthen their spirit, and Rose had to admit that she was glad to see the textile industry preserved, even in such a tiny way.

Sister Isabel oversaw the dying, spinning, and weaving, sometimes doing one of the tasks alone, while Sister Sarah watched over the sewing room on the second floor. Other sisters were assigned to help when they could be spared from the daily tasks of cooking and laundry. So here it was November, and there was still wool to be dyed.

Isabel leaned over a large pot, holding a wet clump of yarn of a light brownish hue. She grinned at Rose. "Be sure to tell Wilhelm about this," she said. "It will please him."

"Brown yarn?"

"Nay, not just any brown yarn," Isabel said. "This is true butternut dye, like the sisters used so many years ago. Thought I'd experiment and see if I could make some. Collected the bark myself late spring, but I didn't get to it until now, so I had to use it dry instead of fresh. But it doesn't look bad, I'd say." She hung the yarn on a peg to dry thoroughly and wiped her hands on her apron. "This is my second batch. The first came out a bit dark, so Sarah had the idea of using it to make Shaker sister dolls to sell in Languor come Christmas time. She's already made half a dozen. Andrew said he'd place them with some shops."

"That's a lovely idea," Rose said.

"But that's not why you're here." Isabel gathered up an armful of undyed yarn. "Let me just get another batch going, then we'll have a talk," she said.

Rose understood the need to keep the work moving, so she occupied herself by admiring the skeins of dyed yarns hanging around the room. Isabel had been busy. Wilhelm would, indeed, be pleased to see the old Shaker dyes and dyeing methods resurrected with such skill. It pleased Rose, too, yet she couldn't help but wonder if they were going the right direction. Certainly there was something about reviving the old ways that gave Rose and other Believers a strong sense of being apart from the world, but wasn't it truly their faith that set them apart? Surely they could maintain that faith and still adapt to the world around them. They had always been leaders in the adoption and even the invention of new labor-saving devices—anything that would make the work quicker and leave more time for worship. Wilhelm believed that life had gotten too luxurious; was he right?

"There!" said Isabel. "We'll let that cook a spell. I'm ready to sit. How about you?"

In answer, Rose lifted a ladder-back chair from two wall pegs, where it hung upside down to keep its seat free of dust. She handed the chair to Isabel, then lifted another for herself.

"I'm glad you're here, Rose," Isabel said. "I'd thought I should tell you about Celia Griffiths' little visit with us this morning, but I didn't want to gossip. I was mighty disturbed, I don't mind telling you. That woman has some odd notions in her head."

"Like what?"

"Well, she seemed quite put out when she dropped into the Sisters' Shop and saw us all doing what she called 'female tasks.' She wondered why there weren't any brethren in here weaving and sewing, and she was nasty about it. Sarah tried to explain it to her—Sarah's so gentle, you know—that we work and eat and live separately from the brethren, so we divide up tasks in a reasonable way, but Celia just laughed. I pointed out that we do help the brethren in the fields during the harvest, and she said, 'Oh, so you do men's work, but they refuse to help with your work!' Honestly. I wanted to ask her to leave, but that would have been rude." Isabel jumped up to check on her soaking yarn, gave it a stir with a long stick, and sat down again.

"All that was irritating, but there was even more. That's when I began to worry." Isabel's smooth forehead creased. "I suppose I could be making too much of it, but . . ."

"Tell me," Rose said.

"She started talking about her own group, those New-Owenites, or whatever they call themselves. I wasn't sure I was understanding her right, but it sounded like they marry, but they don't really believe in marriage, or something like that. But they believe in having children and educating them very carefully so the boys and the girls are equal. I said that we believe boys and girls are equal, too, but she said we obviously didn't, and that our not marrying was unnatural and would kill us!"

"We've heard these things before," Rose said. "Somehow we always survive."

"True, but then Celia started going around to each of the sisters, one by one, spending a lot more time with the younger sisters and the older girls, asking why they weren't still in school, learning to do important work, like science."

"You're afraid she was swaying some of the sisters away from the Society?"

"I've seen it happen," Isabel said. "The younger ones fall in love and want families; they lose their way, listen to all sorts of nonsense. I was susceptible myself, when I was young." Isabel was no more than thirty, but responsibility had given her purpose and self-assurance.

"Do you believe she succeeded in convincing any of the sisters?"

"I have my doubts about Lottie and Frieda. They seemed to listen intently, and they didn't question. Afterward, I noticed them whispering together. The other sisters were polite but went about their work as though Celia did not trouble them. Among the young girls, Hannah seemed most taken with Celia's arguments."

Rose shrugged. "I've seen signs in Hannah of longing to be in the world, so I'm not surprised. She'd make a good Shaker, if she made up her mind to, but her strong will may be leading her in a different direction. As for the other girls, they so rarely sign the Covenant these days, and we can't blame Celia for that. I'll try to keep watch on Lottie and Frieda, though. Did Celia say anything else I should know about?"

Isabel squirmed on her chair. She swept over to the cauldron and gave her yarn a quick stir again. Finally she turned back to Rose and said, "She had two more things to say, but they were so outrageous that I'm sure no one took them seriously in the least. I suppose you should know about them, though. I heard a couple of the things she said to Frieda and Lottie. I was worried, and I'm not ashamed to say I followed behind when I saw Celia go after the sisters as they went to do some weaving. I stood outside the door a bit and listened, and if Mother Ann had been there, she'd've done the same!"

Isabel squared her shoulders and looked Rose in the eyes. "Celia Griffiths told those poor sisters they were being duped by their leaders—that religion was being used to control them, not to help them become more like the angels. She said they'd become better people through education, not by being told what to think and believe. That much alone clear broke my heart, but then . . ." Isabel glanced back at her cauldron as if she'd like to jump in it herself, but with a deep breath, she continued. "Then she said that celibacy is the biggest trick of all. She said that . . . that you and Elder Wilhelm live together in the same house, with no one watching over you, and did the sisters really think you lived chastely?"

Rose felt her mouth open and heard nothing come out. Her feelings were a jumble of protests and disbelief and even some amusement. Surely no sisters would believe that she and Wilhelm . . . surely not. She became aware of Isabel watching her anxiously.

"Isabel, I assure you, these suggestions are false, completely false. I don't yet know Celia Griffiths very well, but it seems she has something in mind that she hopes to accomplish with such vile rumors. I intend to find out what it is."

Relief flooded Isabel's face. "I was sure she couldn't be right, of course, but I'll admit I've been worried. It did seem as though some of the others were listening altogether too carefully. That's why I'd determined to speak to you privately, even if you hadn't come to me first. Sarah and I talked afterward and felt you should know. It wasn't just tale-telling on our part."

Rose forced herself to smile with confident reassurance. "Of course not. You did the right thing. I'll take care of this, don't worry."

The wood bars had been removed from the door of the long-unused Carpenters' Shop, and once again the sounds of sawing wood and brethren's voices drifted from the windows. Rose approached the shop with some misgiving, since it held unpleasant memories for her. She almost turned back to follow her strong urge to have a little talk with Celia Griffiths; she looked forward to the chat with something close to pleasure. But instinct told her to find Gilbert Griffiths first. She suspected he would be easier to talk to, and she wanted to find out if the New-Owenites were hiding their true mission from North Homage.

Rose slowly pulled open the door, aware that she was entering a male domain. A brother might often be seen repairing equipment in the kitchen or the Sisters' Shop, but it was unusual for a sister, even an eldress, to visit the shops where the brethren worked.

Conversation stopped and three men turned their heads as Rose entered. Two were young brethren, Matthew and Archibald, and the third man was Gilbert Griffiths. The brothers quickly lowered their eyes to their work. Gilbert smiled broadly. His few remaining hairs were slicked back on his bony scalp, and he reminded Rose of a hawker of patent medicines.

"I'm sorry to interrupt," Rose said, "but I was hoping to have a word with you, Mr. Griffiths. Could we walk a spell?"

"Gil, call me Gil." He hopped off his perch on top of a maple workbench, scattering sawdust as his feet hit the floor. "At your service." He followed her to the front door.

Matthew and Archibald paid no heed as they repaired an old apple peeler that hadn't been used in the kitchen for decades. *Another of Wilhelm's brainstorms,* Rose thought. He was forever ordering ancient equipment pulled out of storage, repaired, and put back to use. Archibald was stirring a pail of light orange liquid; Wilhelm must have demanded the apple peeler be stripped and returned to its original color. As if they didn't all have enough work to do already.

"What was that?" Gilbert asked, as they walked around to the backyard of the Carpenters' Shop. He pointed toward a burned patch of ground that still held pieces of an iron staircase emerging from a good-sized hole. "I thought you folks were always so quick to clean up a mess and rebuild."

Rose clenched her teeth and silently repeated her well-worn prayer for patience before answering evenly, "That was the old Waterhouse. It burned down, and we didn't bother to rebuild, since we have a new water and sewer system."

"Seems a mighty good location, though. You could expand the Carpenters' Shop, maybe even build a new one, right there close to the maple grove." Gilbert eyed the land as if he owned it.

"I've had very little chance to talk with you about your plans," Rose said. "Since it has come to my attention that your group does not see any benefit in faith and worship, I'm wondering what, precisely, you're hoping to learn from your visit to North Homage." She strolled back toward the center of the village, away from the burned-out Waterhouse and the too-secluded maple grove. Given the rumors already flying, it would not do to be completely alone with a man from the world. Gilbert followed along beside her, a shade too close, and she edged away. He gave no hint that he noticed.

"Well, Wilhelm did mention you seem to spend more time with the women than with him, so I'll be glad to fill you in. Do you know much about our predecessors, the original Owenites?"

"Only a bit," Rose said. "I know they lived in New Harmony, Indiana, starting somewhere in the 1820s or so, just when we were growing in strength, and I know there was some contact then between our communities."

"Indeed. The example of the Pleasant Hill Shakers was very helpful to New Harmony when it was just getting under way, but unfortunately it wasn't enough. The Owenites lasted as a community for only a few years. They were never able to achieve the peaceful, ordered life you all have enjoyed for well over a century. My idea is that this time we'll do it right. We've spent several years planning and obtaining resources. Now we need to study how you live and work together much more thoroughly, learn everything we can, before we plunge into trying our own utopia again. Does that answer your question?"

"It raises other questions," Rose said. They had reached the back of the Schoolhouse. Normal life had resumed for the children, and the rhythmic murmur of voices reciting in unison drifted from a partially open window. "If religion is mere superstition to you, what can you really learn from us? Everything about our life is guided by our faith. For us, work is worship. From the time we get up in the morning, we try to live as the angels, to create a heaven on earth. How can you achieve a life like ours, yet reject its foundation in faith?"

Gilbert stared off into the distant fields belonging to the Shakers and pursed his lips several times as if practicing a response in his mind. For a moment, a small smile played on his lips, and Rose felt a prick of anxiety. What did any of them really know about this group and their plans?

The drone from the Schoolhouse window stopped, which seemed to bring Gilbert out of his silence. "You are right," he said, "that my predecessor, Robert Owen, was quite opposed to the practice of religion, but did you know that in his later years, he became a convert to spiritualism? I believe you Shakers came under the same influence, did you not?"

It was not a period of Shaker history with which Rose was entirely comfortable, so she nodded but said nothing.

"He was open to new ideas, you see. And so are we." His smile broadened.

Rose felt an uncomfortable lurch in her stomach, as if she had eaten a bite of meat just beyond its freshest. She had no time to analyze her reaction, though, as the back door of the Schoolhouse opened, and a small group of children burst onto the brown lawn, running around each other in circles like puppies released from a pen. The air filled with shouts and giggles.

As Rose and Gilbert turned to watch, Mairin's tiny figure emerged alone, lagging far behind the rest of the children. She stopped just outside the door and watched the others at play.

"I wasn't aware you had taken over Mairin's education," Gilbert said, coldness hardening his voice.

"We certainly aren't 'taking over,'" Rose said. "Mairin seems lost and alone here. I thought she would benefit from being with other children for a while. It doesn't look as if she is used to playmates. Does she spend most of her time by herself?"

Gilbert hesitated. Rose studied his face and thought she saw irritation under the scholarly mask.

"She has come a long way," he said. "When we took her in, she did not speak at all, did not know how to bathe, and she ate only with her hands. Celia was horrified. I think she has never really forgiven Mairin for being so like an animal at first, but really, it isn't the child's fault; it was the conditions of her upbringing. The proper environment will turn her around in time. We just have to be patient and keep working with her."

"What is Mairin's background?"

Gilbert watched as Mairin slid to the ground, her back against the Schoolhouse. She didn't join in with the raucous, joyous play of the other children. "All we know is, she saw her parents die when she was five or so. Her mother was a Kentucky girl, Negro, I believe, and the daughter of freed slaves. Father was an Irish immigrant, so her people were uneducated. The child can't have had much of an education herself. I wish we could have taken her into our care much earlier. But there's still hope. Certainly Hugh thought so, or he wouldn't have asked Celia to tutor her."

"And did she tutor Mairin?"

"Well, I . . . that is, I didn't keep watch over her or anything, but I assume she did."

"Did she take care of Mairin's meals?"

"She was Hugh's wife, after all," Gilbert said.

"I see." What Rose did see was that Gilbert had paid no

attention to the girl so in need of the proper environment.

"Hugh was fond of Mairin?" Rose asked.

"Yes, very. At first I think he felt sorry for her, poor little orphan."

"What happened after her parents died?"

"She has never been very clear about that. Apparently she was shunted around from relative to relative, probably starved. My guess is that she ran away at some point, though she won't admit it, and who knows how long she roamed the streets on her own before Hugh found her."

A boy ran up to Mairin. Rose didn't know the boy by name, but he was a child of one of the farm families living near North Homage, brought daily to the village for schooling. He put his hands on his hips and seemed to be scolding the girl. Nine-year-old Nora stopped her play and watched the two. She ran toward them as the boy started wagging his finger at Mairin, who shrank back against the wall. Soon Nora and the boy were arguing, and Mairin slipped away from them, back into the Schoolhouse.

Rose picked up her skirts and ran toward the building. She could hear Gilbert hurrying behind her. The back door of the Schoolhouse led to a small storage room, then on to the schoolroom. In one corner of the storage room, behind a row of unused desks, Mairin had curled herself into a ball. Charlotte knelt beside her, but the child cowered away from her.

"Rose, what has happened?" Charlotte asked. "Mairin seems terrified, but I can't get a word out of her. Has she been hurt? I wish I'd been out there, but I had some work to do, and I thought the children would be fine on their own for a while, with the older ones watching the younger ones."

"Don't blame yourself," Rose said. "It looked as if one of the local boys was teasing Mairin, and she became frightened."

"Did he hurt her? Oh dear, Wilhelm will insist we teach the boys and girls separately again, and we have no one else to help."

"Don't worry yourself now," Gilbert said. "It looked to me like the normal sort of nonsense little boys get into when they

haven't been trained in the proper environment." He seemed
oblivious to the sharp stares Rose and Charlotte aimed at him.
"He needs civilizing, but he did no actual harm. And Mairin
is a bit over-sensitive."

"Did it occur to you she might have been hurt in the past
and is easily frightened because of it?" Rose asked, not mask-
ing the irritation in her voice. She, too, knelt near Mairin and
lightly stroked her hair. Mairin jumped as she felt the touch.
Rose was troubled by the girl's trembling, which was severe
enough to seem almost like a seizure.

"We know very little of Mairin's experiences before she
came to us. I'm sure you noticed she isn't very communica-
tive," Gilbert said, ignoring the fact that Mairin could hear
him. "No doubt she was treated roughly on the streets, but
now she has been well cared for these past two years, with
the very best environment, so I'm afraid what we are wit-
nessing is an innate weakness in her. She may never achieve
a fully civilized state, though I believe she can be made better."

Rose sat back on her heels and stopped stroking Mairin, for
fear the sizzling anger she felt would charge through her veins
and into the child's awareness. Nor could she chance a look
at Charlotte, whose rage, she knew, would be at least equal to
her own.

"Perhaps, Mr. Griffiths, you would be good enough to leave
us alone with Mairin for a spell. Although she knows and
surely trusts you, the company of women might be more
soothing to her just now." She forced herself to smile.

Far from taking offense, Gilbert seemed relieved. "Of
course, I'll leave her with you two." He backed away too
quickly and tripped on one of the stored desks, but managed
to right himself without damage.

"Before you leave, I have one other suggestion," Rose said.
"If you would be willing to let me, I would like to try my
hand at—civilizing, you said?—civilizing Mairin for the remainder of your visit. She has seemed to respond well to me,
and I would like to know her better. It would free you to spend

your time most productively learning what you hope to about living together in a community. Would you and Celia be agreeable?"

The storeroom was dim, but Rose thought Gilbert's eyes lit up. "Well, we are quite fond of Mairin, of course, but if you'd like to try your hand with her, I'm sure Celia would not object. I'll talk to her right away. We'll want to know how she's doing, of course."

"Of course."

Gilbert left so fast that Rose laughed out loud.

"I'm sure he hopes Mairin will be redeemed—especially if someone else does it for him," Charlotte murmured, as she stood and brushed off her long skirt. "I'd really better go out and check on the children. Will you two be all right?"

"Yea, go on ahead."

Mairin had stopped trembling and fastened her bright eyes on Rose, who leaned toward her and reached out a hand. "Can you stand up?"

Mairin slipped her hand into Rose's and allowed herself to be pulled to her feet.

"Have you been hurt?" Rose asked.

Mairin shook her head.

"Is it all right with you if you stay in my care for a bit?"

The girl nodded.

"Good. We'll go to the kitchen and have a treat soon. But first, would you tell me what that little boy said to you? I promise you'll feel much better if you talk about it."

Mairin was silent for a few moments. When she spoke, Rose was again taken aback by her strangely mature voice. "He called me a little monkey," she said. "He said my mama must have swung from trees, and that's why I'm a brown runt with no manners."

"I'm so sorry that was said to you," Rose said. She blinked back tears as she sought the right words. "You know you aren't . . . what he said, don't you?"

Mairin shrugged. "Other people have said those things to me. They don't bother me so much anymore."

"But you were frightened, Mairin. What frightened you?"

Mairin shrugged again.

"Who were the 'other people'? Families you lived with after your parents died?"

"Sometimes."

"Mairin, did those people ever say or do other things, too?"

A wave of fear washed over the girl's face. She pulled her hand back and stepped away from Rose. "I'm hungry. Can we get a treat now?"

"I know it's hard to think about times when people hurt you, but it'll help if you tell me. I promise. Did anyone beat you?"

Mairin's face went blank, as if she had stepped into another world. "I'm bad a lot," she said, without emotion.

Rose sensed Mairin had reached her limit. "We can talk about this more at another time," she said. "Let's go get something to eat, shall we?" As she took Mairin's limp hand and led her into the sunshine, one more question haunted her. She couldn't put it off. "Mairin, when you said you are bad a lot, do you mean . . . now? Do you still think you are bad a lot?"

"Yes, a lot."

Rose's jaw tightened, and the tears that hovered on her eyelids were tears of fury.

SEVEN

A BRISK WIND HAD KICKED UP BEFORE THE EVENING MEAL, AND Wilhelm's announcement of a worship service indoors was greeted by the Believers with pleasure. Though a man had died, a service also meant staying warm and together, rather than trudging off alone or in small groups for another hour or two of chores. In recent years North Homage had struggled to keep going with too few Believers and too much work. They continued to feed and assist visitors, neighbors, anyone who needed their help, but their own strength and resources were dwindling. Little was said about the end many feared was coming. Worship held them together and reconnected them with the heaven they longed for.

With Rose's help, Sister Charlotte had settled the children, including Mairin, in the Children's Dwelling House, with the older ones watching over bedtime preparations and prayers. The wind had died down by the time they'd left for the Center Family Dwelling House, but their wool cloaks felt good in the crisp air. More than likely it would be warm again by the next afternoon; autumn was a long and glorious season, inching its way into the damp, overcast days of winter.

Rose and Charlotte were the last to arrive at the Center Family Dwelling House. The large meeting room, where the service was to be held, was divided in half by an open space which separated rows of chairs. Women sat on one side, men on the other, facing each other. Most of the worshipers still wore their loose Shaker work clothes, giving the room the look of a sketch from an earlier century. Old-fashioned dress was part of Wilhelm's plan to pull North Homage back to the days when it was growing and vibrant. So far, his scheme had seen little effect; the village continued to dwindle, and setting themselves apart from the world only seemed to make their neighbors less tolerant of the Shakers, despite their reputation for honesty and high quality products.

Among the long, drab dresses with white kerchiefs crisscrossed over the bodice, Rose spotted some worldly clothing. She had informed the New-Owenite women that the worship service would honor Hugh Griffiths, as Wilhelm had asked her to, and they had all shown up. She skimmed the men's side of the room and saw all the male New-Owenites in attendance. As her gaze moved from Gilbert Griffiths, she met the eyes of Brother Andrew. They gave one another a brief nod, then looked away, so as not to give the wrong impression to the monitors assigned to watch for "special looks" between sisters and brethren.

Rose and Charlotte slipped into two chairs in the back row. Both were tall enough to see the room over the heads of others. The Believers bowed their heads in silent prayer, easing themselves into a worshipful state, while the New-Owenites fidgeted. After several moments, Wilhelm rose from his first-row chair and walked to the center of the room.

"Believers and friends," he said, "I am pleased that we have this time to worship together. I believe we have a common purpose and that the Holy Father has brought us here in one place for a reason. Everything that has happened, even when it appears as evil, has happened for the good of our joint mission. We are all called to work together, as spiritual friends and allies." Wilhelm's rough features softened into a benign smile.

Rose felt a jolt of confusion, of disorientation, as if she had suddenly been whisked to another world where everything was the opposite of her own. Where was the fiery righteousness she had come to expect from Wilhelm's speeches? Where was the impatience, the intolerance of anything carnal? Perhaps his conciliatory manner was meant to be respectful, but it sounded like a welcome to newly committed Believers.

She glanced over at Andrew, whose open mouth told her that he was as puzzled as she was. Next to him, however, Gilbert Griffiths had a smirk on his face. Before any response was possible, Wilhelm beckoned the singers to the middle of the room and cued them to begin a welcoming hymn, which they sang with less verve than usual.

Instead of calling for dancing worship, which he usually did, Wilhelm nodded to the singers to be seated when they had finished, and he moved again to the center of the room, apparently gathering steam for another announcement or perhaps a homily. A movement on the men's side caught Rose's attention, and she turned to see Gilbert stand and work his way toward Wilhelm. The scowl on Wilhelm's face said clearly that he had not planned this. However, Gilbert stood with a confident smile beside Wilhelm, who was taller and broader and fiercer by far.

Moments dragged by in silence while Wilhelm struggled to overcome his surprise and regain momentum. Rose might have enjoyed seeing Wilhelm caught off guard had she not been so worried about what was going to happen.

Gilbert drew in his breath as if to speak, but Wilhelm took a step forward and spread open his arms.

"Brethren and sisters," Wilhelm said, "I urge thee to open thy hearts and welcome our visitors from the world. Though they may dress differently from us, and talk and work differently from us, we are both called by God for the same purpose. I say this to them, as much as to thee. Though we are apart from the world, and they are, as yet, still of it, we reach for the same stars. We all seek to build a heaven on earth, a place where we can dwell like the angels. And we can create that heaven by working together, all of us, with our eyes on the task, and our hearts free of earthly distractions."

Gilbert raised his eyebrows, and Rose knew why. Wilhelm had just urged the New-Owenites to give up their carnal lives and become Shakers, celibate and faith-centered. His plan was transparent: the Shakers could survive and flourish if they absorbed the New-Owenites, especially the strong, young men who were the leadership.

Rose found herself clutching the sides of her chair seat, steadying herself for the fight ahead.

Gilbert stepped forward, just a shade in front of Wilhelm. "I must agree with our pious friend," he said. The tautness of his wiry body belied his casual, conciliatory tone. "We have much in common with our Shaker hosts, and a great deal to learn from them. I believe, too, that we have some strengths we can share with them." He looked out over the audience, lingering on the faces of the two young brethren, Archibald and Matthew.

"Yea, indeed," Wilhelm boomed so powerfully that Gilbert flinched. "We will be glad to learn from thee as well, during thy brief visit."

Gilbert turned as if to engage Wilhelm in private, friendly conversation. "I'd be more than happy to take some time right now, as we are all gathered—"

"During worship," Wilhelm said, "it is our habit to worship."

"Naturally. I only thought, because you'd asked us to be together . . ."

"I asked us to be together for the sake of worship." Wilhelm's voice was dipping dangerously low, a warning to those who knew him. He fixed Gilbert with a fierce stare. Several moments passed in silence.

"Ah," said Gilbert, his tone still light but with a new undercurrent of authority. "But you see, we New-Owenites do not worship, even to say farewell to a friend. Perhaps we had not made that clear. We understand your need to do so, of course, but we have no need of such a . . . comforting fantasy. We understand human nature and what it takes to make a man happy and good. We have—"

"This is worship!" Wilhelm roared.

This time Gilbert did not flinch; instead, his smug smile implied he had won a point in the debate. "Of course, Wilhelm. We are sorry for the misunderstanding, and we will leave immediately." He bowed slightly, turned, and nodded at the other New-Owenites to follow him out the door. The tall man named Earl Weston watched one of the sisters as he left the room. Rose saw three Believers squirm and bob, as if tempted to leave with the New-Owenites. Two were brethren, Archibald and Matthew. She could not immediately recognize the third, since she could see only the back of her white-capped head in the front row on the sisters' side. As the sister's head swiveled to watch the visitors exit, Rose saw that the apparent sympathizer was Gretchen, the young Laundry deaconess.

Rose twitched under her blanket, unable to fall asleep yet unwilling to leave the warm comfort of her bed. She was still edgy from the tense worship service that evening. She was beginning to understand that both Wilhelm and the New-Owenites had come to their cooperation with hidden purposes, only now coming to the surface. The possibilities alarmed her.

She tossed off her covers and reached for her bedside clock. Eleven P.M.—not late by the world's standards, but well along into the night for the Shakers, who were out of bed by 5:30 in the fall and winter months. Well, if she couldn't sleep, she might as well be up and doing something useful.

Now that she was eldress, Rose shared the Ministry House, occupying the entire second floor, while Wilhelm lived on the ground floor. A century earlier, when North Homage had peaked at two hundred Believers, two elders and two eldresses had lived in the Ministry House, eating their meals together in the small dining room, where they discussed the spiritual and often practical direction of the village. Now, for fewer than forty Believers, it was not really necessary to have both an elder and an eldress, but Rose was glad to provide a balance to the powerful, zealous Wilhelm. At times, though, she grew weary of the constant struggle. This promised to be one of those times.

During the past few months, Rose had been setting up a workshop for herself in the empty room on her floor. She rarely used it since she had very little time alone, but it was helpful for a sleepless night. She pulled a workdress over her nightgown for extra warmth and left her retiring room, carrying her journal with her.

The workshop was sparsely furnished with a small desk and ladder-back chair, an old worktable, and a lamp. The aged ironcast wood-burning stove stood off to one side, still in working order. Perhaps when this Depression ended, the Society could find the money to install a more modern heating system, but for now, and to Wilhelm's satisfaction, they had to make do with the old methods.

Rose opened the door of a cupboard recessed in the thick wall. Inside was a small pile of books she had selected for study, mostly Shaker theology from the Ministry library. However, on her way to bed that evening she'd also pulled *Robert Owen*, by Frank Podmore, and a couple of pamphlets about New Harmony that had been brought by Believers moving to North Homage after the demise of the Pleasant Hill community. She took the Owenite materials to her desk and began skimming through them.

It wasn't long before Rose understood why Wilhelm thought his plan to convert the New-Owenites might work. Like the Shakers, Robert Owen had believed deeply in the importance of communal living, doing away with private property, and granting equality to all, no matter what class or race or gender they'd been born into. He denounced traditional marriage. He believed in educating children and treating them with kindness. He even envisioned severing parental bonds and housing the children together, as the Shakers did.

Her eyelids started to droop, but she kept on reading. The more she read, the more convinced she became that Wilhelm and Gilbert were surely both fighting a losing battle. Their differences overwhelmed their similarities. In fact, as far as she could see, Robert Owen had been like Wilhelm in one respect only—they both had a yen for martyrdom. As a follower of Owen, Gilbert Griffiths would never accept the strict celibacy and profoundly religious basis of Shakerism, and Wilhelm would not give them up if he were the last Shaker left breathing. Nay, she wasn't worried about them. If anything, their fruitless struggle would keep them both occupied. However, her worry reappeared when she pondered the effects on other Believers.

The young brothers, Archibald and Matthew—had they been swayed by Gilbert's rhetoric? Was Gretchen in danger? Lottie and Frieda? All were in their mid to late twenties. All had put aside what might be strong urges for families of their own for life in the Society. Might they come to see New-Owenism as a way to live in community, work for a higher purpose, and still have families?

Rose paced across the room as disturbing thoughts came to her mind. She thought of Andrew. Might she, too, feel tempted if she were younger and less experienced? Her thoughts were reaching a fever pitch when a tentative knock on the door brought her back to her surroundings. It must be nearly midnight. Surely Wilhelm would not be on her floor at such a late hour. A telephone system connected the entire village and both floors of the Ministry House; if an emergency required her presence, he would have phoned.

"Who is it?"

"It's me, Rose." Josie peeked her head around the door. "I won't ask what you're doing up at this hour, if you'll let me in."

"I will ask what *you* are doing up and wandering about the village," Rose said, beckoning her inside.

"You know me, I'm up and about all times of the night."

"Is someone seriously ill?"

"Nay," Josie said, "but it has been an interesting night nonetheless. I saw your light on from the Infirmary, so I decided to bring you into it." She untied the top of her cloak, which she hadn't bothered to remove before dropping her round body into the largest visitor's chair.

"I've just sent Elsa back to her retiring room," Josie said. Sister Elsa Pike, an ambitious supporter of Wilhelm's, often made life difficult for Rose and the other sisters.

"I'm almost afraid to ask what she was doing at this hour," Rose said, pulling her desk chair closer to Josie.

"And so you should be. Elsa seems to have become overly concerned with our worldly visitors and their comings and goings. Apparently the New-Owenites do not keep the same hours we do. They roam about at night, meeting together and exploring the village. Elsa claims she's been following them, or some of them, to see what they're up to."

"She confided in you? That surprises me."

Josie let out a long, tired sigh. "My guess is she sees herself as Wilhelm's eyes and ears. So, nay, she did not rush to confide in me. I saw her from the Infirmary window, as I was checking on my patients. I looked out and what should I see but Elsa sneaking around the corner of the Laundry—I always know her walk. She was following two people who were heading toward the barn. I had no idea what was going on, since I couldn't see who was who in the dark, so I went outside and caught up with Elsa. Normally she would have saved her story for Wilhelm's ears, but she was bursting to tell someone who the couple she was following were. I'll admit, it did disturb me."

"What disturbed you? Who were they?" Rose dreaded the answer. North Homage had been so quiet when she'd left for the East, with no one falling into the flesh, at least that she knew of. The New-Owenites had brought the peace to an end.

"According to Elsa, it was Gretchen and a young New-Owenite fellow, I think his name is Earl. Mind you, I couldn't see them clearly myself, and I can't say I trust Elsa."

"Nor do I," Rose said, "but she may well be right. I thought they might have exchanged a special look at worship last night. I told myself it couldn't be any such thing—after all, I'm not sure they've even spoken together—but it lingered far longer than it should have, at least on his part. I hate to admit it, but Elsa may be right that our visitors are up to something. Did she see where they went?"

Josie's full cheeks blushed pink. "Well, in fact, we both did—though, as I said, I only saw their backs, and from a distance. I'm quite fond of Gretchen, you know, and she's been distracted of late. So I'm ashamed to admit that I followed them, alongside Elsa. They went into the barn. I was horrified and wanted to turn back at that point, but Elsa refused to stop, so I went with her. When we went into the barn, though, no one was there! Elsa was certain they were . . . sequestered somewhere together, but we explored the whole barn, and we didn't hear a sound."

"Did you actually see them go in the barn door?"

"We thought so. Though now I think of it, the area in front of the door was dark. We saw them walk toward the door, but then they faded into the shadows. I suppose they could have kept going around back or into the fields."

"Or on into the orchard," Rose mused. "I would never have thought to mistrust Gretchen. She has been a Believer for at least five years, since well before I became eldress, and she has always seemed at peace in North Homage. Have you ever known Gretchen to have problems here?"

"Nay, never," Josie said.

"There must be more to the story, surely. Did you and Elsa go after them any farther?"

Josie shook her head. "I must admit, I was curious, but I wasn't about to encourage Elsa to sneak around spying on the sisters. Not that she needs any encouragement. I talked her into coming back to the Infirmary with me, so I could keep an eye on her. Then I sent her along to bed."

"Just as well," Rose said. "Best to keep Elsa out of it, if we can. I'll have a talk with Gretchen. Meanwhile, we'd both better try to get some sleep."

"Amen to that," Josie said. She hoisted herself out of her chair and swung it upside down on a couple of wall pegs.

Rose gathered up the book she'd been skimming and put it back in the wall cupboard. As Josie opened the work room door, Rose said, "Josie, I was just wondering . . . I don't remember Gretchen or any of her people living in Languor, do you? Is she from this area?"

"Nay," said Josie. "I believe she came from somewhere in Indiana or Ohio, but I'm not certain. Is it important?"

"I'm not sure," Rose said.

EIGHT

"GOOD OF THEE TO TAKE TIME FOR A BREAKFAST AT THE MIN-istry House," Wilhelm said, as Rose sat in the chair across from him. She had expected him to give her a dose of irony, so she made no response. She bowed her head in prayer, silently thanking the Father and Holy Mother Wisdom for food and for the wide, strong trestle table that stood between her and Wilhelm.

Though she'd had only a few hours sleep, Rose was eager to track down all the information she could about their visitors before the situation worsened.

"I assume there is a reason for thy rare visit?" Wilhelm asked.

Rose smiled. "Have some baked apple?" She was learning, finally, to rise to his bait only when it really mattered. However, she had to admit he could still irritate her.

"I thought it would be useful for us to chat about our visitors," she said, scooping some of the sweet fruit onto her own plate.

It was Wilhelm's turn to say nothing, as he took a large bite of apple. By the time he had torn off a hunk of bread and begun slathering it with apple butter, Rose understood that she would receive no encouragement from him.

"What do you know about these New-Owenites?" she asked.

Wilhelm frowned. "All I need to. They would make good

Shakers. What is thy specific concern about them?"

"I have numerous concerns," Rose said. "But I'll start with the worship service last night. It was a disaster."

Wilhelm's bushy eyebrows drew dangerously close together, but Rose ignored the portent and continued.

"You and Gilbert Griffiths are both deluded if you think you can join our two communities. Your vision of the New-Owenites suddenly devoting themselves to the teachings of Mother Ann is as ridiculous as Gilbert's notion that somehow he can convince us to forget the faith that we breathe every moment of our lives. All you two will accomplish is a rift within both groups. Disgruntled New-Owenites might become Shakers, but unhappy Shakers will replace them. Gilbert won't change, and neither will you. What possible good can this do?"

Wilhelm took another bite of bread and chewed slowly, staring at the wall behind her. She knew there was nothing there to contemplate but her palm bonnet hanging from a wall peg. With a lazy blink, he brought his gaze to her face. His deliberateness was meant to rattle her, and to her frustration it was beginning to succeed. She steeled herself to stay calm.

"Thy faith is poor and weak," he said. "I believe that Mother Ann watches over us always. The arrival of these visitors from the world is her doing. They are meant to become Believers. They need faith, and they have been sent to us to find it. Surely that must have occurred to thee."

"But, Wilhelm, the New-Owenites are just as convinced they can turn us into their followers. Neither group will win, you must see that. It will be a constant struggle. We'll be arguing with them and with each other, and the last thing we need is to be fighting among ourselves."

Wilhelm's lips curved in a way that Rose had come to dread. "There is no need for thee to worry," he said. "The way is clear. More apple butter?"

Rose crossed the central road and walked toward the Laundry, enjoying the crisp warmth of an Indian summer morning. She was still worried about the effect of the New-Owenites on the village, but her breakfast chat with Wilhelm had set her mind at rest on one issue—he did not yet know that Sister Gretchen had been seen out at night with a man from the world. If he had known, he could not have resisted blaming Rose for Gretchen's behavior. Elsa would surely tell him soon, though, and Rose intended to be armed with knowledge if Wilhelm saw fit to confront her.

Many of the sisters worked by rotation, spending six weeks helping with the laundry, then moving on to the kitchen or the gardening, or any of a dozen other jobs. However, as Laundry deaconess, Gretchen spent most of her working time either washing the Society's clothing in the huge washing machines on the Laundry's ground floor, or drying or ironing on the top floor. It seemed grueling work to Rose, and occasionally she would offer Gretchen a different rotation, to give her a change. But Gretchen always said she was content and rather enjoyed laundry work. Rose hoped she hadn't been hiding a growing discontent with her Shaker life.

The steamy Laundry air smelled of soap and lavender rinse. Rose found Gretchen upstairs, ironing a blue Sabbathday sur-coat. The weather was still warm enough for the other laundry sisters to hang clothes to dry outdoors, a job preferable to ironing, so Gretchen was alone. She held the heavy iron poised over a sleeve as she saw Rose top the stairs.

"Has there been a problem with the laundry?" Gretchen asked. Her normally cheerful face was pinched with worry.

"Nay, the laundry is fine, as always," Rose said. "Stop a moment and talk with me." She lifted down two chairs. Gretchen watched, her iron still hovering in the air. "It's all right, Gretchen. I just want to chat with you." Rose had never felt so aware before of Gretchen's youth; she couldn't be more than twenty-five or twenty-six. She was so competent and devoted, she seemed much older. But now she looked young and frightened.

"Elsa saw us, didn't she." Gretchen up-ended the iron and slid into the chair next to Rose. "She was hinting like crazy this morning before we went in to breakfast, so I'm not surprised you found out. Does Wilhelm know?"

"Not yet, though I'm sure he will soon. Let me help you, Gretchen. Tell me what there is to know, and I'll see what I can do to shield you."

"I'd like this to be my confession," Gretchen said, sitting straight in her chair.

Rose nodded her assent, and Gretchen took a few moments to compose herself. No matter what was coming, Rose was grateful it would be revealed without too much fuss. Now that she was eldress, she was learning to handle torrents of tears, but she surely did not regret their absence.

"I do not make a habit of speaking to men alone at night, I want you to understand that," Gretchen began. "But I confess that I did so yesterday. I had no idea Elsa would be out spying on me, instead of in her own bed." Her voice hardened.

"Leave Elsa to me."

"Of course, I'm sorry. This is my confession, and my own behavior deserves reproach. I met with a man from the world, alone, after dark. But that is all I did, Rose, truly."

"Who is the man, Gretchen?"

Gretchen's right hand began kneading the fingers of her left hand, as if in soothing reminder of rubbing a stain out of cloth. "It's not what you think, Rose."

Gretchen bit her lower lip, increasing Rose's fear that "it" was even worse than she'd thought.

"He . . . the man I was talking to . . . Gretchen closed her eyes and inhaled deeply. "It was Earl Weston. We grew up together. We were the best of friends. Over time our friendship . . . well, we were engaged to be married." A pleading note slipped into her voice. "You were engaged once, weren't you, Rose? During your time in the world? You understand. We broke the engagement years and years ago, but he was a special part of my life, and I can't just forget that. I know I should, but I can't. When I saw him again . . ." Gretchen frowned at the floor as if it were responsible for her misery.

"Seeing him again stirred old feelings?" Rose asked.

"Nay, I promise, those feelings are gone. My heart belongs to Mother Ann and the Society, yet . . . I suppose there is a little piece of it that still belongs to him. Can you understand that?"

"Yea, I do understand," Rose said. And she did. "Is that why you met with him? Because that little piece of your heart called to him?"

"Because I thought I could do some good."

Rose raised her eyebrows in a question.

"Earl was a good man," Gretchen said. "I hated to see him so involved with those Godless people. He wasn't like that when I knew him. He refused to become a Shaker, but he was still a believer. Now it hurts my heart to listen to him talk. He thinks God is a lie, and faith is just ignorant superstition."

"So you hoped to convince him otherwise?"

Gretchen nodded.

"And was he receptive?"

"Nay." Gretchen grimaced. "He tried very hard to convince me that *I* was wrong to believe as I do."

"Did he attempt to convert you to his way of thinking?"

"Well, a little, maybe. But there's no need for you to worry on my account, Rose. I would never leave. You know that, don't you?"

Rose was silent for a moment. She was fairly certain that Gretchen was devoted; that wasn't what worried her. Gretchen was indeed unlikely to leave. But would Earl Weston know that?

"You mustn't see him again," Rose said.

Gretchen looked stricken. "But he was such a good friend, and I want so to help him."

"Just as he wants to help you. Don't you see it is pointless? You won't change your mind, nor will he change his, but neither of you will give up, so you'll argue until even the good memories of your friendship are gone. And you will be setting a bad example for the other sisters. What good could possibly come from seeing him again, even in broad daylight?"

"He trusts me," Gretchen said.

"But what does that—"

"He tells me things."

"What things?" Rose felt her hopes stir.

"About his people, those New-Owenites. I know you are

worried about Hugh Griffiths' suicide—whether it really was a suicide. After hearing Earl talk, I think you are right to worry. Those folks aren't the close friends they pretend to be, and Hugh wasn't as liked as everyone says."

Rose leaned forward. "Tell me exactly what Earl told you."

Gretchen leaned, also, her misery blotted out by eagerness to share a good story. "He said that Celia didn't really love Hugh. She only married him to be near Gilbert, who only cares about his ideas. Hugh was besotted with her, though, and he was terribly jealous because he was convinced that Celia and Gilbert were . . . together." Gretchen paused in her enthusiasm to look embarrassed, but it didn't last. "Earl was trying to prove to me that men and women should be able to just change around and divorce and remarry all they want, and then there wouldn't be this sort of jealousy. Of course, I told him it only proved that men and women are much better off not marrying at all!"

Rose was torn between pride in Gretchen and alarm that the conversation had become so intimate. She was also, she had to admit, grateful for the information. So she swallowed her reprimand and asked, "Did he mention anything else?"

"Nay, nothing in particular," Gretchen said with obvious regret. "But I could find more out."

"Gretchen!"

"I only meant . . . Rose, you must know I wouldn't break my vows. I'll keep my ears open, and I'll let you know immediately if I hear anything more about our visitors."

Rose still felt uneasy, but she decided to leave Gretchen's behavior to her conscience. Surely she had learned her lesson.

Rose trusted Gretchen's intentions, but not Earl Weston's understanding of the need for distance between them. She lost no time in tracking Earl down. One of the brethren had seen him enter the West Dwelling House, another of North Homage's unoccupied buildings. *It must be pleasant to have the leisure to wander around aimlessly,* she thought, as she climbed the wooden steps to the single front door. She was not in the most tolerant of moods.

The unused dwelling house was cold and dim inside, and Rose entered carefully, not sure what condition it might be in. Eight or nine years earlier, the brethren had begun renovations, hoping to turn the house into a shop for Shaker goods, but times had gotten too bad, both for the Shakers and for their customers.

Rose left the door ajar to admit fresh air and some light. She'd hoped to find Earl near the front of the house, but sounds from just overhead told her he was on the second floor. Reluctantly, she left the circle of light and climbed the stairs, holding fast to the railing, just in case. But the brethren must have been keeping an eye on the building, because the staircase was sound.

The old pine steps were creaky enough that she was sure Earl would be at the top to greet her, but the hallway was empty when she reached it. She went directly to the room she'd heard footsteps in, a retiring room on the east side. The door hung open. Earl stood at the window, which gave him a panoramic view of most of the village of North Homage, as well as the acres and acres of land beyond.

"It's a breathtaking sight, isn't it?" Rose said.

Earl whirled around so fast that he stumbled back against the deep window frame. Unable to steady himself in time, he sat with a plunk on the wide sill.

Earl stared at Rose as if he couldn't place her. He couldn't be much older than Gretchen, if they'd been childhood pals, but he looked closer to forty. Unlike the Griffiths cousins, he was taller than average. Rose supposed he might be considered handsome, but the telltale signs of a dissolute life had already added extra inches to his girth and dark pockets under his eyes, which were deep brown and hard to read. Rose must have given him a severe shock, because his breathing was rapid and red splotches formed on his already florid face.

"I'm sorry, I didn't mean to frighten you so. I've no idea what shape those sills are in."

Earl stood up and rearranged his expression into one of affability. "I'm fine, just fine. Rose, is it? You just startled me, is all. I, uh, was having a look-see around the house, just out of curiosity. If I may ask, why aren't you using this place?" He scanned the large, empty room as if he could already see it filled with elegant, and probably expensive, furniture.

"You may have noticed when you entered that this dwelling house has only one door," Rose said. "Decades ago, when we were a much larger community, this was where our gathering order lived—people who had not signed the covenant. Since they were still outside the faith, they lived apart from the Shaker families, and took care of their own affairs. Some of them decided to sign the covenant, but others never did. Such folks just don't show up much anymore. It's wasteful to keep this dwelling habitable for one or two people."

Rose didn't go on to tell him about their various other plans for the house. After asking his question, he'd seemed to lose interest, inspecting the woodwork instead of looking at her as she spoke.

"I came to find you for a purpose, Mr. Weston," she said.

His attention snapped back to her face. "Oh? Is there anything I can do for you?"

"Yea," Rose said, "you can stay away from my sisters."

"Your sisters? I don't think I . . ." The splotching reappeared, and he gazed down at the dusty floor. "I see," he said. "You're talking about Gretchen. I meant no harm, I assure you."

"I'll accept your assurances, Mr. Weston, but I must insist that it never happen again. Will you promise me that?"

"I wouldn't dream of causing problems for Gretchen, I was only . . . well, she's an old friend, you see."

"I know all about that."

"Ah. Well, I'm glad you brought this to my attention." He was edging toward the door. "I certainly understand. If you'll excuse me, I promised to meet with Gilbert." He was out the door and thudding down the stairs so fast Rose had no chance to respond. From the window, she saw him trudge through the dormant Kentucky bluegrass toward the South Family Dwelling House. He was halfway there before she realized that he had not actually promised to stay away from Gretchen.

NINE

DURING THE SILENCE OF THE NOON MEAL, ROSE HAD TIME TO gather her thoughts. Gretchen's tidbits about the Griffiths sparked her curiosity. She wanted to find out more, as fast as possible. However, she did not dare say so to Gretchen, who would surely conclude she had permission to talk again with Earl Weston. The Griffiths themselves would probably be secretive, if she were to ask them her questions directly. She could talk to Matthew and Archibald, but no doubt Wilhelm would consider her questioning the brethren an invasion of his responsibility. Still, it might be worth a rebuke.

The gentle slurping of soup and an occasional sniffle were the only sounds in the Center Family dining room. Across the room at the brethren's table, two heads were not bobbing over their soup bowls—Matthew and Archibald leaned slightly toward each other as if whispering a message. Rose noted that the chairs on either side of them were occupied by Earl Weston and Gilbert Griffiths.

Archibald nodded. As his wide, round face turned forward, he caught Rose staring at him. His gaze dropped to his plate. Matthew seemed not to have noticed. Rose made her decision—she would question them.

The brethren were first to finish their meal, and they left silently. Rose squirmed with impatience. As soon as the last morsel at the sisters' table had been eaten—by Elsa, as usual—Rose placed her napkin over her empty plate and stood. All the sisters—and, more slowly, the New-Owenite women—followed her lead.

As Rose lifted her chair and swung it upside down onto its wall pegs, she noticed that one of the front rungs was cracked. She remembered that the stool in the kitchen, the one she had plunked Mairin on top of, had been in need of repair, too. Why shouldn't she bring them to the attention of the brethren at the Carpenters' Shop? Surely that would not irritate Wilhelm.

The sisters who had sat on benches pushed them under the table and waited as the others re-hung their chairs. They all followed Rose from the room, silent and in single-file. The chattering began as soon as they emerged into the sunshine and parted for their afternoon work assignments. Rose took advantage of her long legs to scurry ahead and avoid conversation as she made for the Carpenters' Shop.

Matthew and Archibald were deep in their work by the time Rose opened the shop door. She noted, with disapproval, that they were also deep in wood chips and shavings, which they had not cleaned up from the morning and probably before that, as well.

Both men glanced up at her, then went back to their tasks. They were mending and refinishing furniture, and other pieces lay about the workroom, in various stages of disrepair. All the objects were old, some probably dating back a century or more, when the Shakers made most of their own furniture and tools, often developing new, more efficient designs. Archibald smoothed the nicks out of an oval candle stand, the tip of his tongue protruding from his mouth. Matthew's long, thin fingers worked at the more difficult repair of a table swift with a cracked slat. Rose knew the weaving sisters still used table swifts to wind yarn into balls, but surely they had several newer, unused ones in storage in the Sisters' Shop.

"I see you are mending one of those lovely old maple candle stands," she said to Archibald, whom she knew to be the more pliable of the two brethren. "We don't use them so much anymore, do we?"

Archibald started when she spoke, and he took several moments after she'd finished to digest her words. Though he was a young man, no more than twenty, his face looked puffy, as if he were unhealthy or not sleeping well. Matthew paused to listen.

"Some want 'em again, I guess," Archibald said.

"Oh really? Who?"

Archibald shrugged. Matthew bent again over the new slat he was shaping.

"Did Wilhelm suggest that you fix these old things?"

"Yea," Archibald said. He cast a furtive glance at Matthew.

"They are such wonderful pieces," Rose said. "I'm glad to see them used again. You are bringing that table to a lovely shine, Archibald."

"Thank you, Eldress." Archibald flashed a quick, nervous smile, clearly pleased. For once, he showed no need to check his response with Matthew. Rose wanted a chance to talk with Archibald alone, and she had an idea.

"Matthew," she said, "there are a couple of repairs that need to be done in the Family Center Dwelling House."

"We'll get to them later."

"I know you're busy, but I was hoping you could go over now and at least retrieve the items. I believe they might be unsafe to sit on, and they are both in frequent use." Rose explained the cracks in the chair and stool, knowing that only Matthew had the skill to assess and complete such repairs. "If you could even just take time to examine them—you would know better than I how dangerous they really are."

Rose had reached for just the right combination of deference and command, and apparently she'd succeeded. Without a word, Matthew put down his work and left, surly but obedient. He would likely give the items a cursory look and carry them back to the Carpenters' Shop. She had perhaps fifteen minutes.

As soon as she was sure Matthew was out of earshot, Rose turned to Archibald, who watched the door with the panic of an abandoned puppy.

"I'd love to see what you are doing," Rose said brightly. "How are you getting the wood so smooth?"

The fear faded from Archibald's face as he ran his hand

over the top of the candle stand. "I just keep at it, is all," he said, with a touch of pride.

"Do you think Wilhelm might use it himself?"

Archibald shook his head. "What he told us was, we needed to get all the old stuff fixed up for the South Family Dwelling House."

"You mean the building our visitors are staying in?"

"Yea."

"But there are only seven of them now, and they will be leaving soon, won't they? Is Wilhelm hoping to use the dwelling house for future guests?" With anyone else, Rose would worry she was giving the impression that she and Wilhelm never consulted one another, but Archibald was unlikely to notice anything amiss.

Archibald looked confused for a moment, then brightened. "Elder Wilhelm said them folks might stay," he said.

"Stay? Do you mean, permanently?"

"I guess."

So Wilhelm was certain he could convert the New-Owenites en masse to Shakerism. He was so confident that he had begun to furnish a dwelling house for them to live in. Rose wondered if the New-Owenites were aware of the steps being taken for their future.

"Archibald, you've had dealings with our guests, so let me ask you. What do you think of them?" Rose asked.

"What do you mean?"

Rose hesitated. Questions to Archibald would have to be simple, so she needed to be sure what she was after. "Do you believe they are good people or bad people?"

"Oh, good people, very good. Gilbert is really nice, and Celia is mighty pretty."

"And Hugh? I was gone until Monday evening, so I never got to meet him. What was he like?"

"He was a nice man. He used to talk to me a lot."

"Oh? What did you talk about?"

Archibald looked scared and guilty and confused, as if he might have broken a vow but wasn't sure. "Well," he said, "I guess it was about learning and religion and such." He smiled shyly. "Hugh said I was smarter than I thought, and I ought to get some learning. I only went through the second grade, and once I come here, I was too old to get more schooling."

"Would you like more schooling?"

Archibald nodded. "But there ain't much chance of that. Matthew says I'm too slow. Second grade's about the best I could do."

"We can arrange for more schooling, Archibald. Matthew just isn't aware of that. You could take a few hours a week to study with one of the brethren. Would you like me to talk to Wilhelm about it?"

Archibald's face lit up, and he nodded vigorously.

"Then I'll do so at the first opportunity," Rose said. "Is that what Hugh suggested? That you ask for more learning?"

Archibald frowned in concentration. "Sort of," he said. "But Hugh said I'd never get more learning with the Shakers, and I could come to him if that's what I really wanted. He said he'd give me lessons. Matthew said he'd give me some time away from the shop to do my learning, even though he didn't think it would make much difference."

So Matthew was encouraging contact between Archibald and the New-Owenites, even at the expense of work. Rose wondered just what Matthew's own ties with the group might be. "Did Matthew say why he thought you should study with Hugh?"

Archibald grimaced, as if trying to remember. "Well, just that Hugh was smart and a good person to know. I wanted him to help me be smarter. I always wished I'd've been born smarter. That's why my ma and pa left me here, because I couldn't pick up schooling like my brothers, and they figured I wasn't smart enough to be on my own." Archibald's tone was matter-of-fact, as though he thought it understandable that his parents would abandon him to strangers rather than go to the trouble of raising a slow child.

"Did you spend any time in lessons with Hugh?" Rose asked.

Archibald looked guilty. "Yea, some. You won't tell Wilhelm, will you? Matthew said Wilhelm shouldn't know."

"Nay, I won't tell Wilhelm, but I urge you to consider confessing to him yourself." It was the right thing to do—and it wouldn't hurt if Wilhelm began to understand that conversion can work both ways.

Archibald nodded and averted his eyes. Rose doubted he'd ever work up the courage to confess to Wilhelm.

"What did Hugh teach you?" she asked.

Archibald brightened. "Well, mostly he would tell me how I could've been smarter if I'd've been raised up in a different place, but I can still get smarter anyway." Archibald seemed unaware of how insulting to the Shakers Hugh's words had been.

"We only had two real lessons," Archibald said. "He told me about some rocks and plants and . . ." The guilty look returned. With jerky motions, Archibald started pushing around the woodworking tools on the workbench.

"It's all right," Rose said. "You can tell me anything Hugh said, and I won't be angry or upset, I promise. Just tell the truth, and God will smile on you."

Archibald hunched on a stool, and his broad face puckered as if he might cry. Instead, he took a deep breath and said, "Hugh was really nice to me, but sometimes I didn't understand what he was saying. Like when he talked about Wilhelm—you and Wilhelm."

"What did he say about us?" Rose's voice was sharper than she'd intended, and Archibald flinched. "I'm not angry with you; I'm sorry if it sounded that way," she added, softening her voice.

"That's okay. It's just I think what he said was really bad, but I didn't understand it. I wish I were smarter."

"You're fine as God made you," Rose said. She fought to control her impatience. "Can you remember the words he used?"

Archibald frowned. "Sort of. He said that we weren't being treated like real Americans."

"How? How were you not being treated as Americans?"

"He said it was y'all, you and Wilhelm, and the Lead Ministry. Y'all just took over, he said, without a 'lection."

Rose puzzled through Archibald's words, her mind searching for meaning.

"Did he mean . . . an election?" she asked.

"Yea," said Archibald, with a broad smile. "I knew you'd understand." His smile faded. "What's a e-lection?"

"It's when people vote for who they want to be their leaders."

Archibald nodded, but the crease between his eyebrows told Rose he was still confused. Perhaps Hugh had been right that the Shakers had failed Archibald, Rose thought. He knew so little; perhaps they had given up on him too quickly, assuming he would always be secure in the Society. She would talk to Wilhelm about some special lessons for Archibald.

Meanwhile, she had her answer. The New-Owenites were trying to discredit the Shaker leadership. Celia had intimated to the sisters that Rose and Wilhelm might be living in the flesh together, and Hugh had openly criticized them for not being elected democratically. Rose wondered how democratic Gilbert Griffiths' ascension to leadership had been.

Rose had just left the Carpenters' Shop when she decided a walk through the nearby maple grove would give her a chance to think. She spun around and headed back past the side of the shop. The rasping sound of wood being sanded reached her through an open window. It was good to hear woodworking sounds again.

"Off for a leisurely stroll?" said an all-too-familiar voice behind her. She turned with reluctance to find Wilhelm and Matthew walking through the grass toward her. Matthew was empty-handed. Of course, Rose thought, Matthew never had any intention of fixing broken chairs. He wanted to get rid of her influence, and the easiest way to do that was to fetch Wilhelm. Rose stood her ground and waited as the men approached.

"The sisters should keep thee busy enough," Wilhelm said. "There is no need to waste thy time giving work orders to the brethren. A word in my ear would have sufficed to get those chairs fixed."

Years of living in the same community as Wilhelm had taught Rose that to explain herself was to add kindling to his fire. She waited in silence.

Wilhelm crossed his arms over his thick chest. "Or was thy purpose in visiting the Carpenters' Shop more subtle? Matthew tells me thy questions were critical of our visitors. When he tried not to encourage thy gossip, he was sent away."

"Is that what he told you?"

Matthew stood a few steps back from Wilhelm, shifting from one foot to another. He stiffened as Rose glanced at him.

This time, Wilhelm said nothing, and Rose let the silence stretch on. Matthew removed his broad-brimmed work hat and replaced it in the same movement. "Elder," he said, "I got a lot of work to do, so if you don't need me here . . ."

Wilhelm started, as if he'd forgotten the brother's presence. "I'll handle this, thank you, Matthew. By all means, hands to work . . . and hearts to God," he finished, in an undertone only Rose could hear.

Matthew took off at a trot, and Rose steeled herself for an argument with Wilhelm. He no longer intimidated her, but neither did she enjoy these sparring matches. She decided to take the lead.

"I, too, have much work to do," she said, "and I haven't time for a long chat. If you have a concern, speak your piece."

Rose wasn't normally curt with Wilhelm, and he took a few moments to recover. But recover he did.

"Need I remind thee that the New-Owenites are our guests, and—"

"They are *your* guests," Rose said, "not mine. I was not consulted."

"Thine absence, of course, made it—"

"My absence made it easier for you to direct the village as you saw fit, without my interference. These New-Owenites seem to have caused nothing but trouble since they arrived. They roam around the village at will, turning Believers away from their faith, stirring up discontent, and for all we know, killing one another under our eyes. It is time for them to leave."

Rose didn't flinch as Wilhelm's jaw tightened and his fists clenched. Let him struggle to keep his vow of nonviolence. It would be good for his soul. Within moments, however, Wilhelm's muscles relaxed, and Rose's confidence oozed away. She felt herself tighten as if the tension had shifted from his body to hers.

"It might interest thee to know," he said, "that Hugh Griffiths' death was most certainly a suicide." His lips bent into the shadow of a smile. "His cousin found a suicide note in Hugh's room, while packing up his belongings. So thy suspicions are false. Our visitors have suffered a tragedy, but it is Hugh alone who must answer to God for his sin. The others are merely trying to accept their loss and carry on with their higher purpose."

Rose was so filled with questions that she thought she might burst before sorting them out. The triumphant glint in Wilhelm's eyes wasn't helping.

"How do you know it was the suicide note?" she finally managed to ask. "Why didn't Hugh bring it with him to the orchard?"

Wilhelm shrugged. "Who can explain the actions of lost souls? Perhaps he made and unmade his mind several times before the deed. But suicide was plainly in his mind."

"What did the note say? I want to see it."

"As to that, I'm afraid I can't satisfy thy curiosity by offering thee a peek at the note. Gilbert took it at once to Sheriff Brock, after phoning me from the South Family Dwelling House. He read me the note. It was obviously written by a man bent on destroying himself, but I paid no attention to the actual words."

Too angry to trust herself to speak, Rose spun away from Wilhelm and headed toward the South Family Dwelling House. Wilhelm may have had the last word, but he couldn't stop her from finding out all she could about that note.

TEN

CELIA SHRUGGED HER WELL-SHAPED SHOULDERS. "SORRY, CAN'T help you. Gilbert's the only one of us who saw Hugh's note, and he's gone off to Languor to deliver it personally to the Sheriff's Office." With a quick and dancerlike grace, she swung herself onto a ladder-back chair and crossed her trouser-clad legs in one smooth movement. Bright sunlight shone through the parlor windows of the South Family Dwelling House and on Celia's blue-black hair. If she was a grieving widow, she hid it well.

"When did Gilbert leave?"

"Oh, I'd say about an hour ago, but he won't be back until sometime tomorrow, probably late. He had some errands or something."

"Did he show you the note?"

"Nope." Celia arched her foot and examined the toe of her red leather shoe.

"I suppose he thought it might be too upsetting for you," Rose said.

"Well, yes, as a matter of fact," Celia said, squaring her shoulders. "I certainly didn't want to see the thing. It's bad enough that Hugh would do such a thing to me. I don't need to read his feeble excuses." Celia glided to her feet and shook her trouser legs straight. "I'm feeling bushed. I'm going to lie down for a time."

As Celia reached for the parlor door, Rose said, "Mairin

seems to be doing tolerably well. I thought you'd want to know."

Celia spun around. A faint flush on her cheeks was the first sign she'd shown of emotion. Likely it was guilt, Rose guessed. Surely Celia regretted her callousness toward the child.

"Yeah, thanks," Celia said.

"She seems to be eating well," Rose said.

"I can imagine." One of Celia's perfectly shaped eyebrows arched above a crystalline blue eye.

"I suppose you've had to work with her quite a bit—to help with her eating, I mean." Rose chose her words with great care. In the long run, information would help her more than the brief satisfaction she might get from taking Celia to task for her apparent neglect of Mairin.

"Hah! As if it helped. I saw right away how hopeless that child was, but I tried my best. There was no point in subjecting others to her at meal time; she was such a pig, we'd all have lost our appetites."

"So you took your meals alone with her?"

Celia's other eyebrow joined the first. "I have to eat, too, you know. I had someone bring her some food—when she was even there. Most of the time, she was out running around who knows where, and we had to throw the food away." Celia yawned and stretched. She made for the parlor door, then stopped and turned back to Rose. Both eyebrows were back in place.

"Is Mairin . . . has she said anything yet about—you know, whether she saw what happened to Hugh?"

"Nay, she has said nothing."

"So maybe she really didn't see anything?"

"Perhaps." So Celia's real concern was not for Mairin, Rose thought, as she watched the slender figure sway from the room. Celia had figured out that Mairin might be a witness. She'd used the phrase "what *happened* to Hugh." That didn't sound quite like a reference to suicide. Did she have reason to fear what Mairin might have seen?

* * *

"The Sheriff? Lemme check, Miss Callahan." The telephone receiver clanked as the officer dropped it to go look for Sheriff Brock.

Rose scanned the room while she waited. She was alone in the South Family parlor and had been surprised to find the phone hooked up, as if the residents were expected to stay and conduct business from home. Moreover, the parlor was well furnished. At least half of the wall pegs encircling the room had been put to use holding ladder-back chairs, a flat broom, small bookshelves, and a moveable cabinet. A long wool coat, clearly a design from the world, hung crookedly from a peg as if tossed from a distance. Her gaze paused at a table in the corner. It was littered with books and magazines, so she couldn't be sure, but it looked oval in shape.

Clattering over the phone line was followed by throat clearing. "Uh, Miss Callahan? The Sheriff ain't able to talk right now. Important meeting. Take all afternoon, more'n likely. You might try back tomorrow."

Rose wasn't surprised. "Fine," she said. "And perhaps you could ask him to call me if he gets done early with his meeting." She knew he wouldn't, of course.

"Yeah, sure thing."

"Before you go, would you be kind enough to see if Deputy O'Neal is available?"

"Nah, Grady's off on family business or something for a few days."

"He's at home with his family?"

"Lexington, I think. Or Louisville. Can't remember right offhand." After a pause, he added, "I'll be sure and mention you called, when he's back."

"Thank you," Rose said, as the receiver clicked.

She hadn't really expected help from the world, of course, and she loved being a Shaker, but sometimes she wished Wilhelm didn't toil ceaselessly to remind the world of their differences. At his insistence, they had reverted to nineteenth century dress and the old forms of dancing worship, all to avoid being absorbed by a world which viewed them as those strange people who lived all together but never married, who went into trances and worshiped a woman.

Rose had no time for dejection. She needed to clear her head. She untied her thin white indoor cap, shook out her tangled mass of red curls, and stuffed them back into the cap. As she tied it snugly at the nape of her neck, the table in the corner caught her eye again. She walked over to it.

Of course, she thought, as she lifted up a stack of books, *it's one of the old oval candle stands—like the one Archibald had been sanding in the Carpenters' Shop.* She ran her fingertips across the smooth surface. Recently restored.

Rose circled the room, touching the pieces hanging from wall pegs. All were very old, but beautiful, carefully repaired and refinished. The room was filled with such treasures. Matthew and Archibald must have been working on them steadily ever since the New-Owenites first arrived.

A small, round side table held an oval box, freshly painted in forest green. Rose picked it up. Of the oval boxes made by Shakers decades earlier, many had become cracked or warped through extensive use. This one was still lovely, its seams tight and the swallowtail joints smooth. She held it upside down. The lid stayed on—a snug fit, as it should be.

Rose set the box back on the table; with a spark of guilt, she grabbed it again and slid off the lid. There was nothing inside. She didn't know what she'd been expecting, but it wasn't this. Believers used oval boxes for storing small items—buttons, sewing implements, herbs—but never just for decoration. *This box is not empty,* Rose thought, as she replaced the lid and arranged the box on the table. *It holds the vast distance between us and the world.* Wilhelm was blind if he thought he could ever turn these people into true Shakers.

A creaking in the floor above her head reminded Rose that she'd stayed alone in the parlor far too long for easy explanation. She retied her cloak and slipped out the door.

*   *   *

The schoolhouse door burst open to lively children like a dandelion releasing its seeds to the wind. The Languor children raced to their waiting parents, while the Shaker children, only slightly more restrained, twirled and skipped in the grass in playful imitation of Shaker dancing. They slowed down as Charlotte emerged, followed by a somber Mairin.

Rose watched the girl move through the grass, her hair puffed around her expressionless face. What memories hid behind those striking eyes? Were they buried so deep they could never come to the surface?

Mairin looked across the lawn and saw Rose. She gave a faint smile and changed course, now walking toward Rose at the same deliberate pace.

"Let's go for a walk, shall we?" Rose suggested, as the girl approached. Mairin placed her hand in Rose's outstretched one.

"You aren't cold, are you? Good, then we needn't go back for our cloaks and miss any sunlight. I want to show you some of the herbs we have planted around the village. Do you know what an herb is?"

Mairin nodded but did not elaborate.

Rose let the silence rest between them as she led the way past the west side of the Trustees' Office and toward a wooded area. A narrow path wound among the thick trees. Mairin showed no fear as they left the sunlight behind. They came to a meandering creek, where they stopped.

"This area has been special to us Shakers for a long time," Rose said. "Just off that direction is a hill that is holy to us. Many years ago we used to gather there for feast days, when we would worship for hours on end."

Mairin stared up at Rose as if she were speaking an unintelligible language.

"Sometimes we would speak to the angels and receive special gifts from them."

Mairin's expression took on a hint of animation.

"Do you know who the angels are?" Rose asked.

"Mama used to talk to angels," Mairin said. "They're little

people, aren't they? Mama said they were special, and I couldn't see them, so I thought they must be really little." Her eyes lit up. "Am I an angel? Is that why I'm so little?"

Rose's heart was not behaving normally. She dropped down on the grass beside the girl. She wanted to throw her arms around Mairin, but instinct told her the gesture might be alarming.

"Someday," Rose said, "I've no doubt you will be an angel. But for now you are a girl who has suffered enough for a lifetime. You lost your mama and your papa far too young, and you have gone without for too long."

For a moment, the mask cracked open. Mairin's features twisted, and her eyes flashed like hot metal before filling with tears. The reaction was gone so fast, Rose wondered if she'd imagined it. A few blinks, and the tears vanished, along with the startling array of emotions.

Mairin skittered away without a word. By the time Rose had pushed to her feet, the girl was leaning close to a small plant that was enjoying a narrow ray of late-day sunlight in a clearing. It was one of the few plants that hadn't given up and turned brown as winter approached.

"Nay, Mairin, you mustn't!" Rose cried, as the child broke off a stem and began to rip off the leaves with her teeth.

"It's okay," Mairin said, still chewing. "I've eaten this before."

Rose reached her side and recognized the plants as sage, an edible perennial, and a pungent one. She was surprised Mairin was willing to eat it.

"Do you know the name of this plant?" she asked.

Mairin shook her head.

"It's called sage. If you didn't know what it was, how did you know you could eat it?"

"Is it suppertime yet? I'm really hungry."

"Mairin, did someone tell you it was safe to eat this?"

"I can figure things out. I don't need someone to tell me."

"Do you understand how dangerous it is to eat plants when

you don't know what they are? Now please tell me, how did you know this would not make you sick?"

"Because it didn't. I tried a little, and I was fine. If a little bit makes me sick, I don't eat it again."

Rose sank to her knees and, this time, gave in to the impulse to fold Mairin in her arms. The girl neither responded nor resisted. Rose released her, but held her by the shoulders and looked in her eyes.

"Tell me truly, Mairin. How much time do you spend outdoors?"

"Oh, lots. That's how I know about what to eat. I get hungry."

"Didn't Celia and Hugh ever come looking for you? Didn't they worry?"

Mairin shrugged and pointed to another nearby plant, a wild bergamot. "I can eat that one, too," she said.

"Mairin, listen to me." Rose took the girl by the shoulders. "Bad things happen to everybody. Bad things happen even when you haven't done anything wrong. Sometimes, people are just mean to others, to people who don't deserve to be treated meanly. Do you have any idea what I'm talking about?"

Mairin hung her head as if she'd been caught in a lie. Rose released the girl's shoulders with a frustrated sigh. She searched her mind for other words, other phrases that Mairin might understand better. Her mind went blank.

She began to back away from the girl, then changed her mind and slid her arm around the small shoulders. She pulled Mairin close and whispered in her ear. "You will surely be an angel someday. You are good, I promise you." She made a silent prayer to Holy Mother Wisdom to help Mairin believe and trust her before it was too late.

ELEVEN

"ROSE, CAN I TELL YOU SOMETHING IN SECRET?" NORA glanced sidelong at her retiring room door, through which Mairin had just left.

"Of course you can, Nora. It will take Mairin a few minutes to freshen up for the evening meal. Go ahead."

Nora closed the door and seemed to relax a little. She settled herself cross-legged on her bed, and Rose perched on the side, next to her.

"What's the problem?"

"It's Mairin. I'm worried about her." Though two years younger, Nora had appointed herself Mairin's guardian. "She has terrible, awful nightmares. Last night she woke me up twice."

"Did you ask her what the dreams were about?" Rose tried not to appear too eager.

"Well . . . first I listened for a while, but all she said was, 'No, no, no!' So I shook her and she woke up, but she said she didn't remember what she was dreaming, which didn't make sense to me, 'cause I always remember my dreams when I first wake up, 'specially the bad ones, but Mairin said she didn't remember a thing." Nora cocked her head to one side. "She seems awfully sad a lot, doesn't she? She hardly ever wants to play. I wish I could get her to play more."

Rose laughed and tousled Nora's short-cropped blond hair. "You're doing just fine, Mother Nora. You did right to tell me this. I'll see what I can do to help her. Meanwhile, keep an eye on her, okay?"

It had been dark for hours when Rose slipped out of the Ministry House. Wilhelm's ground floor retiring room was far enough back that she hoped she wouldn't waken him. She'd rather not have to explain her actions to Wilhelm, who already viewed her as lost to the world.

Her long wool cloak and heavy palm bonnet felt good against the damp chill. All other Believers were in bed by now, exhausted by long hours of work, so the buildings housing them were dark and quiet, as was the path through the middle of the village. Times being what they were, North Homage didn't waste money on outdoor lamps. Shakers weren't expected to be out after dark, anyway.

Rose couldn't help a twinge of guilt, but it didn't stop her. Up ahead, to the left of the central path, stood the South Family Dwelling House, its entire ground floor ablaze with light. The New-Owenites clearly weren't worried about the Shakers' electricity costs.

As she walked the path to the women's entrance, Rose whispered a less-than-wholehearted prayer for patience. She was keyed up for a fight. It was one thing to provide succor for visitors from the world, but quite another to sit back and let them stir up trouble as they ate up your stores and drained your cash.

Rose entered the building without knocking. After all, the dwelling house belonged to the Shakers. Her plan was to corner Celia for a private talk about Mairin. The hallway was empty and so was the parlor. A rumble came from behind the closed doors of the family meeting room.

An eruption of angry voices interrupting each other drew Rose a few steps closer to the meeting room doors. She struggled with herself. Listening outside closed doors was appalling behavior for any Shaker, and hardly a good example for an eldress to set. Yet, if these visitors were up to something that

might involve her village—and it seemed as if they were—
Rose needed to know.

She headed for a rear staircase as her mind flashed back
more than two decades to her early adolescence. She was four-
teen, had just finished her Shaker schooling, and was ready to
begin work rotations, helping the sisters. Agatha wanted her
to try everything at least once, so she'd worked several times
with the South Family, spending one of the rotations in this
very building.

The South Family Dwelling House had a special feature,
the brainstorm of a South Family kitchen sister. She'd known
of the Laundry, where steam from the boiler was piped upstairs to racks so clothes could be dried indoors during foul
weather. The sister had wondered if the same principle could
be used to direct excess heat generated in the kitchen, located
in the basement level, up to the room above—the family meeting room. Her idea had worked beautifully to keep the meeting
room toasty during winter evening union meetings and family
worship services.

One night, Rose and one kitchen sister had worked late
because the kitchen needed more cleaning. Since work was a
form of worship for Believers, they'd decided to skip the service. That's when they discovered that the heating pipes went
both ways—heat drifted upstairs, and sound came downstairs.
The kitchen crew was able to sing along with the service and
even fit in a few dance steps.

Rose was fairly certain no one was around to hear as she
hurried down the old wooden stairs to the basement, but she
trod quietly anyway. A door at the bottom, slightly ajar, led
into the dim kitchen. One light had been left on, and Rose
saw why—for the casual snackers who must be frequent visitors. The kitchen was a shambles, by Shaker standards. A
stained, filthy cloth hung over the worktable, which was piled
with dirty crockery and utensils, dried hunks of cheese, bread
crumbs, and several open jars of Shaker preserves. Pans caked
with grease spilled over the edges of the sink, rather than
hanging, clean and shiny, from the wall pegs. In fact, only one

item still hung, unused, from a wall peg—the flat broom.

Rose couldn't stifle a grunt of disgust as she picked her way across the sticky floor to the heat pipes. She would deal with this mess later, since Wilhelm obviously did not concern himself with his guests' living habits.

By now, Rose's anger had bubbled near its boiling point. She felt that Mother Ann and every last angel would forgive her eavesdropping, and if they didn't, she would just have to pay the price. She would not allow her community to be tromped on by these strangers. If she had to defy Wilhelm, she would do so. But first she needed to know what was happening in this dwelling house.

She brushed some crumbs off a chair and pulled it close to the heating pipes. The voices were clear enough, and she hoped to identify speakers, if she could. The more she knew about each of them, the better.

"No!" A familiar male voice shouted. Despite the emotion, Rose recognized Earl Weston's deep tones. "I say we confront Gil as soon as he returns. We need to act fast. If they haven't already found us, they probably will soon. Lord knows we haven't kept very quiet."

"Look, it was Hugh's problem, not ours, and he's gone," said another male voice, higher and more nasal than the first.

"A lot you care!" Rose recognized Celia's strident voice. "I was unlucky enough to be married to that fool. You can bet that his problems will somehow get dumped on my shoulders."

"Come on, Cel, we'll stand by you, you know that. We won't let anything happen to you," Earl said.

"Yeah, so long as you get the money," Celia retorted.

"We *need* that money," said Earl. "It's the only way to make all this happen. But we can't hang around indefinitely, biding our time. We've got Wilhelm with us, at least for now, but once that eldress came back, the situation changed. She's a suspicious witch. We can't keep her off the scent forever."

"Try harder, dear boy," Celia said, in silky tones. "We all know you can do it."

There was general snickering, and then the discussion be-

came unintelligible, the voices fainter. *They must be too far
away from the pipes.* The singing had been so easy to hear,
Rose realized, because it had been done by six strong voices
located near the pipes. She leaned in and bent forward, intent
on catching even a word.

A scraping sound came from the opposite corner of the
kitchen. Or was it closer? Rose scanned the room, alert to the
slightest movement. The meeting room voices, even her own
breathing, now distracted her, so she stood up and held her
breath as her eyes darted from corner to corner. Despite the
poor light, surely she would have seen another person enter
the room.

Nothing moved. She released her breath. Perhaps the sound
had come from the meeting room, after all. Unless. Her stomach flip-flopped as she surveyed the piles of refuse outlined in
the dimness. Unless all this filth had attracted rats. She would
not be surprised.

The thought that the sloth of worldly visitors had triggered
a rat infestation fueled Rose's simmering rage. She was mad
enough to catch the rat bare-handed, and then present it to the
inhabitants of the meeting room.

She had left the kitchen as she had found it, dimly lit to
avoid attracting attention at the top of the stairs. Now she
switched on every lamp in sight, while she kept an eye out
for scurrying creatures. To her surprise, nothing scooted toward the walls or under the furniture. She didn't see so much
as an insect.

The voices from upstairs were coming through clearer
again. Rose could hear them from across the room. She gave
up on hunting rats and started back, her eyes on her chair,
when she stepped right on a half-eaten hunk of bread covered
with raspberry preserves. Her right foot slipped out from under
her, and she landed sharply on her left knee.

Rose slid off the injured knee and sat on the filthy floor,
breathing in shallow bursts as the throbbing subsided to barely
tolerable. She touched the area gingerly. Hot pain stabbed
through her leg. She cried out and squeezed her eyes shut.

Again she waited, biting her lip to keep from screaming. Slowly she relaxed her muscles and allowed her eyelids to open. She was looking directly into a worried pair of coppery green eyes.

"You are hurt," Mairin said.

Rose started and jerked her leg. She groaned. Mairin's hand hovered over the injured knee as if to soothe without a painful touch.

Rose drew in a ragged breath. "Mairin, what . . . what are you doing here? You should never, ever wander around alone after dark, no matter where you are. I'm very upset with you." She might have spoken more gently had her knee not been on fire.

Mairin shrank away as if she'd been struck, and Rose almost forgot her pain. She reached her own hand out toward the girl, palm upward. "Forgive me, Mairin. It was wrong of me to raise my voice to you. I know I sounded angry, but I'm just startled and hurt—and very, very worried. Come back over here, and let's talk."

Mairin inched back toward her. Rose opened her mouth to speak, and in that moment she realized that something had changed. Except for their breathing, the kitchen was silent. Voices no longer murmured through the heat pipes. Then Rose remembered a tidbit she had discovered with the kitchen sisters all those years ago—if they'd sung along with too much gusto, they could be heard in the meeting room above them. It hadn't been much of a disturbance because there had been enough noise upstairs to drown out their contributions, but now and then a worshiper who had sat near the pipes had later teased the kitchen sisters, so they had learned to participate discreetly.

Rose's recent cries of pain and her outburst at Mairin had been far from discreet. Had the New-Owenites heard her and realized they were not alone in the dwelling house? Or perhaps the meeting had ended—in which case, judging by the well-used condition of the kitchen, hungry New-Owenites might soon wander down for a snack.

"We have to get out of here," Rose whispered. Her urgency sent Mairin scooting back under the table. "It's all right, you needn't hide," Rose said, reaching her arm toward the girl. "Neither of us is supposed to be here, you know, but nothing bad will happen if we are found. Only it would be so much simpler, wouldn't it, if we left before anyone came down here?" The last thing she wanted to do was frighten Mairin into even deeper reticence.

"I'm afraid I'm going to need your help getting out of here, because of my knee. I don't think it's broken," she whispered, with more hope than conviction, "but I'm a bit wobbly." She rolled onto her good knee and winced as the swollen left knee moved. An inch at a time, she bent the damaged joint until, though she was whimpering with pain, she was relatively certain it was only bruised, not cracked. She stretched it out again. She slid over to the sturdy table leg, sat on her good knee, and pulled herself up on her right foot. Mairin clung to another table leg and watched, expressionless, as Rose straightened.

Holding her breath to stifle a scream, Rose eased some weight onto her injured leg. It wasn't as bad as she'd feared, but it was bad. As she winced in pain, she noticed Mairin flinch, and she rejoiced at yet another sign that the girl's heart could be touched. Hope for Mairin gave Rose the strength to endure her own pain.

"I'll be all right," Rose assured the girl. "But I could use a hand. Let's get home and to bed, shall we?"

Quick as a chipmunk, Mairin scooted out from her hiding place and flipped off the lights, leaving the kitchen as it had been, lit by one small lamp. Before Rose's eyes had adjusted, Mairin was at her side, prying one of her hands loose from her tabletop anchor.

Voices floated down from the top of the stairs, and Mairin froze.

"I know another way," the girl whispered. "Come on, come *on.*" She had already reached the south end of the kitchen when she turned back with impatience to a limping Rose.

"It's back here," Mairin said. "It leads right outside."

She pointed to a plain, narrow doorway that blended so well with the white walls that it was barely visible in the dimness. Rose remembered that it led to a series of rooms where vegetables and canned goods used to be stored to help the South Family survive the winter. She'd forgotten that the storerooms ended with a door leading to a few earthen steps and a cellar door. During the fall harvest, the brethren used to carry squash, onions, potatoes, and other storable crops directly down to the cool storerooms.

How many other forgotten passageways and hiding places had Mairin discovered during her brief time in North Homage? More disturbing, how many other secret meetings had she listened to, and what else might she have seen that she shouldn't have? It was then, as she limped after Mairin through dank, dark storerooms, that Rose vowed never to let the girl return to the life she'd been leading—either before the Griffiths or with them. Rose felt oddly confident that she would succeed in keeping Mairin with her, with the Shakers. Mother Ann would help her. Mother Ann would understand.

"I'm so very sorry, Rose," Sister Charlotte whispered over the telephone line. Rose had taken the risk of calling her and awakening the children, rather than leave Mairin unsupervised again. "I had no idea she'd left the Children's Dwelling House, or even how she could have managed it. Nora must have been exhausted to have slept through it. She feels so responsible for watching over Mairin."

"Don't even bother to blame yourself, and make sure Nora doesn't hold herself responsible, either. Mairin is far more clever and resourceful than Celia or Gilbert gives her credit for being. I wouldn't be surprised if she's found a secret way out of all the buildings in the village."

"Heavens!"

"Indeed. But don't worry, I've got her with me, and I intend to keep her. I'll bring her to school tomorrow and pick her up after. Now I have just one more favor to ask of you, then go back to bed. Please call Josie at the Infirmary and ask her to come to the Ministry House right away. I'll meet her at the door in ten minutes so we don't awaken Wilhelm."

"Oh, Rose, don't tell me Mairin is hurt!"

"Nay, it was my clumsy self. I've twisted my knee, that's all. A poultice will fix me up."

Rose replaced the receiver and limped back into her retiring room.

Mairin's tiny figure, curled up and fast asleep, looked like a small downy ball on Rose's narrow bed. Despite the ferocious ache in her knee, Rose did not dare crawl in next to the child. She'd just have to crawl out again to meet Josie downstairs, and besides, she didn't want to risk awakening Mairin.

Rose slipped out into the hallway again, softly closing the door behind her. The trip down the staircase took her several times as long as usual, but she told herself her knee would improve with the exercise.

She reached the front door only moments before Josie, who arrived out of breath and worried, carrying two baskets full of tins, bottles, bandages, and chunks of ice from an ice box. She knew enough not to speak, beyond a cluck at Rose's limp. In silence, they worked their way up the staircase. After a quick peek at the sleeping Mairin, the sisters closed themselves in Rose's workshop.

"Promise me you will stay in bed tomorrow," Josie said. "And don't use heat. No matter what the doctors say, cold is best." She removed the melting ice pack from Rose's knee and peered at the puffy, darkening skin. "It isn't broken, thank goodness, but that's a nasty bruise. Knees are tricky; one wonders what God could have been thinking. If you don't take proper care, you'll cause permanent damage, and you'll have no one to blame but yourself."

Rose knew better than to object, though she longed to ignore the injury and stay active, to keep Mairin and the village from danger. However, one day shouldn't matter.

"I'm keeping a close eye on Mairin," she said, "so I'll need to take her to and from the Schoolhouse tomorrow."

"Nay, you will not," Josie said, her plump, normally cheerful face puckered in disapproval. "*I* will take Mairin to and from school. It'll not be the slightest problem. I've some extra help these days from one of our visitors. She's trained as a nurse and wants to learn how we stay so healthy and live so long." Josie arched an eyebrow at Rose. "Most of us, anyway."

"Which one is she?" Rose asked, as she hoisted herself to her feet with Josie's help.

"Martha, her name is. Just a child, about your age or so," said Josie, to whom anyone less than her own eighty years was young and untested. "A bit talkative and over-zealous, like all of them, but bright enough."

"Do you sense she is trying to win you over to her side?"

"Convert me, you mean? Here, put your arm around my shoulders and let me bear most of your weight." Rose hoplimped toward the door, leaning on Josie. "Well, she tried mighty hard for a while, but you know me, Rose, I've got my heart set on meeting Mother Ann and spending eternity with you and Agatha. I wouldn't even mind if Wilhelm showed up someday."

Both women were laughing as they opened the workroom door and found themselves face-to-face with the subject of their mirth. Wilhelm had pulled his work pants and shirt over his nightclothes and left his feet bare. His thick white hair had flattened upward on one side of his head, which might have started Rose giggling again, exhausted as she was, had she not noted the glowing coals smoldering in his eyes. Behind Wilhelm, Rose's retiring room door opened and a small figure wandered out, wearing one of Rose's chemises and rubbing her eyes.

Wilhelm noticed that Rose's gaze shifted to Mairin, and he twirled around to face the girl. She shrank against the wall, crossing her arms over her narrow chest as if to create a barrier between her and the frightening man before her. Without a word, Wilhelm spun around to Rose again. His eyes no longer smoldered; they had burst into flame. A swollen artery throbbed down the center of his forehead.

"What is the meaning of all this noise in the middle of the night? Has the Ministry House now become a nursery for the world's lunatic children?"

"Wilhelm, please don't—"

"Shame on you, Wilhelm!" Josie's curt interruption caught Wilhelm off guard, and Rose was glad to let her handle the situation.

"She's a sweet, innocent child," Josie continued, "and she certainly doesn't deserve to be spoken about in that manner. How do *you* feel, for heaven's sake, when someone calls you names?"

Wilhelm's lip trembled with fury, but he kept quiet. Josie was the only one among them who'd ever been able to quell Wilhelm. Despite her soft and cozy exterior, she was every bit as tough as he was. She needed to be. Her charges often balked at putting aside their work to heal their bodies, never mind their belief in healthy living.

Wilhelm changed tactics. "Then tell me, Sister Josie, is thine eldress also an innocent? Just what has she been drinking that she giggles like a foolish girl and needs thy arm to hold her upright?"

Rose had no intention of letting Wilhelm know about her visit to the South Family Dwelling House, but she did not wish to lie, so she said simply, "I've been feeling unwell."

"And I'm here to help her recover," Josie said, "which she'll never do standing about in this drafty hallway. Surely anything you have to say can wait a day or two, Wilhelm. It would be unfortunate if the village found out you'd been wandering around the eldress's quarters late at night. Come along, Rose. And you, too, little one." Josie held out her free hand for Mairin and led her charges into Rose's retiring room.

As Josie closed the door, Rose caught sight of Wilhelm's face reddening at an alarming rate. She half expected him to break down the door, but of course he would never commit such an act of sinful violence. Would he? As the moments passed peacefully, she dared to believe that Josie had, in fact, vanquished Wilhelm. For the time being, anyway.

"Thank you, Josie. I am in your debt."

"Nonsense. It is good for Wilhelm's soul to be reminded now and then that we are all equal in the sight of God. He forgets his humility more than most, I'm afraid." Josie helped Rose limp to her bed, lift off her work dress, and settle down with a rolled-up blanket under her injured knee.

"Now, I assume there's a spare bed or two in the empty rooms? Good, I'll roll one in and make it up in a jiffy for Mairin. Then we'll see to a comfrey poultice for that knee of yours, and some strong valerian tea to help you sleep."

Josie bustled out the door and returned in minutes pushing a narrow bed on wheels, on top of which lay a pile of fresh white linens.

Rose watched groggily, thankful to be who she was, where she was. "Josie, was Wilhelm—"

"Gone, of course, my dear. Even Wilhelm knows when he is hopelessly in the wrong."

"And hopelessly outmaneuvered," Rose said quietly.

"Come along, little one," Josie said to Mairin, "hop into bed. That's a good girl. You can say your prayers from under the covers tonight."

Mairin grimaced. "I don't know how to say prayers," she said.

"Oh, you poor child," Josie said. "Never mind, we'll teach you in no time. You'll wonder how you ever did without them." Then, seeing the child's eyelids flutter and droop, she added, "But we'll save the lessons until another day. Just sleep now." Mairin's eyes closed at once.

"Now we'll set you up with that poultice," Josie whispered, and got to work wrapping Rose's knee. By the time she'd finished, the valerian tea was unnecessary.

TWELVE

ROSE'S DREAMS PILED UPON ONE ANOTHER, ONE GROWING OUT of the last, to form a chaotic tapestry. Her knee was trapped under a fallen tree; the tree was growing out of her knee; she was limping through a wood, frantic to escape some unknown pursuer, gasping, clutching at saplings to pull herself along. Then she was back in the South Family Dwelling House kitchen, lying on the floor and listening to a rat scratch, scratch, scratch at bits of food.

She groaned and awakened herself, and the scratching sound stopped . . . then started again. Rose opened her eyes. Across the room, huddled close to a small circle of light from a bedside lamp, Mairin sat on her bed, her head bent over what looked like a piece of cardboard. Her hand flew over the flat surface in drawing motions.

As if sensing Rose's gaze on her, Mairin's head popped up. The lamplight caught the sparkle of copper in her eyes and transformed her hair into a feathery halo. Still half-submerged in a dream, Rose wondered if Mairin might truly be an angel, sent by Holy Mother Wisdom to guide them through this difficult time.

"I'm sorry," Mairin said, sucking in her lower lip. "I woke you up." Her head moved away from the lamplight, and she became, once again, a shy young girl, scared of being punished.

Rose eased herself to a sitting position. The pain in her knee had subsided to a dull throb, and she was able to shift her leg.

"Nay, I was about to wake up, anyway," she said, not sure if it was the truth or not, and not caring. "What are you doing?"

"Nothing." Mairin tossed her work onto her bed, away from the light. She curled herself into a tight ball, wrapping her arms around her legs, and began rocking herself back and forth.

"Were you drawing? It's quite all right, you know. I'm not the least bit angry with you. If you were drawing, I'd love to see it. Would you bring it over to me? I'd go over there, but my knee still hurts."

Mairin stopped rocking and sucked on her lip a while longer. Without a word, she uncurled and slid off her bed. Holding the cardboard against her chest, she approached Rose. She started to lay the object across Rose's knees but stopped herself, apparently remembering the injury. Instead, she held up a large pad of paper on a cardboard backing, which Rose recognized as coming from the Schoolhouse storeroom. Usually Charlotte wrote lessons on the blackboard, but sometimes she used paper pads for individual tutoring. Mairin probably noticed them as she went through the storeroom from the back door. She must have gone back on her own, when the building was empty, and taken one.

Rose turned on her own lamp and took the pad. Mairin had rummaged through the storeroom and unearthed some precious Crayolas, too, because the paper was covered with colored slashes.

"Mairin, dear, I promise I'm not angry with you, but . . . did you leave this room while I was sleeping?"

Mairin's eyes widened in fear, but this time she did not pull away. After a few moments, she seemed to have come to a decision.

"I just went to the Schoolhouse for a minute. I know I shouldn't be out alone at night, but I'm used to it, and I knew I could get drawing things there." Having taken the risk of confessing, Mairin withdrew into herself.

With an ordinary child, Rose would be very firm in such a situation. With Mairin, however, she held her tongue. She was grateful that the girl trusted her enough to answer her question. The rest would have to wait.

Rose held the pad of paper under her lamp. As she studied it, a shape began to emerge. Her heartbeat picked up speed. The colors were odd—violet and blue—but the design looked very much like a tree in full bloom.

"What made you draw this picture, Mairin?" Rose made her voice as gentle as possible.

"I dreamed it," Mairin said.

"Tonight?"

"Tonight and lots of nights," Mairin said.

"What was the dream—just this picture?"

Mairin's face went blank. She shrugged. "There was other stuff, too, but I don't remember it. This is all I remember."

Rose's mind raced through too many possibilities. The picture could have something to do with what Mairin witnessed in the orchard, but why a strange-colored tree in full bloom? Hugh's lifeless body had hung from a bedraggled and leafless tree. The tree in Mairin's drawing reminded Rose of the old spirit drawings done by Shakers eighty and more years earlier, during the period of Mother Ann's Work. The gifts appeared in dreams to Believers selected by the Heavens. These instruments created pictures filled with images of celestial beauty. Many of the pictures contained elaborate trees, as Rose remembered, though she had not examined the old paintings and drawings in years. Could this crayon drawing be a true gift from Mother Ann? Was Mother watching over Mairin, trying to send messages to help Rose protect the child?

Rose was far too tired to think anymore. If she had to stay quiet for a day, it would be a good time to reacquaint herself with the spirit drawings. The Ministry Library had all she would need; Josie could collect it for her, so she needn't risk an encounter with Wilhelm.

"Could I keep this lovely picture?"

Mairin nodded. Rose tore off the page and returned the pad to Mairin.

"Will you promise me something, Mairin?" Rose looked into the girl's eyes. "Will you promise, truly promise, that you will stay in this room the rest of the night? I get worried, you know."

"I promise."

"Thank you. Now, I'm falling asleep. How about crawling back into bed and doing the same? You can take your pad with you and draw more, if you can't sleep."

Rose turned off her lamp and snuggled back in bed, grateful that the poultice was doing its soothing work on the pain in her knee. As her eyes closed, she saw Mairin climb back on her bed, settle cross-legged next to her lamp, and begin to draw again.

The next morning, Rose slid her legs over the edge of her bed and lowered them with care. She stood on her good right leg and tried putting weight on the other. It was sore, but it held steady. Good. She was irritated by the thought of staying in bed all day, like an invalid. She wanted to sit awhile in a chair, if her knee would take it.

She tried not to limp, and succeeded, as she walked to the rocking chair by her window. She took with her the drawing Mairin had given her, and the pad upon which the girl had made two more drawings. Within reach, on a side table, Josie had placed a stack of books from the Ministry Library. Rose was itching to delve into them. Next to the books was a tray with rose hip and lemon balm tea, a chunk of cheese, and some brown bread. Josie again. Bless her.

She felt a twinge of guilt as she glanced over at Mairin's empty bed, neatly made by the overworked Josie. Mairin had not known how to make a bed. Yet when Rose had awakened, moments before Josie's arrival, Mairin was sitting on her bed, fully dressed and ready for breakfast and school. What a strange child. She was bright, self-reliant, and articulate when she wished to be, yet she didn't know the simplest things. No

wonder Celia considered her uncivilized. Had she been unwilling to learn, or had no one bothered to teach her with
gentleness?

Rose nibbled on a piece of cheese and began to sort through
the materials Josie had brought her, most of which were old
journals and handwritten memoirs of events from the time of
Mother Ann's Work. Rose flipped through pages looking for
drawings or descriptions of spirit gifts. There was very little
of any depth. Perhaps Believers of that time had been so involved in events or so used to extraordinary manifestations
that they only remarked upon them in passing. Or perhaps
North Homage Believers had done more dancing and singing
than drawing. Most likely, though, Believers had been hesitant
to discuss the drawings because they had always been prohib-
ited from displaying art for mere enjoyment.

Finally she came to a section in an eldress's journal, dating
from 1855 and recording her trip to the eastern Societies. The
eldress, whose name was Bertha, thought that eastern Shakers
seemed more readily inclined than western ones to receive gift
drawings. For that reason—and in defense of her own people—Bertha was tempted to dismiss the importance of spirit
drawings as true messages from the celestial realm. But she
was interested enough to describe her observations and sketch
a few of the drawings.

Though it was roughly drawn, Rose recognized the first
sketch as the Tree of Life, drawn by Sister Hannah Cohoon,
who lived in the Hancock Shaker village in Massachusetts.
Rose smoothed her hand over the ink scratches, remembering
a day perhaps twenty-five years earlier when Agatha, vibrant
and wise, had explained to her the meaning of the tree—that
just as the branches brought forth the rich, shimmering red
and green fruit, so were Believers to create a heaven on earth.
That alluring image had stirred the beginnings of Rose's faith.

In all the materials before her, Rose found only two more
pictures. The first contained disturbing images, prophecies of
horrible disasters, such as earthquakes and fires. The artist

wasn't identified, but Rose remembered hearing about such drawings.

The other sketch was more gentle. Though it was drawn to a tiny scale, Rose recognized sweet images of flowers and fruit floating around an elaborate bird. Again, the artist's name wasn't recorded, but the image looked like the lovely gifts drawn by Sister Polly Reed.

Rose remembered one more bit of Shaker history. Agatha had told her that the Era of Manifestations was an exciting time to be a sister, because it was the first time in anyone's memory that Holy Mother Wisdom had visited her children on earth. Many of the gifts had been brought by her and de- livered through a chosen medium. Holy Mother Wisdom was all a mother should be—tender, gentle, loving, and protective of her precious children. Agatha's eyes had shone when she spoke of those times, just ending when she was a young child. An orphan almost since birth, it was, for Agatha, her first experience of a powerful maternal presence, and the feeling of complete safety had never left her.

Rose spread Mairin's three pictures on her lap and studied them. After the strange tree, Mairin had drawn what looked like a long yellow-and-orange serpent that wound around on the page until it had filled almost every space. When Rose traced the labyrinth to its end, it looked as if the head had been hacked off. Rose pulled a blanket around her shoulders against the chill inside her.

Mairin had jammed an elaborate array of food images into her third picture. Rose smiled. Mairin had probably been get- ting hungry. Very hungry, judging from the loving detail on the plump red strawberries, complete with tiny white dots to represent seeds.

Rose was more confused than ever. What could all this mean? Each of Mairin's pictures was reminiscent of the older gift drawings, yet different. Mairin's tree was haunting, rather than lush. The snake image seemed as violent and disturbing as natural disasters, but the severed head implied the evil in- tervention of man.

Again, Rose studied the delectable foods in the third drawing—shiny purple grapes, so juicy they looked about to burst; succulent meats; fancy pies, cakes, and puddings; and even a generous slice of sweet potato bread, such as Rose had fed her the day of Hugh's death. The picture seemed very much a reflection of Mairin herself.

In her excitement, Rose had forgotten her knee, but now it began to throb again. She gathered up the books and drawings, and limped back to her bed. A few minutes of resting with the rolled-up towel under her knee brought the pain to a tolerable level. Rose lifted her nightgown to her thighs and examined her knee. The swelling had lessened, but the skin was an angry black-purple and tender to the touch. She had surely bruised the bone underneath, but with luck, she'd be able to walk more or less normally soon. Not just yet, though. She lay back and closed her eyes to rest until the noon meal arrived.

The persistent ringing of the telephone in the hall awakened Rose after just a few moments. At least, it seemed like only a few moments. A glance at her bedside clock told her it had really been an hour. Rose counted twenty rings before the phone stopped. She'd considered limping out to answer, but she decided not to risk a setback in her recovery. She had no intention of staying in bed for another day.

A firm knock on her retiring room door startled her just as her eyes drifted shut again.

"Rose? It's me, Lydia." The Ministry's kitchen sister swept in, carrying a tray with soup, biscuits, and more tea. She clucked when she saw that Rose still hadn't finished her breakfast.

"You *must* be feeling poorly, to pass up this lovely food," Lydia said, setting the new tray on the bedside table. Lydia herself was small and slight and claimed to be always hungry. Of course, she probably was, given the nature of her work. For each meal, she helped out in the Center Family kitchen, then packed baskets with enough food for Wilhelm—and Rose, too, if she was there—and toted it back to the Ministry, where she warmed and served it. After washing up, she carried empty serving containers back to the main kitchen and helped the kitchen sisters with the final clean-up and whatever additional cooking or preserving projects were scheduled. Lydia insisted she loved the job because it enabled her to eat more.

"You didn't just phone up here, did you, Lydia?" Rose asked.

"Nay, of course not. I wouldn't pull you out of bed like that, and besides, I've never been too lazy to climb one tiny flight of stairs!"

"I wondered because—"

The phone rang again.

"I'll just take care of that right now, Rose. Don't you stir." She bustled into the hall, and the ringing stopped. Rose could hear her puzzled voice but not what she was saying.

"Rose, it's little Nora," Lydia called, poking her head into Rose's outer room. "She wants to come over right away and talk to you."

"Nora! What about?"

"She wouldn't tell me—just that it's 'really, really, really important.' She did sound scared."

"Where was she calling from? Where's Charlotte? Oh, I'd better talk to her." Rose flung aside her blanket and grimaced as she tried to move her leg too fast.

"Nay, you don't move from that bed," Lydia said, holding her down with surprisingly strong arms. "I already told Nora to come on over, so you just sit tight."

"You should be an Infirmary nurse," Rose grumbled.

"Thank you."

"It wasn't meant as a compliment."

Lydia tucked the blanket around Rose and laid the tray on her thighs. "You just have time to eat something before Nora arrives. Get busy, though. If I know Nora, she'll run like a jackrabbit."

"Does Charlotte know you're here?" Rose asked, as Nora squirmed into a rocking chair too big for her.

"Um, sort of."

"What does that mean?"

"Well, I wanted to talk to you first, and I didn't want to get Mairin into trouble, and anyway, maybe she didn't even do anything wrong."

"Did you sneak out again, Nora? Have you been telling Mairin how to get out without being seen?" Rose spoke as firmly as she could manage, tucked in bed with her long hair loose on her shoulders. Even though she'd opposed Wilhelm's edict that they revert to nineteenth century dress, now she felt uncomfortable without it.

"That's not fair!" Nora jerked and set off her rocking chair. "I haven't shown Mairin anything like that—she's been show-ing *me* . . ." The rocking chair slowed to a stop as Nora held her breath.

"Nora, what are we going to do with you?"

Nora looked as if she'd like to offer a helpful suggestion, but she was wise enough to keep silent.

"I want to hear everything Mairin has been showing you. Now tell me what was so urgent that you had to come running over here during the school day."

"It's noon, so there isn't any school right now 'cause every-one is eating." Nora's hungry eyes focused on the tray of food, and Rose handed her a biscuit.

"Go on."

Nora nodded and swallowed a mouthful of biscuit. "Well, we were outside playing, and—"

"When?" Rose tried to keep the exasperation out of her voice.

"This morning, when Charlotte gave us a play break. She said we were too ram . . . rambuc . . ."

"Rambunctious?"

"Uh-huh. So she sent us outside to play for a while, and she corrected our papers. We were playing—Mairin and me— we were playing on the grass in back of the Schoolhouse." Nora's narrow face drooped, as if she were recalling a sad scene. Rose let her collect her thoughts without urging.

"The other kids can be awfully silly," she said, popping the rest of the biscuit in her mouth. "Especially the kids from town. They're kind of afraid of Mairin, so they won't play with her, and they make fun of her, so we just ignore them and play together as far away from them as we can get." Nora paused for breath, and Rose sipped her tea.

"Mostly I always stay with Mairin," Nora said, "but then Betsy called me over—I'm mad at Betsy 'cause she won't play with Mairin and me, but I went over 'cause I thought maybe I could get her to come back with me, and then we could be friends again. I was only gone for a few minutes." Nora's gaze dropped to her small hands, tightly knitted together.

"Just tell me what happened, Nora. Whatever it was, I won't blame you."

"Betsy wouldn't come with me. When I turned back, Mairin wasn't there. I got really scared. I ran all the way around the Schoolhouse, but I couldn't find her anywhere."

"Exactly where had you been playing?" Rose's heart hammered against her ribs as she struggled to free herself from her bed linens.

"Near that thing that burned down," Nora said.

"The Water House? With the trees in back?" Rose winced as she threw her leg over the edge of the bed.

Nora nodded. "That's where she came out of when I got back from running around the Schoolhouse."

Rose froze in confusion. "Mairin isn't missing?"

"Nay. I mean, she was for a while, but then she got found again. When I got back, there she was. I asked where she'd gone, and she just said, 'The woods,' and that's all she'd say, no matter how hard I asked."

Rose pulled her legs back under the blanket and studied Nora for a moment. "What aren't you telling me? Why were you so upset that you had to come racing over here without even telling Charlotte?"

Nora's lower lip slid out. "Because *Mairin* was so scared, that's why. She made me promise not to tell Charlotte she'd been gone." Nora grinned. "But she didn't say I couldn't tell you."

"Where do you think she had gone—into the woods to climb a tree? Was she bruised or mussed up?"

Nora shook her head and shrugged. With a shiver, she snuggled back against the blanket hung over the back of the rocking chair. She pulled the corners around her shoulders. "Mairin is very brave, you know. Something really bad must have happened to her, but she won't tell me. So I decided to tell you, 'cause you're watching out for her now." She gazed at Rose with a child's confidence that the adult in charge could fix anything, even if that adult could barely limp across the room.

"You did the right thing." Rose spoke with calmness, to hide her confusion and fear. "I'll find out what happened. You've been a big help. Now, you'd better head back to the Schoolhouse—but on your way, stop down in the kitchen and tell Lydia I sent you to get something to eat. She always has some extra."

Nora slid off her chair and gave Rose's hand an impulsive squeeze before running out of the room. Rose's smile faded as soon as the door closed. For the first time since finding Hugh's body, she was truly frightened. Until now, Mairin's fear had always been associated with her terror of punishment. Otherwise, even violent death did not seem to touch her emotions. Something had happened in those woods, something terrifying enough to pierce even Mairin's armor.

THIRTEEN

AFTER A NAP AND ANOTHER POULTICE, ROSE COULDN'T BEAR to stay in bed any longer. There was too much to be done. She poked at her knee. Its color was still ugly, but the swelling had subsided entirely, and if she was careful, she could move her leg with minimal pain. She eased to her feet and walked a few steps. With concentration, she could avoid limping.

A plan began to form in her mind as she slipped her loose work dress over her head. Mairin must stay with the Shakers, to be raised and educated and cared for in the village. Rose had not felt so determined since the day she'd realized she was being called from the world back to the Society. Life with the New-Owenites would doom the girl; the Shakers could help her.

She would talk to Celia, who was Mairin's guardian—she'd probably be glad to see her go. Rose gathered up the journals and books she'd been studying, planning to return them to the Ministry library on her way out.

She took the stairs slowly, leaning on the banister to lighten the load on her knee. Bringing along the stack of books had not been her wisest decision. Sometimes her Shaker neatness overwhelmed her common sense. At least she needn't be too worried that Wilhelm might find her and question her reading material. During the afternoon, he usually preferred active work to spiritual study.

A few steps from the bottom, the toe of her shoe caught on

the hem of her long dress. She let the books fall. She had to, it was the only way she could grab the banister with both hands and keep from tumbling down the stairs. The volumes scattered. The largest, a book of memoirs, fell open and some colorful pages slid out. Mairin's drawings. Rose must have stuffed them in a book without thinking.

Rose steadied herself and caught her breath. She tested some weight on her injured knee. No additional damage. After thanking Holy Mother Wisdom for watching over her, Rose berated herself. Now she'd have to take the drawings back upstairs. Honestly, one would think she'd fallen on her head instead of her knee.

The click of the front door startled her in mid-step. A forceful arm swept the door open to a blast of crisp air—and to Wilhelm. He saw Rose, frowned, saw the clutter of books on the floor, and frowned more deeply. Then he saw the drawings, and his expression cleared. He grabbed the pages, his wind-roughened features lit with excitement.

"I doubt these are *thy* work," he said. "Where did they come from?"

Rose hesitated. She recognized the light in Wilhelm's eyes—the fire of zealotry. In this mood, he was capable of anything. If he learned Mairin had drawn the pictures, the child would become his tool. He would use her to further his own ends, and never mind the consequences. Her sanity would be a small price to pay.

"They are not what you think, Wilhelm." She held out her hand for their return. "They are of no use to you."

"On the contrary, they interest me greatly." Wilhelm ignored Rose's hand and took the drawings into the library.

Rose followed, avoiding the books still scattered at the foot of the stairs. When she caught up to him, Wilhelm had spread the drawings across the desk and was leaning close to them.

"Where did you find these?" he demanded. "In one of those journals? They look like the work of a child; perhaps one of our own sisters was chosen as an instrument at a young age. Is there no hint as to the artist?" Wilhelm picked up the purple tree drawing and flipped it over. A crease appeared between his bushy, white eyebrows. "This paper is new. What kind of trick is this? Is this thy notion of a proper way to pass the time during thy convalescence?"

Rose noted that it never entered his mind to wonder if she could be a chosen instrument. If it was her work, he assumed it was only time-wasting play. She sank into a chair, wishing she'd followed Josie's orders and stayed in bed.

"Unless . . ." The glint returned to Wilhelm's eyes. "That girl in thy room, that New-Owenite child. Did *she* draw these?" He ran his blunt fingertips across the surface of all three pictures.

"Perhaps," he said, "she is not the lunatic she seemed to me. In my poor human blindness, I could not see. Chosen instruments have often been called mad by the world. Because the girl has been *of* the world, I failed to grasp the message sent so clearly by the Heavens—God has chosen her to carry out His will. She is to bring our two groups together and make us one. Only one of their own could lead the New-Owenites into the light of Mother Ann. A *child* shall lead them."

Wilhelm was no longer aware of Rose. His eyes devoured Mairin's drawings, squinting at every detail. Rose slipped from the room. She closed the door behind her and released her breath in a long sigh.

"Are you certain this isn't too much for you?" Rose asked. "If you aren't feeling strong enough, you have only to say so."

"Don't fret, now," Agatha said, waving her thin hand with a flash of her old impatience. "The girls and I will have a wonderful time. Gertrude can bring us tea and some of that lovely cider cake she keeps in a tin." Nora's and Mairin's faces lit up at the mention of cider cake.

"You know Gertrude is a terrible gossip," Rose said.

"Not if I tell her how important silence is for protecting the children."

"You're probably right," Rose said. Gertrude would enjoy

keeping silent more than having a good gossip, as long as she believed it was for the higher good.

"Hand me that basket, would you, Rose?" Agatha's thin hand waved toward her desk, where a basket lay covered with a piece of scrap cloth. Rose set it on Agatha's lap.

"My dears, look what Sarah brought for you." Agatha pulled aside the cloth and lifted out two dolls, identical except for the colors of their dresses and their hair. They were made entirely of cloth, hand-sewn, with smiling embroidered faces. Agatha handed to Nora a doll in a dark blue Shaker work dress with a white kerchief pinned over its bodice. A few strands of embroidered black hair showed beneath the doll's thin white cap. Nora squealed and held the doll to her chest.

Agatha handed the second doll to Mairin. Its dress was of fine butternut wool, also covered across the bodice with a white kerchief. One red curl had been embroidered on the doll's head, so that it peaked out from under her cap.

Mairin held the doll delicately, as if she feared it would break. She looked up at Agatha.

"Do I have to give it back?"

"Nay, child, the doll is yours forever."

Nora had already begun telling a story with her doll. Mairin placed hers on her lap and began to rock gently.

"I suggested to Sarah that she make a doll for each of the girls," Agatha said. "They've had so little in their lives, and it's not as if they've signed the Covenant and vowed to share everything in common. They are only children, after all."

"The dolls are lovely," Rose said. "Was it your idea that Mairin's should look a bit like me?"

Agatha merely smiled.

"Run along now, Rose. Do what you need to do."

"I'll leave them in your hands, then. Nora, Mairin, do you solemnly promise me you will stay here with Agatha until I come to get you?"

Both girls nodded, and Rose left. It was the best she could do, to keep Mairin safely out of sight for a time. She hoped it was enough. But worry plagued her as she set out for the

South Family Dwelling House. When she had picked up Mairin after school, the girl had been as blank as a new ledger page—no sign of the fear Nora had reported, nor of any other emotion. She had not seemed to notice Rose's outstretched hand. Perhaps the new doll, and Agatha's influence, would bring Mairin back.

Then there was the problem of Wilhelm. Rose was fairly certain she knew what he would be planning, now that he had Mairin's drawings. He'd called a Union Meeting for that evening, and she'd had no justifiable reason to object. He had already sent word to the New-Owenites to attend, as an opportunity to learn. She knew what he would attempt to teach them. She also believed the New-Owenites would never agree to leave Mairin with the Shakers, once they saw her as a pawn for Wilhelm. She could see only one option at the moment—she had to convince the New-Owenites that she did not agree with Wilhelm, that she would support the New-Owenites in their resistance to conversion. She could start by warning them, at least indirectly, about Wilhelm's probable plans for the Union Meeting and by urging them not to attend.

The foyer, parlor, and family meeting room of the South Family Dwelling House were all empty—messy, but uninhabited. Rose heard a murmur of voices coming from upstairs, so she resisted the temptation to clean, and she climbed toward the second-floor retiring rooms, resting her knee every few steps. She looked into the first room, on her right at the top of the stairs. It had once held eight beds, and surely it had seemed less crowded than now, when it contained only two beds and three people. The air reeked of cigarette smoke and unwashed linens.

In addition to the built-in drawers, two large dressers stood along the wall, obscuring the window. Drawers hung open to show unfolded clothing piled inside. Rose counted five ladder-back chairs and two rockers, all serving as clothes hangers. The wall pegs were empty. A full-length mirror leaned against the wall facing the doorway, throwing Rose into momentary confusion. She had never seen herself in a full-length mirror, wearing traditional Shaker garb. Only her pale, freckled face and her hands showed, in stark contrast to the other female inhabitant of the room.

Celia Griffiths sat cross-legged on an unmade bed, her feet bare and her loose trouser legs hiked up to her knees, revealing shapely calves. Her ivory silk blouse was unbuttoned about an inch below the point of modesty. She stared at Rose as she took a long drag on a cigarette and stubbed it out in an empty jam jar.

Gilbert Griffiths and Earl Weston occupied the two rockers. They, too, were smoking, and they shared, as an ashtray, one of the Society's white soup bowls perched on an ash-dusted oval candle table.

Over the years, Rose had come to know and accept her human flaws, even as she strove for perfection, as did all Believers. But the one trait that still conquered her will was her temper. Agatha had taught her dozens of prayers pleading for patience, and she knew them all by heart. The litany raced through her mind, as it had on other trying occasions. She felt herself calming down. Then Earl allowed his cigarette ash to drop on the pine floor. Rose gave up her prayers.

"Is this how you care for your own belongings, or do you reserve such behavior for when you are guests in another's home?" Rose tried to keep her voice low and steady, but the fury was unmistakable. Celia and Earl were surprised into silence, while Gilbert jumped to his feet and stubbed out his cigarette.

"So very sorry," he said. "We forgot you folks don't smoke. Earl, put that thing out. Vile habit, of course, but I'm afraid we're just more lax about such things. We become so engrossed in our struggle to bring education and happiness to mankind that I suppose we do tend to forget the niceties."

Perhaps he meant for his smile to be engaging, but it sent Rose's temper into the danger zone. Her hand jerked, as if to express her impulse to slap his self-satisfied face. Her own surge of anger alarmed her, and this time she prayed harder. She threw herself on the mercy of Holy Mother Wisdom and felt, finally, a blessed calm quench her rage. She breathed in deeply.

"We no longer smoke or drink alcohol," she said, "out of concern for our health, but we certainly do not tell others that they must do the same. However, we must insist that you not smoke inside our buildings. Most of them are old and susceptible to fire. We don't want you to be hurt."

"Of course, of course," Gilbert said. "We will do our smoking out of doors from now on, I can assure you of that."

Rose was not assured, but she merely nodded.

Gilbert cocked his narrow head like a thin bird. "May I ask to what we owe the pleasure of this unexpected visit?"

Rose blinked rapidly. Did this man ever speak from his heart? She trusted Wilhelm more—at least she knew his true dreams. But Gilbert—was he a zealot, or just an irritating but clever con artist? She regretted the need to warn these people of Wilhelm's plan, but it had to be done. There was no chance at all that they might be tempted to become Believers, and heaven forbid that they should!

Gilbert swept some papers off the woven seat of a ladderback chair and offered it to Rose, who shook her head.

"Nay, I'll only be a minute. I'm here to bring you a warning of sorts. As you may or may not already know, Wilhelm hopes you will all choose to become Believers."

Gilbert's eyebrows rose slightly, but otherwise none of the New-Owenites showed much reaction. Earl seemed to be suppressing a smile.

"You've heard that Wilhelm has called a Union Meeting for tonight, after the evening meal, and he is urging you to attend. I urge you not to."

"And yet we've never actually seen one of your Union Meetings," Gilbert said, "though we've heard about them, of course."

Earl broke into a smile. "Yes, I imagine they are quite a relief, given how little contact is allowed between your men and women."

In fact, the meetings did provide sisters and brethren a way to chat in a safe and chaste setting, but Rose was not about to feed Earl's worldly amusement at the Shakers' expense.

"Normally, it would not be worth your while to attend, but believe me, this evening's meeting is likely to be unpleasant for you. I'll leave it at that." Rose retied her bonnet and turned to leave.

Gilbert rushed forward to hold the door for her. Rose paused to gather her cloak more tightly around her skirt, so she wouldn't brush against him on the way out.

"Thank you for the warning," he said. "We will certainly keep your words in mind." An undertone in Gilbert's matter-of-fact voice brought Rose's gaze to his face. His smile was pleasant, his gray eyes absent of malice. But Rose was glad to leave.

FOURTEEN

By some miracle, Mairin and Nora had worn out before Agatha. When Rose checked on them, just before the Union Meeting, both girls were wrapped in blankets and snoozing on Agatha's bed. Mairin's Shaker sister doll lay against her cheek. Gertrude had returned to lend a hand, which kept her from revealing Mairin's whereabouts, while allowing her a chance to gossip to Agatha. Rose excused Gertrude from the meeting and asked her to stay in Agatha's retiring room until Josie arrived to put the girls to bed.

As soon as she entered the Center Family meeting room, Rose was thankful she'd tucked Mairin away out of sight. The New-Owenites, all of them, had arrived and were clustered together at one end of the room.

Rows of ladder-back chairs faced each other across a space large enough to prevent contact, but small enough for voices to carry to aging ears. The windows were shuttered against the damp chill of the November evening. To save electricity, as few lamps as possible were lit, and shapeless shadows of Shaker clothing flowed across the walls.

In the old days, the elders and eldresses would have assigned Believers to specific seats, to prevent romances, but in North Homage such strictness hadn't been necessary for years. Conversation with the dwindling number of brethren was shared without jealousy or favoritism by the sisters. Tonight, however, the New-Owenites added a new wrinkle. Many of the sisters, especially the older ones, were shy about talking with men of the world, so they quickly seated themselves across from brethren. Two or three sisters would lean together nervously, clearly planning to share one brother.

The New-Owenites seemed to be biding their time. At first Rose feared they would refuse to sit down. Perhaps they would actually try to take over the meeting. Then they began, one at a time, to find seats, always after it had become clear which Shaker would be in the opposite seat.

Andrew sat at the end of the brethren's row, and at once Celia glided across the room to sit facing him. A sister heading his direction changed her mind, leaving the seat next to Celia unoccupied. Celia wore an evening-length gray silk dress that clung to her body and formed a soft drape outlining her thigh as she crossed her legs. Andrew looked startled but not alarmed. He was, after all, used to conversing with women from the world. Rose felt a twinge of emotion that she did not care to identify. She thought it best not to sit next to Celia and appear to be vying for Andrew's attention.

Gretchen settled herself toward the middle of the sisters' row, separating two clusters of sisters with their backs turned to her chair. She blushed slightly as Earl claimed the chair across from her. This time Rose was sure of her emotion—she was growing anxious. The other four New-Owenites made equally deliberate seat choices, while Gilbert hung back. Was he hoping somehow to sit next to Wilhelm? Nay, Gilbert still didn't move when Wilhelm, with a triumphant stride, chose a seat for himself.

Several sisters, out of courtesy, were waiting for Rose to take her place, so she settled beside Theresa, for comfort. She nodded to the sisters, sat down, and looked across to the brethren to find Gilbert smiling at her. He continued to smile, unconcerned, as Wilhelm stood, holding several bright drawings.

"We are greatly honored this evening in two ways. We are privileged to share our Union Meeting with our guests. And we have been favored by Holy Mother Wisdom with a rare treasure—three new gift drawings." He held up the drawings, one by one, and panned the room so everyone could see them. There were gasps of awe from the Shakers, but Gilbert and his followers showed no reaction.

"Normally our meetings are reserved for social discourse," Wilhelm said. "But as always, we Believers are open to any opportunities to discuss our faith, and this is an important time to do so. These drawings were made by a little girl, sent by Mother Ann to show us all the way. The drawings provide proof. The girl may seem to be of the world, but she is, in fact, a messenger; otherwise, she would not so clearly have re-created Mother Ann's Work, here and now. So, Believers and friends, I urge thee to put aside thy mundane, petty chats for this one evening and to explore the meaning of these gifts, for all of us in this room. God is with us." He laid out the drawings on the long, narrow rug that covered the space between the men and the women.

For a few moments, curious participants leaned toward the drawings, studying them in silence. Rose watched the faces of the New-Owenites. They showed interest, but no surprise, no shock or alarm or anger.

Conversations began, halting at first, then with growing intensity. Rose wanted to be everywhere at once, especially with Gretchen and with Andrew, but she realized Gilbert had spoken to her.

"I said, I imagine this is what you tried to warn us about," Gilbert repeated.

"And I imagine there was no need for me to do so."

Gilbert shrugged. "We do appreciate your concern, but we are well aware of Wilhelm's hopes for us. Moreover, this is not the first time Mairin has made her night drawings. Celia tried to cure her of it by taking away her pencils and paper, but she always found more. Some of her drawings have been quite alarming."

"Did it occur to you to try to find out what was causing her to make these 'alarming' drawings?" Theresa, sitting next to Rose, shot her a sideways glance, and she realized her tone had become sarcastic. But Gilbert seemed not to notice.

"I understand them quite well," he said. "Celia never has, unfortunately, but Hugh and I were in complete agreement." Gilbert tilted his head, turning his smile crooked. "Robert Owen was not without his spiritual instincts, you know."

"I beg your pardon?"

"Of course, he was not religious, in the strictest sense. Quite opposed to organized religion, in fact. But later in his life he came to believe in spiritualism, as Hugh and I have come to as well."

Rose cast her mind back many years to conversations with Agatha about spiritualism. Communication with the dead was important to Believers—it was how they received guidance and comfort—but during the period just following Mother Ann's Work, such communications had become almost overwhelming. Agatha had been a young child at the time. She'd been frightened yet fascinated by the mysterious rappings that answered questions Believers posed to the spirit world. Mediums from the world often visited and conducted seances, which Agatha had now and then sneaked away to watch. Even though some of the mediums were less than honest, to the Society these manifestations proved the existence of the afterlife and reassured them that death was not final.

"So then, you agree with Wilhelm?" Rose asked, astonished. "You believe Mother Ann is speaking through Mairin for the purpose of uniting our two groups?"

"After a fashion," Gilbert said. He pursed his thin lips. "Hugh and I always believed Mairin is a natural medium. She may or may not be communicating with your Mother Ann— personally, I doubt it. I do, however, firmly believe that Mairin's drawings are messages, perhaps warnings, from the spirit world."

"Warnings?"

"Indeed," Gilbert said. "We New-Owenites are being warned of danger, imminent danger."

"From us?"

Gilbert shrugged. "Possibly."

"Yet Mairin's pictures are so similar to our own gift drawings from the time of Mother Ann's Work. Why would Mother Ann warn you of danger from us?"

"Ah, I wasn't aware of the similarity in style. Intriguing. That would explain the violent colors and the frightening nature of the images."

"How?"

"Well, of course, now it is clearer than ever. We are *all* being warned, Shaker and New-Owenite alike, of the dire consequences for all of us if our people join with you in the Shaker faith. You look skeptical, but just examine those drawings. Look at that tree with its funereal coloring. If that is an image of the Shaker community, then I'd worry it has become diseased from the inside. And that unfortunate snake, once so powerful, and now its head has been ripped off. Well, the message is certainly clear to me."

Rose quelled a series of impulses, from walking away to laughing. Surely Gilbert was playing a game with her. He couldn't be serious, could he?

"You see," Gilbert continued, "Mairin is serving as a medium from concerned spirits, who want to tell us that in fact Shaker ways are contrary to the laws of nature. We New-Owenites must not be absorbed into what is—forgive me—a rotting way of life, rapidly losing its strength. I know this is painful for you to hear, Rose, but believe me, I am concerned for your future. The best and most immediate way for you to save yourselves from inevitable destruction—" Gilbert leaned toward Rose and gazed in her eyes with an intensity that sent a shiver through her body. "—Is for you to join *us,* to drop these religious superstitions of yours. Give up this foolish denial of natural human urges and become New-Owenites."

He shifted to the edge of his chair and opened his hand toward her. For a nervous moment, Rose feared he would reach over and touch her knee. She pushed her spine against the slats of her chair. She could think of nothing to say.

As if coming out of a trance, Gilbert relaxed and sat back in his chair, his intensity wiped clear away and replaced by his usual faint smile. "Wilhelm doesn't worry me," he said, keeping his voice low, so it would not attract attention. "Wilhelm's faith blinds him and makes him a predictable opponent." Gilbert stood and buttoned his jacket. "Think about what I've said, my dear. You would do very well as one of us. I have been searching for years for my intellectual equal in the body of a woman. I regret I have work to do, so I'll bid you good night."

He stood, bowed to her, and strode from the room, signaling to the other New-Owenites to remain seated. Rose's face felt like she'd just leaned into the steam from a boiling kettle, and she didn't dare look around to see if anyone was watching. She comforted herself that at least she could hear the sisters on either side of her engaged in pleasant and engrossing conversation with brethren across from them. Perhaps her humiliation had gone unnoticed.

Rose had just seen a side of Gilbert Griffiths that repelled and alarmed her. She almost pitied Wilhelm. No longer could they dismiss Gilbert as a pedantic dreamer. He was ruthless. And he was smart.

Gretchen lifted down a ladder-back chair for herself and offered her rocker to Rose. Gretchen's retiring room was much like every other sister's room—neat and meagerly furnished, with a narrow bed, small desk, built-in drawers, and a tiny mirror over a washstand. To Rose, though, the room seemed cozy and safe, after her experience in the Union Meeting.

Rose struggled between her duties as eldress and her avid curiosity.

"I promise all he did was talk about the New-Owenites," Gretchen said. "Earl was very respectful. I think he's just getting fed up with those people. Earl really, truly believes in all those ideas Gilbert keeps talking about. But Gilbert—well, Earl said Gilbert talks a lot better than he acts. And Hugh wasn't any better."

Rose decided that giving in to her avid curiosity might just be her duty as eldress. "All right," she said, "you'd better tell me everything you learned from Earl. Start with his opinion about Mairin's drawings."

Gretchen hitched her chair closer and leaned toward Rose like an excited schoolgirl about to share some luscious gossip about a despised fellow student.

"Well, Earl hardly paid any attention to those drawings, just said that if Wilhelm thought he could use them to influence Gilbert, he'd get nowhere fast."

Rose nodded. Earl's comment supported her own observation that Gilbert was cleverer than he appeared.

"Earl had a *lot* more to say about Gilbert," Gretchen said. "And about Hugh and Celia, too, although he thinks Celia's been treated badly."

"Who has treated Celia badly?" Rose's eldress instincts alerted her to the hint of jealousy in Gretchen's voice. A confession would be in order. But not just now.

"Both of them, Earl said—Gilbert and Hugh. Earl said Hugh was very rich and was funding Gilbert's whole dream."

"Why would he do that?"

"Because of Celia. Earl said Celia was hopelessly in love with Gilbert, though he couldn't figure why, and Gilbert pressured her to marry Hugh, so the New-Owenites could get hold of his money. She went through with it, even though she didn't love him. Hugh was very jealous of her and practically kept her a prisoner."

Rose had difficulty imagining Celia as anyone's prisoner. Perhaps she adored Gilbert so much she'd do anything for him—but that, too, was hard to imagine. Celia did not seem capable of forgetting herself long enough to love so deeply.

"Earl said Hugh was practically a monster," Gretchen said. "He had a drinking problem, you know, and he gambled a lot when he was away on business. It made Gilbert very angry, the gambling did, because he was afraid Hugh would lose all his money, and then he wouldn't be able to finance Gilbert's dream community."

Rose's head was spinning with too much information. Her absent-minded rocking only confused her more, and it was beginning to bother her knee, so she wandered around Gretchen's retiring room. A small part of her mind noted with

approval the dust-free surfaces as she sorted through what
Gretchen had told her.

"Did he mention anything about unpaid gambling debts?"
Rose asked, remembering Earl's comments during the discus-
sion she'd overheard through the South Family Dwelling
House heating pipes.

"He said Hugh had lots of them, and everyone had been worried that gangsters might come after him." Gretchen's eyes
glowed with excitement. "Do such things really happen, Rose?"

"In the world, anything is possible. Let's hope our guests
have left such evil behind them and far away from us."

"There's more, too," Gretchen said, "and you won't like this
at all. Hugh used to whip Mairin—that's why she keeps running away, Earl said."

"I suppose I shouldn't be surprised or shocked," Rose said,
a now-familiar fierce protectiveness surging through her, "but
I am. Still, I can't see any of the New-Owenites killing Hugh
to stop him from beating Mairin, nor can I believe Hugh
hanged himself out of guilt for his behavior. There does seem
to be a consistency in Hugh's behavior. But why have the
New-Owenites been telling me that Hugh was soft-hearted, if
not terribly responsible?"

Gretchen shrugged.

"Although, if they were involved in Hugh's death, it makes
sense . . ." Rose muttered, as she paced the room. They certainly would want to keep any possible motives for murder to
themselves, and a soft-hearted Hugh would be more likely to
kill himself. But why would they believe they could get away
with the falsehood? Did they assume Rose was too stupid or
too unworldly to find out Hugh's true nature?

She was starting to feel that pain behind her eyes that usually only Wilhelm could trigger. Dropping back into the rocking chair, she said, "I'm grateful for one thing, at least—that
this time no Believers can be suspected of violence."

"Well . . ." Gretchen wriggled in her chair.

"Nay, it can't be," Rose said, leaning her head back with a
sigh. "Tell me."

"You know the brethren who've been fixing up furniture for the New-Owenites, Matthew and Archibald? It seems they are overfond of Celia. She's been to visit them in the Carpenters' Shop several times, which she should never have done, of course, but she did, and I guess she cried on their shoulders a bit about how Hugh was treating her, and you know how kind most brethren are, and I guess they just felt more and more sympathy for her, and—"

"Matthew and Archibald are *both* in love with Celia Griffiths? Have they fallen into the flesh?"

"Not . . . not that I know of," Gretchen said, reddening at Rose's bluntness.

Rose hated to believe that the two brethren could be so susceptible, though she'd seen some evidence of it herself. Matthew and Archibald were quick to defend Celia against criticism.

"Thank you for telling me, Gretchen—for all of it. I'll see if I can sort it out. You stay clear of Earl, do you understand?"

"Yea."

"Get some sleep now." Rose squeezed Gretchen's shoulder. "Heaven knows I need some myself."

"I was just wondering . . ." Gretchen said, as Rose reached for the door. "Should Wilhelm know? About Matthew and Archibald, I mean."

"I suppose he should. Let's wait, though. I'll warn the brethren to avoid further contact with Celia and to confess, if their consciences are impure. You can drop it from your mind, Gretchen. Sleep tight."

Rose hurried back to the Ministry House under a dark sky punctuated by bright stars. A chill north wind pushed her from behind, plastering her cloak to her back. Her weary mind resisted, but she had to decide what to tell Wilhelm. Despite her temptation to tarnish Wilhelm's belief that the New-Owenites would make excellent Shakers, she simply could not trust him to resist using the information somehow to further his own plans. For now, she would tell him nothing.

FIFTEEN

"SHE DROPPED RIGHT OFF, POOR SWEET," JOSIE WHISPERED.

Rose hung her cloak on a wall peg and sank into a chair. "Thanks for putting her to bed and watching over her, Josie. You must be exhausted."

"No more than you, from the looks of it. Are you sure you don't want me to keep Mairin in the Infirmary for a spell?"

"Nay, I'm happier when she's under my eye, especially at night. There's so much going on inside that little head, and I want to be around if it starts emerging. You run along and get to bed."

"Call if you need me, dear," Josie said. "I'll be up much of the night, anyway, with Sister Viola down with her autumn cough and fever. She's so frail, I keep expecting it to carry her off, but she always pulls through. Rose, you're falling asleep in your chair. Get to bed this instant."

Josie helped Rose out of her work dress and into bed, then fussed over the blankets. Rose was asleep within seconds, in the middle of Josie's whispered chatter.

When Rose's eyes opened again, the room was dark. She heard a mumbled voice. At first, Rose thought Josie must have decided to stay after all, and was chattering with herself to keep awake. But as she listened more carefully, the muttering made no sense.

Rose hoisted herself up on her elbow and listened. It was Mairin, babbling, undoubtedly in her sleep. Rose wanted to awaken her, to hold and comfort her, but some instinct told her to be still, to listen for words, clues to Mairin's fears.

Minutes inched past, and Mairin said no more than a few mumbled syllables. Rose's knee began to ache. She lowered herself back under the covers, her head on the pillow, and tried to stay awake to listen. If it hadn't been for the persistent ache in her knee, Rose might have lost her struggle and been fast asleep within seconds. If she had done so, she might have leaped out of bed and done her poor knee lasting damage when Mairin screamed in anguish.

"No, no, no! No, don't!" Her pleas subsided into staccato cries that sounded at times like a sobbing child's, at times more like a frightened animal's.

Rose was alarmed, yet disappointed. Mairin's outcries could easily be related to the ongoing abuse she had experienced. Rose had hoped Mairin's nightmares would provide more direct access to whatever was buried in the girl's memory, but even in sleep, she was hidden. Rose decided to try another tactic. She slid out of bed and went to Mairin, staying quiet, to avoid rousing her too early. The crayons and paper lay on the table set next to Mairin's bed.

"Mairin." Rose shook the sleeping girl's shoulder. Mairin's eyelids flew open. She whimpered and curled in a tight ball, like a cornered animal expecting an attack. She clutched her doll against her chest.

"It's me—Rose. I'm sorry I startled you. You were having a bad dream, and I was worried about you."

Mairin's body loosened, but she kept her distance. Rose switched on the bedside lamp. The girl's stillness and wide pupils gave her the look of a startled fawn.

Rose picked up the paper and crayons, and laid them on the bed in front of Mairin. "I was thinking, if your dream frightened you, it might help if you drew for a while. It has helped before, hasn't it?"

Mairin's gaze shifted to the paper, and she reached out a hand for the crayons. She picked them up, then dropped them again, as if she expected to be punished.

"Draw all you want," Rose said. "I'll crawl back into bed and not bother you. Keep the light on. If you need me, just call out. Good night, now." She slid back into her own bed and turned on her side, so her back would be to Mairin. She waited, trying to stay alert and failing. Just as she was relaxing into sleep, she heard the faint rat-scratches that told her Mairin was drawing. She pushed herself to stay awake, in case Mairin was so upset she might sneak out; but in the end, sleep took her.

When she awakened again, gray light streaked in her window, and the room was silent—too silent. Ignoring the warning twinge in her knee, Rose twisted around to find Mairin's bed tousled and empty. She tossed off her covers and leaped out of bed, but then she wasn't sure what to do. Get dressed. If Mairin had taken off again, Rose couldn't mount a search in her nightclothes. She grabbed the same work dress she'd worn the day before, carefully hung on a wall peg by Josie, and slipped it over her head.

As she went toward her built-in drawers to find a fresh kerchief to crisscross over her bodice, she passed close to Mairin's bed and saw several sheets of paper crumpled along with the bedsheets and the girl's nightgown. She turned one over and smoothed it out. Mairin had drawn another tree. This one was even more disturbing than her first. The deep hues were broken by lightning slashes of red and orange, and the headless snake coiled its way up the violet trunk.

Rose turned over two more rumpled pages. The first was a lovely bird with green eyes and bejeweled wings spreading forward as if to surround whoever held the drawing. The image did not strike Rose as frightening, but she supposed it might have a different effect on a child.

The third drawing looked like Mairin's attempt to impose order on the terrifying chaos of her imagination. A checkerboard, each square outlined with precision in black crayon, covered the page. Perhaps this drawing had been her last, because she hadn't filled in any colors. Or perhaps she hadn't needed colors, just order.

Aware of a sense of urgency, Rose rolled up the drawings and stowed them in a small cupboard built into the wall of her retiring room. If she could, she wanted to keep both Wilhelm and Gilbert from learning about the sketches. They would only encourage the two leaders to keep using Mairin as a pawn in their struggle for power. She'd been tossed about all her life. Perhaps that was the reason she'd drawn a checkerboard, though it seemed a sophisticated image for a child who lived in the trees.

Rose had just shut the drawings in the cupboard when a click told her the retiring room door had opened. She whirled around. Mairin stood in the doorway, fully dressed and holding her doll.

"Mairin! I thought . . . I got very worried when I woke up and saw your bed empty."

"I'm sorry. I just went to the bathroom."

"Well, I noticed you'd dressed, so I was afraid you'd left."

"I'm sorry," Mairin repeated. But she neither cowered nor ran away. Instead, she stepped inside and closed the door behind her. *It doesn't matter where she's been,* Rose thought. *It only matters that she's come back.*

"I'm glad you're here," Rose said. "Let's leave your doll on your bed during school time, shall we? That way the other children won't feel left out."

Mairin nodded and placed her doll on her pillow.

"It'll be breakfast time soon. Are you hungry?"

This time Mairin's nod was more vigorous. "Can we eat with Agatha again?" she asked.

"I'm sure she would love it," Rose said.

Mairin had slipped easily into her role as Agatha's helper. As soon as Polly brought a tray from the kitchen, Mairin pulled a chair near Agatha's and sat on the edge. She always fed Agatha a bite first before eating anything herself. When she did eat, Mairin copied Agatha's slow chewing, almost down to the second. She was rewarded by a warm smile from Agatha. The former eldress was perfectly capable of feeding herself with her left hand, but it was like her to choose a child's growth over her own fierce independence.

Rose remembered, from her own childhood, Agatha's easy ways with young people. When Agatha had listened to her endless prattle, she'd felt like the most important person on earth, and certainly the most interesting. Now she felt just a twinge of jealousy as she watched Mairin unfold in Agatha's sunshine. But she was glad for Mairin, too.

"Mairin, may I tell Agatha about your drawings?"

After Mairin's brief nod, Rose described the three new drawings to Agatha. "Could they truly be spirit gifts, do you think?"

Agatha's cloudy eyes traveled to her small desk. "Rose, dear, look in the drawer. You should find a drawing."

Rose wasn't alone in her curiosity—Mairin hurried to stand next to her as she pulled out a yellowed sheet of paper. The drawing—done in spidery black, blue, and red ink—depicted a garden filled with exquisite and unearthly flowers. Each was drawn with intricacy and precision, and none looked like anything Rose had ever seen. She handed the drawing to Agatha.

"You did drawings, too?" Mairin gazed at Agatha with hope.

Agatha handed the paper to the girl and said, "This is very precious to me. I was about your age when I drew it. I regret it was the only gift drawing I was ever given, but I will always feel blessed for having received it. Tell me, child, when did your own pictures come to you—were you awake, or asleep?"

"Asleep."

"You dreamed the pictures?"

"I guess so. I don't remember dreams, but something woke me up, and I just knew what to draw."

Rose marveled at the ease with which Agatha drew a response from Mairin. However, she also noticed another jealous pang. Clearly a thorough confession was called for, but Rose wasn't sure how she'd explain to Agatha, her confessor, how she, a pampered adult, could feel envy because of the friendship budding between Agatha and Mairin. Could it be that

Rose wanted, for herself alone, the privilege of being Agatha's "daughter" and Mairin's "mother"? This was just the sort of thing she had vowed to forsake—these jealous, exclusive ties. Yea, a confession was in order, and the sooner, the better.

By the time Rose stopped castigating herself, Agatha was explaining her own drawing to Mairin.

"You see, what we want, we Believers, is to create a heaven on earth, a home as pure and glorious as the celestial home we will journey to someday. But we don't always understand how to do that. The celestial world is a paradise beyond our imagining. So sometimes angels, heavenly spirits, come in dreams or when we worship to show us the way. Do you understand that, Mairin?"

The copper in Mairin's eyes had taken on a sheen. "Yes," she said. "I think so. It sounds beautiful."

"Yea, indeed, it is beautiful. That's what I was trying to draw—in my own poor way—the astonishing beauty of the heavens, like exquisite flowers we have never seen on earth."

Agatha's thin face relaxed in a smile, and her tightly stretched skin seemed to loosen. "When I drew this, we were getting fewer and fewer gifts. I think everyone was ready to settle down a bit." Agatha chuckled, and Mairin giggled in response, though she couldn't have known Agatha was remembering a period of Shaker history that went somewhat out of control.

"We weren't dancing so much anymore, which disappointed me, so I was dancing all by myself in some woods. I must admit I sneaked off now and then, but I never stayed away long. This time I twirled and shook and jumped, the way I'd seen the sisters do it, and I felt like I was being taken into another world, an unutterably lovely world. Then suddenly Mother Ann appeared to me, dressed all in white with sparkling jewels sewn into her robe. Hundreds of angels swirled around her."

Agatha leaned her head back on her rocker and closed her eyes. "Mother Ann spoke to me. She said, 'Child, go home and draw flowers, glorious flowers, and look at them whenever you need to remember your true home.' Then she blessed me and was gone."

Agatha opened her eyes. "You never saw a girl run so fast as I did to get home to the Children's Dwelling House. I had red and blue and black ink because I was helping Sister Iris mark the lessons of the younger girls. It took weeks of work, but I never forgot the vision Mother Ann had blessed me with, and I did as she bade me—whenever my faith wavered, I looked at my gift drawing and remembered my true home."

Both Mairin and Rose sat spellbound as Agatha finished her story. Rose had never seen or heard about Agatha's drawing before, perhaps because Rose herself had always been of a more practical bent; she had never received a direct message from Mother Ann, though she knew such experiences were possible. She simply—and to her disappointment—had never been chosen as an instrument.

Agatha leaned toward Mairin and covered the girl's light brown hand with her own thin blue-veined one. "Think, Mairin. Try to remember your dream. How did you know what to draw?"

Mairin's face puckered in concentration. Rose remembered her own childhood and suspected that Mairin wanted desperately to please Agatha. But the girl took her time and seemed to be focusing on her dream. Finally she opened her eyes and frowned.

"I'm not sure," she said, "but I don't remember seeing a beautiful lady and lots of angels. It was scarier than that. The things I drew, I just saw them in my dream, and I knew to draw them. Only I don't remember if Mother Ann told me to draw them." Mairin's pupils widened with fear.

Though her own eyesight was probably too poor to see the anguish in Mairin's eyes, Agatha responded to the tone in her voice. "The visits of Mother Ann are different for everyone," she said. "You have not lived with us for long, so perhaps she came to you in hidden form. Nevertheless, it is very like her to give you pictures to draw."

Agatha sank back in her rocker, spent.

"It is past time to get Mairin to the Schoolhouse," Rose said, planting a light kiss on Agatha's cool forehead. "And time for you to rest."

Agatha clutched Rose's wrist. "Stay just a moment," she said. "Mairin, dear, would you take this tray back to the kitchen? Thank you."

She waited for a moment after the door closed behind Mairin before motioning Rose to sit again.

"I know our experiences were very different," Agatha said, "but my heart tells me that Mairin was visited by Mother Ann."

"You surprise me," Rose said. "I was sure you'd say it was just a bad dream. Why would Mother send such odd messages?"

"Mother does not always send bright and beautiful messages, after all. Remember that she lost all her own children. I truly believe she has come to Mairin's aid because she is a child, and a needy one. Mother Ann has appeared in disguise because the child might not understand—but appear she has. I believe her message is as much for us as it is for Mairin, perhaps even more so. Mairin is in grave danger, I feel it, and those drawings are messages from Mother Ann to warn us. We *must listen.* We are all she has. We must not fail her."

SIXTEEN

WHEN ROSE HAD TOO MUCH TO THINK ABOUT, WORKING IN the Herb House always seemed to help. So, after depositing Mairin at the Schoolhouse, she assigned herself to a morning of packing herbs for sale to the world. The harvest was in, and the Herb House would be bursting with bound bunches of herbs hanging from every possible hook, peg, and rack. Many of them were dry and ready to be crumbled and stuffed into round tins. Maybe she'd allow herself to work on the dried buds collected from the lavender plants during their second flowering in the late summer. It was tedious work, but Rose found the fresh fragrance helped clear her mind.

She swung open the Herb House door to an explosion of heady scents—pungent, sweet, and grassy. But her joy was short-lived. The building was filled not just with herbs, but with people. On the ground floor, a brother repaired a large herb press, while a group of sisters, laughing and chattering, worked at a long table. At one end, two sisters were tying up the last of the harvest for drying, while several other sisters used the remaining space to extract essential oils from several piles of herbs. Rose recognized long stalks of valerian. So some of this work was being done for the medicinal herb industry, which Andrew directed.

Waving a greeting, Rose made for the stairs to the second-floor drying room. The smell of pickles told her that dill seeds were being packed even before she entered the room. Once again, the lifting of her spirits was only momentary. More sisters and a couple of New-Owenite women bustled about the room, asking and answering questions. The Herb House was not a quiet, tranquil place. She would have to do her thinking elsewhere.

She descended the staircase to find Andrew at the worktable, consulting with the sisters extracting herb oils. He made a notation in a journal, closed it and hitched it under his arm, and looked up to see Rose. Though his lips barely moved, Rose felt his smile. They never made any effort to run into one another—that would feel tantamount to breaking their vows—but their friendship grew, and they allowed themselves to enjoy working together, when the task called for them to do so.

"Rose, I'm glad to find you," Andrew said. His expression grew serious. A wave of brown hair, an inch longer than Wilhelm preferred, fell across his forehead. He ignored it. "Have you time to come back to the Trustees' Office with me? I want to show you something."

Rose noticed a sidelong glance or two from the sisters, but assured herself she had no reason for guilt. Nor did Andrew, though his habit of direct speaking sometimes triggered suspicions.

"Is there a problem with the books?"

"It seems so," Andrew said. "It seems that . . . well, it's better if I show you."

Rose followed him from the Herb House, her anxiety increasing with each step. Normally Andrew would have consulted with her immediately, unconcerned that others might hear. Something must be very wrong.

"Gilbert says that Wilhelm approved these expenditures," Andrew said, holding the ledger book out for Rose to examine. She laid it on the desk and bent over it, one hand supporting her chin, the other tracing the columns of numbers. By the time she'd finished, she needed both hands to hold up her head. Her eyes met Andrew's troubled brown ones, and neither of them cared at that moment that they were too close together, seated at the pine double desk that Rose had once occupied.

"We can't go on this way," she said. "Have you spoken with Wilhelm? What does he say?"

"He won't even discuss it. He says it's worth the investment. I thought, with your authority . . ."

Rose stared again at the ledger and shook her head. "Two hundred dollars for furniture? I thought Matthew and Archibald were spending all their time repairing furniture for the South Family Dwelling House. How much furniture can a group of seven visitors need?"

"I asked Gilbert the same question, and he was vague, so I called Si at the Languor Furniture Store and asked him for a list. It seems they bought items such as full-length mirrors and new mattresses. Gilbert told Si he had authorization from Wilhelm to charge what they needed to the Society. Si said they put in an order for a couple of double beds, too. He said he wondered about that, what with our being Shakers and all. I took it upon myself to cancel the order. I haven't told Gilbert or Wilhelm."

"Nor do you need to, Andrew. I will take care of this myself." Anxiety had turned to anger, a more familiar emotion for Rose, and a more welcome one at the moment. "You may call Si, and these other merchants as well, and tell them all not to extend any more credit to any non-Believer. Wilhelm should never have authorized this without consulting with me first. He frequently forgets that I am now eldress."

"Wilhelm has little use for women," Andrew said.

"Wilhelm has little use for me, in particular," Rose said, with a bitter laugh.

"Then he is a fool."

Both sensed danger at this point and scraped their chairs farther apart.

"I'm afraid there's even more bad news," Andrew said, a shade too quickly. "I got worried and began checking around the rest of the village. I borrowed a few journals from the deacons and deaconesses, and this is what I discovered."

He pulled a sheet of paper from his desk drawer and handed it to Rose. It contained two columns—on the left, a list of the village's food and nonfood stores, as recorded by the Shaker deacons and deaconesses in their journals, and on the right, an inventory of those same stores, dated the day before.

"Our stores are disappearing," Rose said. "Don't tell me the New-Owenites have just been helping themselves and not even telling us. I thought surely Wilhelm would have rationed an amount for them, as we would with any guests."

"The deacons and deaconesses were as shocked as we are, though they had noticed that items seemed to be disappearing. They thought they were at fault for not recording accurately."

"But how can this be? We put locks on the storeroom doors. Even Wilhelm agreed we had to do so, given the times." It had been one of Rose's easier victories, once she'd reminded Wilhelm that the Millennial Laws had once called for locking up the stores. "Do you suppose . . . ?"

"Yea, I'm fairly certain," Andrew said. "Somehow the New-Owenites have gotten keys to our storerooms, most probably from Wilhelm. They are draining our reserves. At this rate, we won't have food through the winter, even without guests."

Andrew's long bones seemed to melt against his chair with weariness. "I'm afraid," he said, "this is a battle we will need you to fight. I will do whatever I can to help."

Rose leaned back, as well. In silence, she let her gaze run over the neatly organized cubbyholes stacked on her side of the desk, and their twins on Andrew's side. Andrew was lax about some Society customs, such as hair length and authentic clothing, but his organizing skills were above reproach, as was his devotion to his faith. She could trust him. The seeds of a plan germinated in her mind.

"As trustee, can you come up with a reason to make an immediate trip to Indiana?" Rose asked.

"Indiana? I suppose so, but why . . . Indiana is where the New-Owenites came from, isn't it?"

"Indeed. I heard they've been living somewhere east of Bloomington for the last few years. The rest of them are still there, as I understand it, waiting for word from their leaders about where and when to move. My guess is there are people who know the New-Owenites far better than we do and can give us an accurate accounting."

"And you want me to go there and see what I can find out?"

"Yea, if you can manage it without making Wilhelm or Gilbert suspicious."

"What should I be looking for? Anything in particular?"

"This may sound odd," Rose said, "but I seem to have too much information at the moment. I can't sort my way through it. Some of the stories we've gotten are inconsistent. For instance, was Hugh soft-hearted, or did he beat Mairin and keep his wife a virtual prisoner? Are we to believe that Hugh was despondent over gambling debts and hanged himself? Or was he a monster who invited murder? I can't shake the fear that Mairin saw something terrible and that she is in mortal danger, but I can prove nothing. I need to know what the truth is."

Andrew rubbed his chin and nodded slowly. "That doesn't sound in the least odd. To be honest, I've had some of the same questions. Celia, for instance. And Gilbert. Are they what they seem?" Andrew glanced over at Rose. "I had an uncomfortable conversation with Celia yesterday evening at the Union Meeting."

Rose encouraged him with raised eyebrows.

"I'm afraid she was rather . . ." Andrew fidgeted with a pen. "Well, she was downright worldly."

"I saw how she was dressed. It astonished me that Wilhelm did not object. You seemed untroubled, or I would have intervened."

"Nay, it posed no problem for me, but I was irritated that she would try to distract me. It was so clearly a calculated effort. She showed no respect for our faith."

"If I may ask, what did she say to you?"

Andrew's cheeks reddened. Rose was surprised, since Andrew had once been married and was well accustomed to dealing with the world.

"I want you to know," Andrew said. "She asked about my

background, my marriage and all sorts of highly personal information like that. She paid no attention to the drawings, by the way. It was as if she had rehearsed a part and was going to deliver it, no matter what. After a while, she began speaking in a low voice, and I found myself leaning forward to hear her. She asked if I ever thought about . . ." Andrew took a deep breath. "About being with a woman again. She suggested it was unnatural for a man my age to embrace celibacy when I'd already had a wife and children. I tried to change the subject, but she ignored my efforts. Just after Gilbert got up to leave, she looked into my eyes and told me that she was coming into a lot of money, and she had no one interesting to spend it with. Then she told me to 'think about it' and let her know my feelings soon." Andrew laughed without mirth. "This feels like a confession," he said.

"You've done nothing wrong. Celia treated you with disrespect."

Andrew sauntered toward a window. After a moment of silence, he looked back at Rose.

"What did Gilbert say to you?"

"Gilbert?"

"Yea, at the Union Meeting. Gilbert spoke to you at length. You looked uncomfortable to me, so I was just wondering if he was as insensitive to you as Celia was to me." He gave her a lopsided grin. "I feel much relieved for having told you my experience. Perhaps I can offer you the same relief, if it is necessary. And together we will have more information to work with."

"Ah, you will be an elder someday, Andrew."

"Nay, thank you, but I've no interest. Tell me about Gilbert."

She did. Andrew stayed by the window; he seemed to know that she needed distance from him to talk about Gilbert's impropriety.

"So," Rose concluded, "it seems that both of their performances were orchestrated. But why? Did they plan it together, hoping we were weak links and would convert to their world more easily than some others? Or did each of them behave independently? It sounds as if Celia hopes to leave the New-Owenites, with Hugh's money, whatever is left of it, and in the company of a man. Gilbert would hardly be happy with that plan."

"But he might have instructed her to pretend," Andrew said.

"Perhaps. I still have difficulty believing Celia could be so much under Gilbert's influence." Rose heaved a sigh and pushed out of her chair. "What do you say? Will you go to Indiana and try to find the answers to some of these questions?"

"I wouldn't miss it. It might be awkward to contact you while I'm gone."

"If you learn something important and feel it can't wait," Rose said, "call through the Infirmary. Josie will understand."

SEVENTEEN

WILHELM ARCHED HIS EYEBROWS WHEN ROSE ENTERED THE Ministry House dining room for breakfast the next morning. The sun had just begun to rise and the small room was lit by two candles and a few gray streaks from the windows. Lately Wilhelm seemed to be avoiding the use of electricity whenever possible.

"I am surprised to see thee," he said. "Does this mean thy heavy duties allow thee time to discuss Society matters with me?"

Rose forced a cheerful expression and took a sip of tea. "We do have a few items to discuss, Wilhelm. May I have some bread?"

"Where is the child?" Wilhelm asked, as he pushed serving plates toward her. "The girl should be here with us. I have questions to ask her."

"I'm sure you do, but Mairin is still sleeping."

"Sleeping? I've been up doing chores for an hour. She will never make a Shaker this way."

Rose thought it a good moment to take a bite of bread.

"Has she had more gift drawings?" Wilhelm's expression brightened. "Is that why she is sleeping through the morning—because she was up in the night, drawing?"

Lies did not come easily to Rose, so she chewed slowly and thought quickly. "Mairin has terrible nightmares," she said finally. She had hesitated a moment too long.

133

"So," Wilhelm said, tapping the air with his fork, "the 'nightmares' are her trances, her experience of being an instrument. If she were a Believer, of course, the experience would be blissful, but at least she has been lucky enough to be chosen." He slathered strawberry jam on a second slice of bread. "Bring the drawings here as soon as we've finished. I want to examine them."

"I'll do no such thing. You'll leave that poor child alone." *Tact, Rose, tact,* she thought, as Wilhelm's face tightened in fury. "I don't want to wake her. Her health has been damaged by years of neglect."

"As soon as she has awakened, then. I need to see those drawings as early as possible today, to be prepared."

Rose was losing her appetite. "Prepared?" she asked. "Prepared for what?"

"For the worship service, of course." Wilhelm pushed back his chair and stood. "One is scheduled for tomorrow evening. Do thy plans still allow time for such frivolity as worship?"

"Wilhelm, I know we have a worship service coming up, but I don't see what Mairin's drawings have to do with it. You showed them at the Union Meeting, and the New-Owenites ignored them. The last time you invited them to a worship service, they walked out. I doubt they'd bother to attend another."

"They will if Mairin is there."

"Wilhelm!" Rose stood and faced him, hands on hips. "I will not have you put that child on display, all so·you can win converts!"

Wilhelm leaned over the table on his fists. Instinctively Rose took a half step back, then forced herself forward again. She was not a novitiate; she had survived many battles with Wilhelm. She had seen those eyes turn to blue slits above a grinding jaw. He might startle her, but he no longer frightened her.

"It is not thy place to withhold gifts from the Society—thy sisters and brethren, or does that no longer mean anything to thee? Those drawings are gifts from Mother Ann. They belong to all of us. They are a message to all of us, for our protection and our future. It is thy duty, as eldress, to share those drawings with everyone."

Rose was torn almost beyond endurance. She truly did not know if Mairin's drawings were gifts from Mother Ann or the products of a child's tortured mind. Yet how could she, a Believer, deny that Mother Ann might be speaking through the child, if for nothing else than to save her life? If there was the slightest chance that the drawings were Mother Ann's Work, then they belonged to the whole Society.

"I will bring the drawings to the worship service," Rose said. "But Mairin must stay away."

"She must be there."

"Nay, she is too fragile. I won't allow it."

Rose and Wilhelm were still hissing at one another when the kitchen door swung open and Lydia appeared, holding a folded sheet of paper.

"I'm sorry to interrupt, but . . ."

Two pairs of blazing eyes turned on her. To her credit, though her mouth hung open in alarm, Lydia didn't slink back into the kitchen. She held out the piece of paper toward Wilhelm, who frowned at it as if it were a poison mushroom.

"What's that?"

"A message, Elder. From Andrew."

"Well, why didn't he come in himself?"

"It wasn't him brought the message, it was another one of the brethren."

Wilhelm's frown deepened. "Give it here. And clean up now—we're finished."

Lydia slid over to Rose's side of the table, perhaps thinking it safer, and gathered up an armload of dishes. She hurried back into the kitchen.

Wilhelm read the note, then crumpled it and tossed it on his soiled plate.

"What is it, Wilhelm?"

"Nothing. No concern of thine." He reached the dining room door and turned back to her. "I want to see those drawings *before* the service," he said, and was gone.

Stifling her guilt, Rose reached across the table and grabbed the crumpled paper on Wilhelm's plate. Hearing Lydia push on the kitchen door, Rose stuffed the note inside her kerchief and hurried out of the dining room. The parlor was empty, so she closed the door behind her and smoothed the paper on the desk. It said:

> *Having problems with some customers in Ohio and Indiana not paying as promptly as they should. Given our current financial situation, have decided on quick personal visits. Left by train last night, but didn't want to disturb you. Back in a couple of days.*

> *Andrew*

Rose couldn't help grinning. It was clever of Andrew to slip off so quickly, giving Wilhelm no time to object. It was the sort of plan she would have followed, when she was trustee and more subject to Wilhelm's control. Even more clever was Andrew's pointed reference to the village's financial dilemma, caused by the New-Owenites—and, indirectly, by Wilhelm. No wonder Wilhelm had said it was not her business.

Placing the note back under her kerchief, Rose climbed the stairs to her retiring room to awaken Mairin, get her some breakfast, and deliver her to the Schoolhouse, where Charlotte was waiting to give her some extra Saturday lessons. Rose was eager to pursue her own investigation of the New-Owenites. She did not delude herself that Andrew's note would leave Wilhelm chastened enough to give up his dream. In fact, it was likely to have the opposite effect—Wilhelm might feel increasing pressure to bring the New-Owenites into the fold, so that they would be giving as well as taking.

Hoping not to frighten Mairin, Rose tiptoed through the door and eased it closed behind her. She turned around and saw immediately that Mairin was not in the room. Her small nightgown was once again thrown across her unmade bed, and her clothes were gone. Her Shaker doll, somewhat crumpled from frequent hugging, lay on the pillow. Rose was getting used to Mairin's disappearances, so she calmed herself with the thought that the girl probably was preparing for the day, as she had done before.

Rose went down the hall to the bathroom and called Mairin's name. There was no answer. She phoned downstairs and checked in the kitchen. Nay, Mairin had not been there. Now Rose was ready to panic. Wilhelm had left the dining room in a hurry. What if he had somehow spirited away the sleeping child, while Rose was shut in the parlor? Surely he wouldn't do such a thing. But he might have asked Sister Elsa Pike to do it. Elsa was the one sister who blindly followed Wilhelm and paid little attention to Rose, her eldress.

A call to the Center Family Dwelling House, where Elsa lived, went unanswered, so Rose called the Laundry. Gretchen answered and assured Rose that Elsa had been ironing since breakfast and had not been gone for even a moment.

Rose hung up the wall phone and caught her breath. Mairin had left her doll as she did when she went to school. All right, Rose decided, she'd check one more place. And then she'd panic. There was no point in calling the Schoolhouse. The phone was tucked away in the hallway, and Charlotte often didn't hear it.

The Schoolhouse was quiet as Rose entered the front door. She peeked into the classroom and saw Charlotte's thin white cap and Mairin's light brown fuzz bent close to each other over an open book.

"Mairin!"

The girl's serious look brightened at the sound of Rose's voice. But Rose's relief had unaccountably turned to anger.

"Mairin, you mustn't *ever* leave without telling me." Rose's voice was harsher than she'd intended—harsher than she'd ever used except with Wilhelm, when it was hard to get his attention. She knew instantly she'd made a mistake. Mairin's happiness at seeing her evaporated. The girl's skin was just dark enough to hide a flush, but Rose saw misery dull her eyes as her face became a blank mask.

Rose knelt beside Mairin's chair. "I'm sorry. I shouldn't have spoken to you that way. I was afraid something bad had happened to you, and that made me sound angry. Can you understand that? Please forgive me."

"You were afraid for me?"

"Yea, child, very afraid. I don't want any harm to come to you; that's why I need to know where you are when you aren't with me or Agatha. Okay?"

Mairin's expression cleared.

"I'll tell you what. Promise me that you'll always let me or Josie take you to school. Will you do that?"

"I promise."

"Good. And if you have to visit the bathroom during the night and don't want to wake me, just write me a quick note, okay? Then I won't worry."

To Rose's alarm, Mairin hung her head. Charlotte placed a hand on Mairin's shoulder. "It's all right, dear. No one blames you. Rose, Mairin was never taught to read and write. I only just realized it yesterday, and that's why we've decided to spend extra hours on lessons. Mairin is quite eager, but she was embarrassed to have you know."

Rose lost her temper more easily than she wept, so it surprised both Charlotte and herself when the tears appeared and spilled over her eyelids. "Of course," she said, "take as much time as you need. I'll help, too, when I can, and as you learn, I'm sure Agatha would love to be read to."

"Mairin, would you go to the storeroom and get more paper for me?" Charlotte asked.

"Sorry," Rose said, once Mairin was gone. She pulled a handkerchief from her pocket. "I don't usually blubber like that. If anything, I'm furious. Gilbert Griffiths is always spouting off about the value of education—why on earth didn't he insist Mairin get reading lessons? I'm quite sure she has the ability."

"Oh, she has the ability," Charlotte said. "She learned her

alphabet in one morning. And don't ask me to explain those people. It seems to me they've treated Mairin like some sort of freak show they captured in the wilds. They just want to show her off, but they don't seem to have taken her seriously as a human being. I hope you're planning to put a stop to it."

"Oh, I am," Rose said. "I most certainly am."

Rose squatted in the small Ministry House garden, pulling out dead roots and breaking up the soil. It was a task that didn't truly need to be done, but Rose couldn't just wait and do nothing. She was watching for an opportunity to search the South Family Dwelling House. While waiting for Andrew's report, she intended to find out everything she could about the New-Owenites and their reasons for being in North Homage.

Gertrude had said none of the New-Owenites had shown up for breakfast. She'd called all the workshops, and none of them had reported visitors yet that morning. So the visitors must have slept in; perhaps they were even now deepening the mess in the South Family kitchen.

She counted the New-Owenites one by one as they strolled from the building. Gilbert first, then Earl, followed by Celia and the others. They went in different directions, as if they had assignments. Rose waited until the last one was out of sight before she slipped around to the back of the dwelling house. She entered by way of the cellar door Mairin had shown her. She moved quickly through the storage rooms and even faster through the frightful kitchen and up the stairs to the main floor hallway. There she paused for a few moments, listening. Aside from the tick-tock of the large clock in the hallway, she heard nothing to indicate human presence.

She took the women's staircase out of habit, though she guessed she was as likely to run into a man as a woman on these stairs. She must be getting used to the filth. Mother Ann had told them always to "keep a clean habitation," and Rose had taken the advice to heart, but she was able to stay calm as she noticed the dust gathering in the corners of the stairs. There was more important work to be done. Once this was over, the sisters could give the dwelling house a thorough cleaning, and she would talk with Wilhelm about a sweeping ritual, too, to restore purity.

Most of the first-floor retiring room doors were ajar, which made Rose's task easier. She peeked in the room she had already visited. It was little changed, except that the chairs were empty. The room looked as if it had already been torn apart in a search, so Rose set to work without taking much care to replace items as she'd found them. If anything, she had to stop herself from neatening up as she moved among the drawers and cabinets.

Against the wall, Celia had a large cherry wardrobe, which she must have bought in town. Certainly Shaker sisters never needed such monstrosities; each hung her Sabbathday dress and two work dresses on peg hangers. She opened the wardrobe and caught her breath. It looked like a treasure chest, crammed with bright colors and silky fabrics. Only a few dresses actually hung on hangers; most items clung to the end of a hanger or were piled on the wardrobe floor.

Rose ran her hands through the pile and recognized the feel of fine silk and satin. She picked an item off the top and held it up. It was a ruby red satin negligee, low-cut and form-fitted, with matching red lace barely disguising the décolletage. Rose dropped it on the floor. She looked through the rest of the items of clothing and found elegant sheath evening gowns; casual, but still expensive, silk dresses; and more negligees. She had seen Celia wear none of this clothing. Did she go out at night? The New-Owenites had their own automobile, a white Buick.

The room held two narrow Shaker beds. Under the wrinkled and soiled clothing piled on it, one of the beds was still made—clearly by a Shaker. So Celia was not entertaining at night. However, the single bed also indicated that Celia and Hugh had not shared a bedroom. According to Wilhelm, who believed deeply in the sinfulness of any and all carnal pleasure, the New-Owenites had promised to separate their men from their women, but Rose never believed they would actually do so. For whom had Celia been wearing those negligees? Earl had told Gretchen that Celia was in love with Gilbert; perhaps she'd find further evidence in Gilbert's room.

In Celia's dresser drawers, Rose riffled through delicate underthings, silk stockings, belts, and embroidered handkerchiefs. One entire drawer held jewelry, which had become entangled into a wad of chains and pins. The Shakers took better care of their most worn baskets than Celia did of all these riches.

Closing the last drawer, Rose looked around. Open jars of cold cream, several perfumes, a mirror, and at least a dozen make-up containers littered a table near the full-length mirror. A couple of fashion magazines lay splayed across Celia's unmade bed; otherwise, there was no evidence that she ever read or wrote anything. Next to her bed was a new-looking radio.

If Celia was a prisoner, she was a pampered one. No one had mentioned that she had money of her own, so she must have freely spent Hugh's, perhaps adding to the pressure of the gambling debts. Rose wondered what Gilbert thought of these expenditures, since he must have wanted Hugh's money all for his own vision. So far, Celia seemed the preferable victim, not Hugh—unless Hugh had threatened to cut off Celia's resources. If Celia had been involved in her husband's death, she would have needed an accomplice, someone strong—like the faithful Earl or the besotted Matthew. *Though I suppose,* Rose thought, *she could have driven Hugh to take his own life.*

Time was passing, and Rose hurried through the rest of the rooms on the women's side of the dwelling house. Two more rooms contained women's clothing. Both rooms were neater than Celia's, but far short of Shaker standards. One of the rooms held a new maple double bed. So one of the couples had decided to stay together. To her surprise, though, the drawers contained no men's clothing. Perhaps they were preserving an appearance of propriety, though Rose couldn't see why. Or perhaps one of the women was expecting her husband to arrive soon.

Rose crossed over to the men's retiring rooms. Her heartbeat picked up speed, but not because she shouldn't be there. Every morning, while the brethren were out doing chores, the sisters went to their rooms to air out the beds and do mending. Rose was used to being in the brethren's empty rooms. But now she wished she had started with these rooms first. At any moment, one of the New-Owenites might decide to come back, and there was far more to look at here than on the women's side.

The first room was the opposite of Celia's messy one. Rose recognized Gilbert's walking stick standing in a corner. A map of Kentucky was tacked to the wall above a bookcase filled with scholarly tomes, including several geology and zoology books. The bed was made, if not with precision, at least with neatness.

A leather chair sat in front of a Shaker pine desk. Except for the chair, all the furniture in the room looked like refurbished Shaker items. Gilbert had even hung his work suits on peg hangers, as the Shakers did. His built-in drawers held neatly folded shirts, socks, and underclothes. Rose opened the desk drawer and found a stack of blank paper and several pens. If Gilbert had written anything, he kept it somewhere else.

From time to time, Rose had needed to keep an item concealed, and she had always used her built-in wall cupboard. She scanned the room. Every retiring room had a cupboard—except, apparently, this one. Unless the bookcase was in front of it. Gilbert kept his room so neat, using every amenity almost as the brethren would. It seemed out of character for him to ignore something so useful as a built-in cupboard. The heavy bookcase was already about an inch away from the wall, so Rose edged it out a bit more. The cupboard was there, but Gilbert hadn't ignored it. He had fitted it with a lock, drilled right into the wood, and sealed it tight with a padlock.

Rose replaced the bookcase with care. Unlike Celia, Gilbert was likely to notice any rearrangement of his belongings. She took a last look around. The room showed Gilbert to be secretive, well-organized, and single-minded—there was no evidence of any woman, certainly not one so flamboyant as Celia. If Celia adored Gilbert, it was apparently one-sided.

The next room had to be Earl's. It was similar to Gilbert's but more expressive of personality. A bookcase held more scholarly works, as well as a battered copy of Hemingway's *To Have and Have Not.* He'd thrown his blanket over the bed without smoothing out the sheets underneath. Some clothing hung on pegs, but without hangers. His drawers were neater than Celia's, certainly, but not so precise as Gilbert's.

The built-in cupboard was in plain view, and Rose opened it. Inside she found a stack of novels of the sort she wouldn't have read even during her stay in the world, though it did give her a moment of pleasure to think how Wilhelm would react if he saw them.

Earl's desk held stationery, envelopes, pens, and stamps. The desk itself was another lovely old Shaker product, and it looked natural with its chair, a refinished old ladder-back with a red-and-white woven seat.

The loose, brown work clothes the New-Owenites favored were missing; Earl was probably wearing them. The clothing left in the room looked unfamiliar to Rose. She touched the fabric of a long black coat hanging from a peg. The smooth softness reminded her of the fine wool the sisters used to make Dorothy cloaks. The rest of Earl's wardrobe showed, in Rose's perception, the understated elegance of high-quality clothing. So Celia wasn't the only one who liked expensive things.

Sensing the approach of the noon hour, Rose moved on to the next room, but she hadn't yet slipped through the doorway when the sound of men's voices floated up the stairs. She didn't stop to think. She only knew she mustn't be in one of the occupied rooms. She ran to the far end of the hallway, slipped into a room that was unlikely to be in use, and closed the door behind her. She could hear the voices again as they drew closer. Then they ceased, probably because the men had entered their rooms.

She leaned her back against the door to give her aching knee a rest, and took a look at the room she'd likely be in until everyone left for the noon meal. When she'd entered, the room had seemed small and dark. Now she realized why. Furniture was everywhere—in front of the curtained windows, with pieces piled on top of each other, even on several Shaker beds that had probably been there since the South Family had died out.

Rose didn't dare turn on a light, so she examined the pieces as best she could. They were old, like the ones already in the New-Owenites' rooms—and like the pieces she'd seen Matthew and Archibald working on. The wood felt smooth, refinished. Tapes were stretched tight across the seats of ladder-back chairs. Nothing looked broken or crooked.

Her knee throbbed and her head swam; she dropped into a nearby chair, a rocker, and let her body go limp. How long had the New-Owenites been living here? No more than two weeks at the most. In that short time, Matthew and Archibald must have worked well past dark every night to repair all this furniture, even if some of it hadn't needed much work. But why?

She suspected the answer before she'd finished the question. There must be many more New-Owenites, waiting in their temporary home near Bloomington, perhaps, for word that North Homage was to be renamed New Harmony, and the Shakers were to become industrious, land-rich converts to New-Owenism. Wilhelm was cooperating, of course, because he truly believed the New-Owenites would become Shakers. Perhaps he thought that once they sat in Shaker chairs, they would be unable to resist the spiritual power of the Society. As if a true Believer could be created without a call from within.

All at once, Rose felt a heaviness on her chest, as if the room and the hubris it represented had fallen on top of her. She had to get out. She didn't care if the men had left yet for the noon meal. The thought of a direct confrontation was almost a relief. She left the room, walked openly down the hall, then down the staircase, and out the front door. She encountered no one. Perhaps Mother Ann had been watching over her. Much as she longed to force the battle into the sunlight, it wasn't yet time.

EIGHTEEN

AFTER HER SOJOURN IN THE SOUTH FAMILY DWELLING HOUSE and a quick meal, Rose made straight for the Carpenters' Shop for a talk with Matthew and Archibald. She was in no mood to stop and chat with anyone, so she cut through the grass between the Children's Dwelling House and the Schoolhouse. In so doing, she had a clear view of the area in back of the Carpenters' Shop. She saw someone walking toward the grove of sugar maples, well past their autumn prime. The figure was dressed in trousers and a long coat, but the swaying gait could only be Celia's. There was nothing suspicious about a walk in the woods on a crisp fall afternoon, of course. But Rose was fairly certain Celia was walking from the back door of the Carpenters' Shop; otherwise, she'd have been visible earlier. All the more reason to give the carpenters a serious talking-to, since Wilhelm had on his blinders.

By the time Rose reached the door, it was clear that all was not well inside the shop. She heard no sanding or sawing through the open window, only the unmistakable sounds of an argument.

"I was only thinkin'—" said a protesting voice, which Rose recognized as Archibald's.

"Well, don't, all right? *Don't* think," Matthew responded in a harsher voice. "And for God's sake, don't open that mouth of yours."

Tempting as it was, Rose couldn't stand outside and listen.

She might be discovered at any moment. She could, however, question Matthew and Archibald about Celia's visit. Even if they lied, she would learn something.

She rapped on the door and stepped inside. Both men sat at worktables, in front of partially finished projects, but neither held any tools. As Rose entered, Matthew grabbed a ladder-back chair and examined its splintered leg. Archibald stared at her, his mouth slightly open. Neither of the brethren greeted her.

"Surely our visitors have enough chairs," Rose said. "How much furniture can seven people possibly need?"

"I couldn't say," Matthew said, without looking up. "I just do the work I'm given as best I can."

Rose strolled to a corner of the shop and took a closer look at the jumble waiting to be refurbished. Bookcases, small tables, rocking chairs, desks, and a variety of baskets were stacked precariously.

"Who has been giving all this work to you?"

Matthew bent close to the chair and seemed not to hear her question. Archibald had gone to work on his oval box, but he glanced up when Matthew didn't answer.

"Elder Wilhelm told us, go ahead and fix up what's needed," Archibald said helpfully. When Matthew scowled at him, he cringed and went back to his work.

"I see," Rose said. "I wondered because I saw Celia leaving the shop and thought perhaps she'd come to order more furniture."

She didn't expect an immediate answer, and she was not surprised when neither man spoke. In fact, she was encouraged and even somewhat amused by their discomfort. She might yet convince one of them to blurt out some information. Archibald was the better bet, once he'd recovered from Matthew's rebuke.

To buy time, Rose pulled down a small oval box waiting for repair. It was aged maple with tiny cracks under the swallowtail joints and a few streaks of mustard yellow paint clinging to the top. Across the side the word "nutmeg" was written in careful script. She pulled off the top. If she held it close to her face, she could still smell the spicy-sweet nutmeg, some grains of which had lodged in the seam between the bottom and the curved sides.

Carrying the box, she walked over to Archibald's worktable. He was sanding a larger box, which looked to be of the same vintage. His pudgy fingers worked the surface of the wood as if he were petting a newborn kitten. "You're doing a good job on that," she said. "You've brought out the grain, and I can't tell if it was ever painted."

"Bright red it was," Archibald said, "and cracked worse than that one." There was pride in his voice, for which Rose forgave him, since he seemed unaware of it. She sensed Matthew was watching them, so she continued to chat to keep Archibald's attention away from the other carpenter. Her voice was low and casual, and she hoped Matthew could not hear her.

"By the way, I've spoken with Wilhelm about some special lessons for you, as we discussed. Since the harvest is finished, one of the older brethren could spend some time teaching you. Would you like that?"

Archibald's grin broadened his already round face. "Yea, I would. It might be a while, though," he said, looking at the box in Rose's hands. "We have a lot of work left to do."

"How many of these boxes have you repaired already?"

"A couple dozen, thereabouts," Archibald said. "There was a lot of them in some empty rooms."

"Did Wilhelm send you around to look for unused furniture?"

"He started us off, but he didn't know all the places." This time the pride came through with a shy smile. "We found some on our own, in the South Family Dwelling House, getting the place ready, you know."

Rose nodded. "Of course, when the South Family was gone, we really didn't have room to store all that they'd left behind, so we put most everything into a few rooms and just took out what we could use. Goodness, there was furniture enough for fifty Believers, at least. You must have been working day and night to repair all of it."

Archibald beamed. "Day and night," he agreed. "Matthew's been sleeping here, in the room upstairs, so he can work past bedtime. That's the last of it, over there. That you're holding is the last box, and Matthew, he's doing the last ladder-back."

Archibald's face fell as he glanced up and caught another of Matthew's glowers. But this time his fleshy lips formed a pout, and he turned his attention back to Rose. "Matthew and me, we've been working mighty hard to help out. We got near three rooms full of fixed-up chairs and tables and such-like back at the dwelling house, and those folks've been real grateful."

"I imagine they are. Why else would Celia come over here just to thank you for your work?"

"Oh, she just come to pass the time of day, see how things are going, like she always does." It didn't take Matthew's disapproval to quell him this time. At once he realized what he'd said. He gulped hard and began sanding, just a bit harder than before.

Behind her, Rose heard the clunk as Matthew put down his work, and she knew he was coming in her direction. With a light spin, she faced him.

"Well, it's good to know you will be done with this huge task soon," she said. "There's quite of bit of repair needed elsewhere in the village. When do you suppose you'll be ready to turn to that?"

"Soon," he said. "If we can get some peaceful work time." He stood in the middle of the room, and his tall, gangly body made it seem as if he'd be more comfortable galloping through the pastures. Apparently aware of his rudeness to his eldress, his shoulders hunched forward and he took an awkward shuffling step out of Rose's path.

"I'll be running along, then," she said, with determined cheerfulness. As she headed for the door, she passed the chair Matthew was repairing. It had a cracked leg and a seat woven from red-and-white tape, like the ones she'd seen in the South

Family Dwelling House. This one had dirty streaks across the seat, as if someone had stood on it with muddy shoes, and then slipped off.

Rose pulled out Mairin's three most recent drawings and spread them across her desk. She picked up the checkerboard. Despite the lack of color, it could represent the interwoven tapes used for ladder-back chair seats—like the one she had just seen Matthew repairing—the one that looked as if it had been kicked aside by a man committing suicide. Even old chairs were unlikely to have such scuff marks on them. Shaker furniture was functional but delicate, more easily broken than furniture used by the world. Shaker pieces were made to be treated gently, used with respect. They were crafted for the glory of God and the pleasure of the angels. No Believer would use a ladder-back chair as a step-stool, especially without wiping his feet first.

The chair Matthew had been repairing was surely the one that had disappeared after Hugh's death. She had questioned all the Believers, and no one had admitted to taking it out of the orchard. How did it get to the Carpenters' Shop? Matthew and Archibald had just shrugged when she'd asked them. Had Celia perhaps stopped by on one of her frequent visits and told the brethren there was one more chair to be picked up and fixed? That seemed cold-hearted. She would have known, surely, how it had been used. Or perhaps she had used it herself.

Rose shook her head to clear it. She still had virtually no factual information, but her suspicions were growing. She wished she could just leave it alone and let Hugh be recorded as a suicide. But there was too much at stake. Mairin's serious little face floated into her mind. She could never leave Mairin with the New-Owenites if there was the slightest chance one of them was a murderer, and it was looking more and more as if the New-Owenites would not hand her over to Rose without a fight. Mairin was, at the moment, a valuable possession for Gilbert.

A worse specter popped into her thoughts. What if, by some doubtful miracle, the New-Owenites decided to join with the Shakers? Even if they were only Winter Shakers—using the community's food and shelter for a time, perhaps pretending to be serious novitiates, and leaving in the spring—then Mairin could come, too, but at what cost? Would the Society be taking in Hugh's killer—or killers?

Rose took a sheet of paper and a pen from her desk drawer, set the drawings aside, and settled down to organize her thoughts. She drew three columns, labeled "Murder," "Suicide," and "Oddities/Questions." After half an hour of writing—small, so she could fit everything on one page—she relaxed in her chair and read her lists.

Murder?	*Suicide?*
Celia felt imprisoned by Hugh.	Hugh had gambling debts.
Gilbert wanted Hugh's money,	Suicide note.
could get through Celia?	Chair.
Gambling threatened the $ source.	
Earl disliked Hugh— why?	

Oddities/Questions

Was Hugh gentle or cruel?
Who took the chair from the orchard, and why?

*Why so much furniture? Just how many New-Owenites
   are there?*
What do they want from us?
Is the note real?
*What is Celia's relationship with Gilbert, Earl, Mat-
   thew, and Archibald?*
What did Mairin see in the orchard?
What frightened Mairin outside the Schoolhouse?
*What does Gilbert keep locked up in his wall cup-
   board?*

Despite the lack of factual information, Rose felt more sure,
seeing it all written down, that murder was a stronger possibility than suicide. Mairin's shock proved nothing by itself;
she might have been affected as badly by suicide as by murder.
But something continued to frighten her, as if a threat still
existed.

The amount of furniture being readied disturbed her. She
had understood from Wilhelm that Gilbert had left behind a
handful of followers, far too few to need all that. It was possible that Wilhelm had given the initial instructions to begin
the repairing, and he might not have checked recently to see
how much was being done. It would be like him to lose interest in the details. If that was what had happened, then the
New-Owenites were the ones stockpiling furniture.

She folded the paper and stuffed it in her apron pocket.
When she heard from Andrew, perhaps she could straighten
out some of her questions. In the meantime, the list would
help to guide her efforts. She wanted a look at that so-called
suicide note. Then it would be time for a heart-to-heart talk
with Mairin, and she would need Agatha's help.

NINETEEN

THERE WASN'T TIME FOR A VISIT TO LANGUOR BEFORE PICKING up Mairin from her extra lessons, so Rose asked Charlotte to deliver the girl to Agatha's retiring room. Then she made a quick call to the Languor County Sheriff's Office. Grady O'Neal had returned, and Sheriff Brock was out for the day. Perfect. Rose made an appointment to visit Grady in half an hour.

Andrew usually watched over the Society's black Chrysler, but since he was gone, Rose decided not to tell anyone where she was going—not yet. It was mid-afternoon, and the other Believers were busy at their rotations, so though she might be seen taking the car, especially by a New-Owenite wandering around, no one would know her destination.

She hurried to the parking space beside the Trustees' Office, slipped into the car with more haste than grace, and pressed the starter button. The brethren kept the Chrysler clean and well-maintained, and it was still fairly new, so she began her trip with no difficulties. However, as she pulled onto the un-paved road leading through the village center, she glanced out the driver's window and saw one of the brethren standing out-side the Carpenters' Shop, watching her drive off. From the tall, thin stature, it had to be Matthew.

Rose headed west from the village over the eight miles of hilly, bumpy road to the town of Languor, the county seat. When she'd served as trustee, she had traveled to town regularly to meet with customers and to order supplies. Since she had become eldress, the visits had become rare, though she had more freedom now to travel.

She drove through the outskirts of Languor, where the poorest of the poor lived, and she was reminded that not all the world lived as pleasantly and productively as the Shakers. As this grinding Depression wore on, their neighbors suffered more each day.

The autumn chill had driven the children inside, giving the area an abandoned look. Porches and steps sagged, windows were covered over with paper, and more than one roof had a hole or a patch. And these were the folks who had homes to sleep in. The Society's carpenters shouldn't be wasting their time helping the wealthy New-Owenites stockpile furniture. Right here was where Matthew and Archibald should be working. She was still dreaming about turning all the repaired Shaker furniture over to the Languor poor when she parked near the Sheriff's office.

"Rose, it's good to see you again," Grady said, with genuine pleasure, as he ushered her into his tiny office. "I just spoke with Gennie on the phone, and she sends her love. She's staying on with my family, to help my mother while my father recovers."

"I only knew you were away on family business," Rose said. "I had no idea your father was ill. I should have pressed harder for information. How is he?"

"He's better," Grady said. "He had a heart attack. Gave us a bad scare, but it looks like he's through the worst."

"We will pray for your father and your family," Rose said.

"Thanks." Grady riffled through a stack of papers on his desk, and Rose sensed his discomfort.

"I wouldn't presume upon our friendship at a time like this if it were not a matter of extreme importance—perhaps of life and death." She drew her list from her pocket and handed it to Grady. A crease between his eyebrows deepened as he read it twice.

"I'd heard there'd been a suicide on your land, but nobody

said anything about suspicion of murder," he said.

Rose sighed and closed Grady's office door. "Sheriff Brock does not seem eager to pursue the matter," she said.

"Now, it seems to me, if there'd been any way to pin a murder on you folks, Harry'd be the first to pipe up. So to my way of thinking, that means there wasn't even the slightest evidence pointing to murder. Why are you so concerned about this? Do you all *want* to be accused of murder?"

"Nay, of course not, but . . ." She bobbed her head toward the list in Grady's hand. "There's a child at stake—a sad and hurt little girl named Mairin. I think she witnessed the incident, as you can see on my list of questions. Right now she can't remember, but someday she might. What if it *was* a murder, and she was the only witness? How much will her life be worth? There are so many unanswered questions, so many contradictions. I know I don't have anything solid yet, but something is very wrong, I *know* it."

He scanned her list again. "Is it really so odd that the chair got picked up later?"

"Nay, it's just what a Shaker would have done—but no one will admit to doing so. Given the slovenly habits of our guests, I doubt any of them would have picked it up, just to neaten the orchard. But someone must have carried or sent it to the Carpenters' Shop for quick repair."

Grady tipped his chair back and stared at the yellowed ceiling. Rose noticed dark circles underneath his eyes and a couple days of beard growth. Dragging him into this right now, with his father ill, cost her a guilt pang, but there was no one else to whom she could turn.

"Okay," Grady said, "suppose we assume the possibility of murder. More'n likely it was one of your visitors killing another, for reasons of his own. Why not stay out of it? If any solid evidence comes to light, let us take care of it. Just ask them to leave. You've done it before. Sounds like they'd love to get the kid off their hands, so you could probably keep her."

"I don't believe it's that easy." Rose explained the power

the New-Owenites had over Wilhelm and her fears that Mairin had become a pawn. "Besides," she added, "would *you* want a killer to go free, perhaps to kill again?"

"Of course not, but . . ." Grady let the front of his chair drop forward with a clunk. "All right, what do you want me to do?"

"You can show me the suicide note. Have you seen it?"

Grady shook his head. "I just got back to work last night, and Harry didn't fill me in much." He heaved himself out of his chair, quite unlike the strong, eager young man Rose knew. "We'll go take a look at the note," he said, "but don't you dare tell Harry or anyone who might tell Harry—promise?"

"Promise."

Grady stuck his head out the door. "Ray, you busy? Yeah, it's a slow day. You might as well run out to the Pike place and check on things. The Pike kid's been complaining about that neighbor of his again. Something about broken fences. Thanks. I'll watch things here." He closed the door and waited a few moments. When he reopened it, the outer waiting area was empty.

"Come on," he said to Rose. He led her to a small room that reminded her of the furniture storage rooms back at the South Family Dwelling House, so crammed was it with everything from hunting rifles to clothing. He pulled a string attached to a single bulb, covered with grime, and gray light flickered over their heads.

"This is our evidence room," Grady said with a snort. "The Lexington police would call it a junk closet." He routed around the dusty items until he came to a file cabinet splotched with rust. "We store paper evidence in here. The suicide note is probably just tossed in somewhere, since Harry didn't think there was a crime involved."

He pulled out a stack of papers of all different shapes, sizes, and ages, and he handed half the pile to Rose. "I know what you're thinking, Rose; you don't need to say it. If you Shakers could just get hold of this mess, you'd clean it right up."

"Just give us a couple of hours," Rose said.

"Be careful what you offer," Grady warned. "If I ever become sheriff, I might just take you up on it."

They both found relatively clear surfaces to work on and began their painstaking examination of each item. Since neither had seen the note, they were careful not to toss anything aside too quickly. The minutes crept by, interrupted only by an occasional sneeze from Grady or Rose.

"Ray will be gone for a while, won't he?" Rose asked.

"Yeah, he'll be lucky to get back by suppertime. That feud has survived generations; poor Ray won't be able to make a difference, that's why we usually don't send anyone. At some point, he'll just decide he's had enough and probably go straight home for a couple shots of . . . whiskey." His voice trailed off, and Rose looked over at him.

"What is it?"

"I'll be damned," Grady said. When he didn't automatically apologize for his language, Rose's curiosity doubled. She dropped the paper she was squinting at and went toward him.

"Look at this," he said, some of the old eagerness back in his voice.

She read it aloud: "I'm ashamed and I can't take it anymore. This is the only way." She frowned at Grady. "This can't be it, can it?"

"Yep, sure can. See that little mark in the top right-hand corner? That's Harry's mark, and he wrote the date next to it."

Rose held the paper under the light. "It's dated last Wednesday, the day after Hugh's death. That's when Gilbert said he'd found the note and delivered it to the Sheriff's Office. But I don't understand. This note is printed, and rather sloppily, too. Hugh was an educated man. Why would he have printed his own suicide note?"

"I suppose he might have had unreadable handwriting," Grady said.

"I could certainly check on that," Rose said, "but still, it's written so messily. If he was being careful to make the note readable, wouldn't he have been neater? This is very puzzling."

"No kidding." Grady took the paper from Rose's hand and studied it again. "If someone had delivered this note to me, I'd've been mighty suspicious. You said it was the leader who found it?"

"Gilbert Griffiths, right. But retiring rooms are never locked. Anyone could have put the note in Hugh's room."

"Still, you'd think he would know the deceased's handwriting. I'd expect to see some notes attached to this, something written by Harry saying that the deceased usually printed, and Gilbert vouched for the authenticity, and so on. But there's nothing. Harry just stuffed this in the drawer, and in the middle of the stack, too . . . almost like he didn't want it to come to light easily." Grady shook his head. "No, I just can't believe it. Harry and I don't see eye-to-eye most of the time, but he usually makes a stab at following procedure."

"Maybe he's getting ready to retire," Rose suggested, not without a hint of hopefulness.

"Yeah, maybe. I don't know, I'll have to think about this for a while."

"Will you ask him why he handled this the way he did?"

Grady folded the note and stashed it in his pocket. "I don't know yet."

"I can at least try to find out something about Hugh's handwriting, whether he ever printed," Rose said.

"That would help," Grady said. "Keep me informed."

Rose stopped briefly in her retiring room to pick up the drawings before arriving at Agatha's room. She felt a surge of warmth and hope as she entered to find Mairin standing at Agatha's side, feeding her with care. Mairin responded inconsistently to affection; sometimes she emerged from behind her mask, and other times she withdrew further into her silent world. This was one of the good times.

"Good evening, dear," Agatha said. "Mairin has finished

eating, and I'm almost done, but I asked Gertrude to bring you some soup, in case you returned hungry."

Mairin put down Agatha's spoon and lifted a brimming white bowl from the desk. As she carried it to Rose, she bit her lower lip in concentration, trying not to spill a drop. Rose took it from her with a thank-you.

Rose was very hungry indeed, and the creamy chowder was still warm enough to send its rich fragrance spiraling up as she stirred it. She ate faster than she'd intended and was finished. almost the same time as Agatha.

"Now," said Agatha, easing back in her rocker, "tell us about your day, Rose. You've been running about at top speed, which usually means you're trying to work out a puzzle."

Rose looked from Agatha to Mairin and hesitated. Mairin watched her with bright, coppery eyes, but how much could the girl really handle?

"While you were gone," Agatha said, "Mairin and I had a nice talk—didn't we, child?—about lots of things, such as what she remembers about her younger years and about her bad dreams."

She's telling me the time is right, Rose thought. It was like Agatha to have read her mind and paved the way. She pulled Mairin's drawings from her pocket and unfolded them, watching the girl's face. Mairin's eyes widened but did not dim as she recognized her pictures. Rose took the checkerboard design and held it out to her.

"What is this a picture of, Mairin, can you remember from your dream?" Rose avoided any direct reference to Hugh's death for fear Mairin would withdraw again.

Mairin took the drawing and stared at it, her full lips parted, showing badly stained teeth. Rose silently promised that as soon as she had the right, she would take Mairin on a visit to the dentist.

"Take your time," Rose said. "Close your eyes and let your mind wander." She wrapped a soft blanket around Mairin's shoulders and settled her into a corner of Agatha's bed. Mairin curled into a ball and closed her eyes. Rose returned to her chair and waited.

Minutes passed, and Rose began to wonder if Mairin had fallen asleep. Agatha seemed to be dozing off, as well. Rose's knee began to ache, and she shifted her position. The room grew chilly. Rose was considering finding a blanket for herself when Mairin whimpered. Agatha jolted awake. She struggled out of her rocker, and Rose hurried to help her. Mairin cried out and curled more tightly. With Rose's support, Agatha sat on her bed and began stroking Mairin's forehead with her steadier left hand. She crooned to the child, an old Shaker song, "Love, Oh Love Is Sweetly Flowing." Mairin's body relaxed. But instead of falling into a deep sleep, her eyes opened and focused on the rocking chair Agatha had vacated. Rose moved her own ladder-back chair so that Mairin could see it, too.

Mairin sat up. Rose had lain the drawings and crayons on the bed, within reach. Mairin took the checkerboard drawing and a red crayon and began coloring every other square.

"So it *was* a ladder-back chair," Rose said.

Mairin glanced at her with a puzzled expression.

"Was this what you saw in your dream? Red-and-white checks?"

Mairin nodded.

Rose prepared to take it slowly. So far, she had only confirmation of her guess—that Mairin had been dreaming about Hugh's death scene, where an old red-and-white Shaker chair had lain as if kicked aside. Rose needed more, much more. She touched Mairin's shoulder.

"I know your dreams have been very scary, and that you don't want to have them anymore," she said. "Agatha and I can help you be free of those dreams. Would you like us to try?"

Mairin nodded.

"I used to have bad dreams sometimes when I was your age," Rose said, "and Agatha taught me how to make them go away. She used to hold my hand and let me tell her the entire dream. Whenever I got to a really frightening part, she told me to stop and remind myself that I was not alone and that Mother Ann was watching over me. And do you know what I found out? That even if the dreams didn't stop right away, they got less and less scary the more I talked about them."

Agatha took one of Mairin's hands, and Rose took the other. "You have all three of us to protect you, because I know Mother Ann is here. So would you try to tell us your dream?"

Mairin looked at her hands, securely held. "When I had bad dreams before," she said, "everybody laughed at me. They told me I was just trying to be important."

"You are a child of God," Agatha said. "We will never laugh at you."

"I have the same dream over and over. A snake climbs up a tree and onto a limb, and then its head falls off, and there isn't any blood. But then I look on the ground, and all the blood fell like this." Mairin nodded at the checkerboard drawing.

Rose bit her tongue to keep from leaping in with more direct questions.

"That is a very frightening dream," Agatha said. "I understand why you've been afraid to talk about it. Does it seem as scary now?"

Mairin paused a moment and her pinched features relaxed. "No. It's better. Will it go away now?"

Rose and Agatha exchanged a glance. "Sometimes, with really bad dreams like this one," Rose said, "it helps if we talk about where it came from. Once I had a dream that terrified me, about a monster with huge teeth that was about to chomp on me, and Agatha helped me remember that I'd seen one of the brethren get hurt by a threshing machine. Once we talked about what I'd seen, I stopped having the dream. Perhaps we could think about where your dream is coming from."

To Rose's relief, Mairin seemed to be considering her suggestion.

"Close your eyes again," Agatha said, in a low, soothing

voice. "Think about what the dream reminds you of, and remember that we are here with you. We won't let anything happen to you."

Mairin closed her eyes briefly. Rose expected a severe reaction, but when the girl opened her eyes again, they were dull with misery. "I don't have to think about it," Mairin said. "I remember. But I can't tell."

"Why can't you tell?" Rose asked.

"I just can't," Mairin said. "Are you mad at me?"

"Nay, of course not," Rose said. "Only I don't understand . . . did someone order you not to tell?"

Mairin's mouth tightened in a stubborn pucker, and she said nothing.

In frustration, Rose took a risk. "Mairin, do your pictures bring back the day I first met you? The day Hugh died?"

Mairin pulled her hands back and scooted away from the women.

"That's what your drawings and your dream are about, aren't they?" Rose pressed, despite a warning glance from Agatha.

Mairin pulled her knees up to her chin, and her eyes flashed.

"Mairin, do you understand how important this is? Was someone else there when Hugh died? Did you see someone with him? Please, Mairin, I need to know in order to protect you, to protect all of us."

"Leave me alone! I can't tell!"

TWENTY

Rose brought a silent Mairin back to the Ministry House for the night. As they ascended the stairs to her retiring room, Rose heard a murmur of voices coming from behind the closed doors of the Ministry library. Mairin seemed not to notice, so Rose decided to give the girl a cup of chamomile tea and put her to bed early. Once Mairin was asleep, Rose would make a quick foray down to the library to find out what was going on.

Mairin was settling into bed before she realized her doll wasn't in its usual place. Her sullen silence dissolved into tears of rage. Rose tried to hold the girl, but she squirmed away and crawled under her bed, then under Rose's, looking for the doll. When she couldn't find it, she curled up in a corner, on the cold floor, her small chest heaving.

Rose had no idea what to do. She considered calling Agatha or Josie from the hall phone, but she didn't want to leave the child alone just then. She sat cross-legged on the floor in front of Mairin.

"We will find your doll," she said. "We got clean sheets today, so I bet your doll just became tangled up in the old ones. Gretchen will find her when she shakes out the sheets before washing them. I know you're worried about her, but first thing tomorrow we'll call over to the Laundry and warn them to watch for her." She reached over and pried loose one of Mairin's hands. "This has been a hard day. You'll feel better if you get some sleep."

Mairin sniffled.

"The sooner you go to sleep, the sooner morning will come, and we can call the Laundry about your doll. How about it?"

Mairin allowed herself to be carried to bed, tucked in, and sung to until she slipped into sleep.

Rose was exhausted and cast a longing look at her own crisp, clean sheets, but she had to find out what was happening downstairs in the Ministry library. Assured that Marin was deeply asleep, she went down to investigate. She couldn't mistake the voices. Wilhelm and Gilbert were firing volleys at each other, barely pausing for breath. She thought she heard other voices, too, underneath the verbal battle.

So Wilhelm was holding an evening meeting with the New-Owenites and without her. Her temper flared, and for once she didn't care. She was tired of the subterfuge and especially tired of eavesdropping in her own village. She swung open the door with more force than necessary and stood framed in the doorway. Wilhelm, Gilbert, Earl, and Celia all turned to stare at her.

Without a word, Rose swung down a ladder-back chair and joined the group. She crossed her right hand over her left, as if she were settling down to a Union Meeting, and looked from face to face.

"Do continue," she said. "I'm sure I'll be able to catch up." Rose ignored the exchanged glances and waited.

"We were just discussing ideas for a joint meeting on Sunday evening," Gilbert said.

"Joint worship," Wilhelm said.

"We understood you were busy with your duties," Gilbert said, "or naturally we would have included you, Rose."

"Naturally," Rose said. "So what are the plans so far?"

"Well, you see, we all believe this is a very important time for both our communities—a time of testing, if you will. We feel the need of a guidance that is, shall we say, beyond our poor human understanding. Naturally, as Mairin is so linked—"

"Absolutely not!"

"Rose, just hear us out," Gilbert said. "The girl will come to no harm."

"I won't allow that child to be the rope in your tug of war. She has been through too much already, and she needs to live a normal, quiet life."

"It is not thy decision to make," Wilhelm said. "She is a chosen instrument. It isn't our place to question Mother Ann's Work. She has sent her gifts through this child, and it is up to us to accept them with praise and gratitude."

Celia crossed one slim leg over the other and began to swing it. "Personally," she said, "I don't care if Mairin ever draws another picture. I think you're all making her into something much more important than she really is. You act as if she's some sort of chosen creature, when she's really just an uncivilized runt, impossible to deal with, and I can't believe that Robert Owen or this Mother Ann person of yours would pick her to speak through."

"Robert Owen?" Rose asked. "Do you mean the Robert Owen of a century ago?"

"Really, Gil, I have to agree with Celia." Earl reached over and squeezed Celia's hand. "It's hard for me to believe that Mairin, of all people, would have what it takes to be a medium. Surely, guiding a seance is beyond her meager capabilities. Drawing pictures is a far cry from speaking with the spirit world." He flashed a friendly smile at Rose. "You've been more than kind to her, but I can't help feeling she should be in an institution. She isn't quite right in the head. One never knows what she'll say or do next. Putting her under the strain of a seance would just be cruel."

"You are planning a seance, with Mairin speaking for Robert Owen?" Rose stood up to command attention. "You will do no such thing!"

"Calm thyself," Wilhelm said. "We are discussing a simple worship service, with Mairin attending. If Mother Ann thinks she is not strong enough, then Mother Ann will not continue to choose her as an instrument."

Rose sank back in her chair, despair sapping her strength. Wilhelm and Gilbert had each made up his mind about the nature of the proposed worship service, and no amount of arguing would show them that neither of them could have it all his way. In the ensuing fiasco, Mairin might be destroyed forever.

"I agree with Celia and Earl," Rose said, trying to hide her distaste. "Mairin isn't up to it. Even attending a worship service, or whatever this is, would be too taxing for her. She is frail. She needs quiet and nourishment, to build her strength. I propose we put off this idea until she is truly well enough."

Gilbert flung back his head and stared at the ceiling, deep in thought. Moments of silence passed, and Rose dared to hope that she had persuaded him.

"If we are to delay the seance," Gilbert said, smoothing back his few remaining hairs, "then I want her returned to our care. We will build up her strength. You are far too busy, and it isn't your responsibility, anyway."

"Gilbert, no, not again." Celia's whining voice drowned out Rose's objection. "I don't know what to do with her."

"Now, Cel," Earl said, "it won't be that bad. Tell you what, I'll help. I'm a bit at loose ends now, anyway, with Hugh gone. I'll take her riding—the Shakers have horses, I've seen them—and that'll make her strong in no time. You'll see."

"Oh, must we? Earl, you know how hard I've tried with that girl."

"I know, Cel. You've done your best."

Celia gave her shiny hair a subtle toss. "At least *someone* understands what I've been through."

"What *have* you been through?" Rose asked curtly.

All eyes turned to her.

"You see," Rose explained, "it isn't clear to me that any one of you has bothered to work with Mairin. It seems you've all just passed her on to the next person, and no one has actually kept her. Charlotte has been spending extra hours teaching her—did you know that? Mairin can neither read nor write. Yet she is clearly capable of learning. Agatha and I have made quite a bit of progress with helping her eat at a moderate rate; she has learned quickly. I can't believe that any of you, including Hugh, ever spent more than five minutes with her."

Even Wilhelm sat in stunned silence. Celia's lips were parted over white teeth. *I see she takes care of her own teeth,* Rose thought. Apparently one visit to a doctor, to diagnose her rickets, was all Mairin had ever been allowed.

A slow flush spread up the fair skin of Celia's neck and face. "How *dare* you speak to me that way? What would you know about being a mother? You haven't had to live with the monster for the past two years, with no one to help, and these men who think all they have to do is dump the kid on me, and she'll magically become *like* me. Well, it isn't that easy, you know. That girl will never be like me!"

For which I give profound thanks. Rose was wise enough to keep this prayer to herself.

"We do understand how hard it's been for you, Cel," Earl said gently. "You've been a saint and more."

"Yes, of course," Gilbert murmured.

"No, I don't think you do understand, not really. I tried and tried to get her to eat right, but she gobbled like a wild animal. It was repulsive. She never listened to me, even when I gave her a good slap and sent her to bed without supper."

"You . . . found it necessary to hit her?" Rose asked. "How often?"

"Well, *you* try controlling a wild creature without a whipping! In the beginning, she was so crazy I had to whip her practically every day and keep her locked in her room." Celia's sapphire eyes narrowed into slits. "And before you go judging me, just remember that she's only good with you because of all my work! It's certainly nothing *you've* done."

Fire shot through her muscles, but Rose steadied her voice. "So, the whippings . . . you believe they worked?"

"You bet they did. For a while, anyway. Until she started running away." Celia's harsh laugh almost broke through

Rose's self-control. "Mairin *wants* to be uncivilized. I think it's in her blood—well, I mean, look who her mother was."

"Celia, you don't mean that!" Gilbert said, his hands fluttering.

Rose was distracted from her own shock by what she saw on the faces around her. Celia sulked, and Earl set about soothing her in a low voice. Gilbert seemed more flustered than angry, which puzzled Rose. Supposedly, the New-Owenites agreed with the Shakers that all races were equal, or else why would Gilbert choose Mairin to prove himself as a social reformer? *Unless,* she thought, *Hugh's money—probably soon to be Celia's—is so important to him that he'll cast aside his cherished beliefs to avoid alienating her.*

Wilhelm was grim, and so he should be. Surely he must now see that these people could never be good Shakers.

"We have discussed this enough," Wilhelm said. "Bring Mairin to the worship service tomorrow evening, and we will let Mother Ann decide whether the girl is strong enough or civilized enough to be a chosen instrument."

Rose closed her eyes and took in a deep breath. Wilhelm was too devoted to his plan to see what was before him.

"I agree," Gilbert said. "Whether it's the shade of Robert Owen or Mother Ann, bring Mairin tomorrow evening, and let the spirit world decide."

"Nay," Rose said, "I will not."

"I must remind you," Gilbert said, "that Mairin is not your charge. Since you refuse to cooperate with us, I'm afraid we must demand you give her back to us. She is no longer your concern."

"She is very much my concern, and I will not turn her over to you. If you are truly Mairin's guardians, then you should be able to show me documentation to prove it. Can you?"

The silence answered her question. "Then Mairin stays with me. It is a matter of conscience, since it is clear she has suffered under your so-called care."

"I warn you, we'll call the sheriff and get him out here, if we have to." Gilbert's pedantic style did not lend itself well to authority. He sounded more like a whining little boy.

"Then by all means, do so." Ignoring the painful twinge in her knee, Rose spun around and left the parlor, to prevent herself from saying everything else that was on her mind.

Afraid of wakening Mairin, Rose eased into her dark retiring room and quietly closed the door. She thought she heard a whimpering sound, as if the girl were having bad dreams. She stood a moment and let her eyes adjust until she could make out Marin's bed, with its jumbled pile of sheets and blankets. She tiptoed toward it. The bed was empty.

In panic, Rose switched on the bedside lamp. She heard a cry from the corner, and she turned toward it. As earlier, Mairin was a small, tight ball, her arms thrown protectively over her head.

Rose knelt in front of her. "Did you have a very bad dream, Mairin? Did it frighten you to find me gone when you woke up?"

Mairin breathed in short gasps and said nothing.

"Can't you tell me what is wrong?"

Mairin didn't move.

Rose rolled off her still-tender knee. She didn't dare touch Mairin, let alone pick her up. Perhaps it was time to call Josie.

"I'll be right back," Rose said. "I'll just be out in the hall, if you need me."

Josie promised to come quickly with a strong batch of peppermint-valerian tea, and Rose returned to her room, switching on all the lights as she entered. Across the room from where Mairin still crouched, Rose saw a small pile of fabric on the floor, which she recognized as Mairin's winter cloak, selected for her from the spare clothing the Shakers kept on hand for children. She hadn't needed it yet, and it had been hanging undisturbed, tied snuggly over a wall peg. Rose's ingrained instinct to be tidy sent her toward it.

Rose was surprised it had fallen off. Her gaze shifted automatically to the hanger. It hung askew from its wall peg, pulled off balance by an object tied to one side. It was Mairin's doll. She still wore her butternut Sabbathday dress, but the kerchief had been removed from her chest. One corner squeezed the doll's soft neck like a vise. The other end was knotted to the hanger.

Mairin was still curled tightly across the room, as far from the doll as she could get. Rose watched her, paralyzed by uncertainty—and by fear. Had someone sneaked into the room during the day and arranged the doll so horribly, just to terrify Mairin? Had Mairin awakened, decided to run away, and found the doll like that? Or had the girl hanged the doll herself, out of anger with Rose?

Rose had just pulled down the doll and hidden it in a drawer when Josie arrived. She said nothing as Josie gathered Mairin in her plump arms and guided her back to bed. The girl obediently sipped her tea and closed her eyes when told to, as if her will had broken. After a whispered thanks to Josie, Rose moved her rocker next to Mairin's bed, wrapped herself in a blanket, and watched the child sleep. As her own weary eyes closed, Rose sent a silent plea to Mother Ann to show her how to help Mairin—or to make it clear that she could not.

Mairin spent a restless night, despite the sedating tea. Though Rose had left the paper and crayons near at hand, Mairin did no more drawing. In the morning, she seemed to have withdrawn into herself entirely and did not speak as she dressed. Rose did not push her. Neither mentioned the previous night. The girl's eyes were dull and puffy; Rose wondered if she had only pretended to sleep.

Since the Sunday worship service had been moved to evening at the request of the New-Owenites, the day was open. The Shakers, of course, treated it as a work day, taking the opportunity to tackle projects they needed to catch up on, such as preserving, repairing, and thorough cleaning. Charlotte had planned a morning of school for Mairin and the Shaker children, to make up for the missed hours the morning of Hugh's death. Then she'd scheduled a nature walk. Rose would be free to work on the answers to her list of puzzling questions.

A piercing north wind further discouraged conversation as Rose and Mairin walked toward the Schoolhouse. Mairin had refused to wear her cloak, so Rose had given her a wool kerchief to wrap around her shoulders. The girl kept her head down. Rose had tied another kerchief around the girl's ears to keep them warm. Without the cloud of hair around her face, Mairin looked even tinier than usual. Rose tried to think of something soothing to say. Nothing came to mind. She wished Agatha were with them.

They were late. When they arrived, school had already started. Rose took Mairin around to the back entrance, so she could slip in through the storeroom and into the classroom without drawing attention to herself. On impulse, she gave Mairin a quick hug around the shoulders before sending her inside.

"Stay close to Sister Charlotte and Nora, okay?"

To Rose's surprise, Mairin's eyes glistened for a moment, as if tears threatened. Then she lowered her gaze and closed the door behind her.

Rose stood just outside the women's entrance to the South Family Dwelling House, considering her options. Protecting Mairin from the evening service had been essential, but it had also left Rose with even fewer sources of information. By now, Gilbert would have surely ordered all the New-Owenites to avoid talking with her. Celia might not obey him, especially if she saw a chance to get rid of Mairin forever. And Earl seemed to waver in whichever direction Celia was going.

Hugh's alleged suicide note bothered her. If she could throw its authenticity into doubt, maybe she could get some help resolving this mess—and perhaps even get the police on her side before Gilbert made good his threat to call them.

While walking back from the Schoolhouse, Rose had watched Gilbert leave the South Family Dwelling House and head back toward the Ministry House, probably for another go-round with Wilhelm. Celia and Gilbert were not with him, and the white Buick was parked beside the dwelling house.

Rose felt certain that they would not observe the Sabbath with either work or worship, so they'd most likely be back in the dwelling house, relaxing.

She entered the dwelling house, purposely making noise to make it clear she had a right to be there. She needn't have bothered; the raucous laughter coming from the parlor drowned out her gesture. Celia cackled, apparently at something Earl had said, and other voices joined in. Rose stood quiet and tall in the parlor doorway. It was her second grand entrance in as many days—Agatha would enjoy hearing the story, assuming Rose survived to tell it.

Earl and Celia, along with another man and woman, sat around a table, playing a card game and smoking cigarettes. Their baggy brown work clothes had been replaced by elegant evening wear—at least, that was what it looked like to Rose, though she was ignorant of the world's rules regarding acceptable dress during the day. Celia was especially stunning. An emerald-studded comb held back her glistening hair on one side, and a satin gown of the same shade draped low beneath her neck and skimmed over her narrow hips. A flowery scent blended with the smell of cigarette smoke. The worldly scene, right here in a dwelling house, sent a stabbing pain through Rose's heart as she envisioned a day when the Shakers would no longer be strong enough to hold their community together, and their buildings would be sold off to the world.

The laughter and chattering trailed off as the New-Owenites became aware of Rose's presence. All but Celia hurried to stub out their cigarettes in white teacups. The second couple glanced nervously at each other and at Earl and Celia, then excused themselves. Rose barely had time to step farther into the room before they rushed for the doorway. Celia watched them disappear, took one last drag on her cigarette, then stubbed it out.

Earl wore a pearl gray suit that flowed into place as he stood to greet Rose. "I apologize," he said. "I'm afraid it just slipped our minds that you'd asked us not to smoke in the building. However, there's really little danger of fire when we're just relaxing with a game of cards, so no harm done. Have you information about the meeting tonight?"

Rose made a quick decision. She would waste no more time in subterfuge. "I'm the one who wants information," she said. "Did Hugh ever print, instead of writing in script?"

"I beg your pardon?" Earl glanced at Celia, whose porcelain face had tightened in a frown. "Why do you ask?"

"Was Hugh's handwriting clear and legible? Do you have a sample of it around, Celia?"

Celia reached for another cigarette but didn't light it. "I suppose I might," she said.

"Samples of Hugh's handwriting used to be all over the place," Earl said. "He was always jotting down notes on little bits of paper. We all do."

"I need a smoke," Celia said. "I'm going outside."

"First, as far as you know, did your husband make a habit of printing his notes?"

"I suppose it's possible. I didn't pay much attention."

"Actually," Earl said, "I believe he printed pamphlets and so forth. Our typist kept making mistakes trying to read his script. Isn't that right, Celia?"

"I have a vague memory of that," Celia said, clearly bored.

"I'd like to see a sample of your husband's handwriting." Rose edged toward the doorway, hoping Celia would not just barrel through her.

"Oh, honestly. Earl, would you be a dear and get one from my room? I think I kept one or two of his letters and put them somewhere in my dresser. I simply must have a smoke." She glided from the parlor, and Rose let her.

"I'll just be a few minutes," Earl said. "Although now that I think of it, if you're interested in how legible his handwriting was, love letters are probably not the best test."

Rose had to confess she hadn't thought of that.

"Tell you what, I'll look around and see if any of Hugh's notes were overlooked when we packed up his things and sent them back."

"You sent everything back?"

"Of course. When one of our community dies, we distribute his belongings to the poorest of our members, as a way of creating more equality. Don't you?"

"Those people are impossible," Rose muttered as she left the South Family Dwelling House. She'd get nothing from them, and without Wilhelm's cooperation, she couldn't get rid of them. She flung open the Ministry House door and headed straight for Wilhelm's workshop, where she found him pacing, as he usually did on Sunday mornings, while thinking through his homily.

Rose burst into the room without knocking, which so startled Wilhelm that he was speechless.

"I want Mairin's three drawings back," she said. "I want them right now. Where are they? I'll get them myself."

"Nay, those drawings belong to the Society!"

"And I am just as much the Society as you are, Wilhelm. I haven't time to waste. I want those drawings."

Wilhelm was uncharacteristically calm, which gave Rose her first moment of doubt.

"If I allow thee to see the gift drawings," he said, "then in return, I want thee to bring Mairin to the worship service tonight."

"I will not. Mairin is not a possession, to be exchanged for a favor."

Rose crossed her arms and stood her ground, ready for escalation. However, Wilhelm must have recognized he'd never get back to his homily if he continued to protest.

"How do I know I will get the drawings back in time for the worship service this evening?"

"If you do not give them to me, I will not allow the sisters to attend the service."

Wilhelm's bushy eyebrows flew up. "Mother Ann would—"

"Mother Ann disrupted church services when her conscience told her to. I am quite willing to prevent a service from happening."

Without another word, he opened his built-in cupboard, extracted Mairin's drawings, and handed them to Rose.

TWENTY-ONE

"Mother Ann had a hand in these drawings," Agatha said. "I have no doubt."

"If she did, then there must be a message," Rose said. "A coherent message. You are my only hope for deciphering it." She rearranged the six drawings on Agatha's desk, putting the two trees next to each other, followed by the headless serpent, the red-and-white checkerboard, the bejeweled bird, and the luscious foods.

"These last two don't seem to fit," Rose said.

Agatha leaned close to them, then sat back and closed her eyes. "The angels have often given gifts of celestial food," she said. "This may have been their way of showing Mairin how much richer her life would become as she learned to follow Holy Mother Wisdom. What better picture of heaven could there be for a starved child than inexhaustible, wonderful foods?"

"That makes sense," Rose said. "But what about the bird? I can't imagine that would say anything meaningful to Mairin. She has lived a lot in trees, so she's probably seen lots of birds, but why would she be directed to draw one like this?"

Agatha picked up the bird drawing and studied it. "You truly don't know what this is?" she asked, with a gentle smile.

"Nay."

"This lovely green-eyed bird is you, Rose. You have spread

your protective wings around the child, and she feels safe with you. You are her guardian angel."

"Oh." Rose took the bird drawing. "Agatha, you know these things better than I, but . . . it would be helpful if I were a real angel. I have difficulty understanding her. I hope I don't let her down."

"You've been given the tools, Rose. You have only to use them."

Rose pointed to the remaining four pictures. "What about these, then? What do they tell us?"

"What do *you* think they tell us, Rose?"

Agatha had always been her guide to the world of spirit, and it sounded as if she might be retiring. Rose had not felt so uncertain since she'd first become eldress. With trepidation, she picked up the checkerboard. "Well, I believe we've been shown that this is Mairin's memory of the chair found in the orchard, which was broken and scuffed, either during Hugh's suicide, or by a killer. It tells us only that she probably saw the event."

Rose pulled the two trees and the serpent toward her and studied them together. She changed the order of the drawings, then changed them again.

"There's a sequence here—look." She moved the drawings closer to Agatha's dim eyes. "The tree and the snake combine in the third drawing. They were separate and then somehow together. And the snake lost its head before climbing the tree, not after." Rose frowned at the yellow-and-orange serpent. "We don't have snakes of that color around here, do we? I didn't think so. I wonder . . ." She traced back from the hacked neck to the end. "This isn't a snake," she said. "I'm sure of it. Look at the end—neat but blunt, not tapering off, as a snake's tail would. Now this looks more like a piece of hemp rope, like the one Hugh was hanging from."

Agatha sat back in her rocker and was silent.

"One end has been hacked off crudely, while the other is neatly sliced, just as the brethren would cut it." She shook her head. "But what does that tell us, really? Either Hugh or the killer could have cut the rope, or somebody else could have done it earlier."

"Rose," Agatha said, "the drawings were sent by Mother Ann, if not by Holy Mother Wisdom. They would not send a meaningless gift."

Rose slid back her chair and began to pace the room. She longed to open the window to air out the stuffy room and clear her head, but Agatha's frail body could not tolerate the November chill.

"Quiet will serve better than agitation," Agatha said, barely above a whisper.

Rose forced herself to sit and be still. She closed her eyes and envisioned the scene she had come upon Tuesday morning—Hugh's lifeless body hanging from a branch of a plum tree.

"Something is puzzling me," Rose said, opening her eyes and picking up the drawing of the rope. "It took very little rope to hang Hugh from such a low branch, yet this looks like quite a long rope. So what's pictured climbing the tree must have been cut from a longer length." She jumped from her chair in excitement. "Where's the rest of that rope? If Hugh hacked it off, he would have done it in the orchard, once he saw how much would be needed. So whatever he cut with would have been found in the orchard. Also, the rest of the rope would have been there, too."

She flung herself on Agatha's bed. "I think this is just confusing me more," she said, rubbing her hands over her face. "However," she said, staring at the ceiling, "the rope used on Hugh is with the Sheriff. If I can locate the longer length of hacked rope, it might help convince the police that Hugh was murdered, either in the orchard or somewhere else and then moved to the orchard. Agatha, where do we keep most of our rope—in the barn?"

"We always used to," Agatha said.

"Then I'm off to the barn."

*   *   *

To avoid delay, Rose decided to cut through the medic garden behind the Infirmary. One of these days, someone would notice how often she trod through the grass instead of following the neatly maintained paths. If she was very unlucky, that someone would be Elsa, who would delight in telling Wilhelm what a bad example Rose was setting.

As a reflex, she glanced to her right, toward the central path, and saw three brethren leaving the South Family Dwelling House. They were so engrossed in conversation that they did not look up. Rose's impulse was to slip out of sight behind the Infirmary and go on with her task, but some instinct stronger than curiosity kept her rooted in place until they came close enough for her to be certain of their identity.

The men reached the path and stopped. They seemed wrapped up in their topic, sometimes all talking at once. Rose was certain that the tallest figure was Matthew and the shorter, plumper one was Archibald. The third man kept his back to her, but she guessed it was Benjamin, Andrew's assistant in the Medicinal Herb Shop. Now her instincts were screaming at her. Benjamin had been disgruntled since the day he'd arrived. If those three had gone together to visit the New-Owenites, it did not bode well for village harmony.

Rose longed to hear their conversation. Their intensity was escalating, and it looked as if Benjamin and Matthew were arguing with Archibald. Matthew poked an angry finger in Archibald's chest, pushing him backward a step. It was more than Rose could tolerate—Believers nearly coming to blows with each other. So much for their vow of nonviolence.

She began to walk toward them. She'd gone no more than a few steps when the door to the men's entrance opened a crack and a sleek black head appeared. Celia called something that Rose couldn't make out, and Matthew sprinted back to her. They conferred briefly—with their heads much too close together—and Matthew spun around. Rose realized he was looking directly at her. The other two men turned, as well. The dwelling house door closed. Rose stood her ground, refusing to sneak away as if this were not her village.

Something distracted her, perhaps a slight movement above the brethren's heads, and Rose glanced up at the second-floor windows. She had only a moment, before the light curtain fell back into place, to see someone's face behind the wavery glass. She hadn't been able to make out the features, but whoever it was had been watching her. With a shiver, she wondered how many times before she'd been observed as she'd gone about her search for the truth.

Since it was Sabbathday morning, only one of the brethren was in the barn, doing some long-delayed tidying. The others were probably using the extra time to catch up on projects elsewhere. The barn wasn't one of Rose's usual haunts, so the brother started in surprise at seeing her. Without questioning her, he showed her where they kept the spare rope, then went back to his cleaning.

The ropes had not yet been straightened, so they were tangled in a pile. Rose set about disentangling them, one by one. She was used to a certain amount of manual labor, since the Ministry was expected to work alongside other Believers, as an act of humility; however, her hands began to blister after twenty minutes or so of sliding them over ropes, searching for the ends. So far, each end was neatly sliced. Just as she reached the bottom of the pile, she found it—a long length of rope with one neat end and one frayed, as if it had been hacked off with a dull blade. She rolled it up and hung it over her shoulder. Sheriff Brock might criticize her for taking it, but she feared that if she left it, the rope wouldn't be there the next time she came to look.

She walked a little too fast toward the barn door and caught her left foot on the edge of a rut in the hard dirt floor. Once she'd righted herself and waited for her knee to calm down, she noticed the ruts ran deep from the side of the barn to a spot near the middle, in full view of the door. Puzzled, she called the brother away from his work and asked what might have caused the gouges.

"Sorry we haven't had a chance to fill those in," he said.

"We noticed them, too. Looked like they might've come from a wooden box that was stored over against the wall there, but none of us remembers moving it, and it's not something we'd forget easy."

Rose looked above her head at the rafters. A person could certainly hang himself—or someone else—from those rafters, she thought, but why here? And if here, why move the body and hang it in the orchard? Her head was beginning to spin again.

"Rose?" Charlotte peeked inside the barn door. "I'm so glad I found you. The children are having a play break, so I thought I'd seek you out. Agatha said you might be here."

Charlotte seemed calm, but Rose's stomach tightened. Something wasn't right.

"I was just wondering," Charlotte said, "if you were planning to bring Mairin in for the lessons this morning—the ones to make up for Tuesday, do you remember?"

Rose stared at her, hoping she wasn't hearing correctly.

"Rose?" Charlotte's eyes widened.

"I brought her this morning," Rose said, her voice husky with fear. "We were just a bit late, so I sent her in the back way. I watched her close the back door behind her."

"She never made it to the classroom," Charlotte said.

TWENTY-TWO

MAIRIN HAD NOT SOUGHT COMFORT EITHER IN AGATHA'S RE-
tiring room or in Rose's. From the Ministry House, Rose
called all the other buildings and managed to catch everyone
just before they left for the noon meal. No one had seen the
little girl. The Believers promised to watch for her, while the
New-Owenites in the South Family Dwelling House showed
no surprise and no concern.

"Sure, we'll keep an eye out," Gilbert had said, too casually,
"but she does this all the time. Just give her a few hours or a
day, and she'll be back. She always is. She takes it into her
head to disappear sometimes, and we have no idea why."

Rose called the Sheriff's Office, hoping to get Grady, but
she was disappointed to hear Sheriff Brock's impatient voice.

"Well, what is it now? Y'all come up with another body
out there?"

Rose told him about Mairin's disappearance.

"The kid makes a habit of disappearing, doesn't she?"

"Yea, but—"

"I don't have time or near enough men to go off looking
for a runaway, especially when she isn't even one of ours."
Brock slammed the phone down before she could ask for
Grady. Not that it mattered; Brock would have said Grady was
out, anyway.

Rose was on her own. Her distrust was running high, and
so was her fear. She decided to do a thorough search, with or

without help. It was the perfect time to search the South Family Dwelling House, with everyone in the communal dining room. If anyone was still in the dwelling house, Rose didn't care; she intended to search every corner of that building, and she wasn't about to let anyone stop her.

The wind cut through the village with a warning of winter, and Rose was glad she'd remembered to grab her long cloak as she'd rushed out of the Ministry House. Since morning, the air had dipped from crisp to shivery, which meant a cold night—far too cold for a little girl to be outdoors or in some damp basement. Mairin was a bright child; perhaps she had found a cozy corner in a dwelling house to stash herself. Rose tried to fend off the other, more terrifying alternative—that Mairin's disappearance might not have been her own choice.

Perhaps her luck had changed; the South Family Dwelling House seemed empty, though of course all the lights had been left burning. The effort to leave them on cost Rose a stab of pain through her head. She reminded herself that her most important goal was to find Mairin, and lights might help. She began with the closets and all the unoccupied rooms, hoping Mairin had opted for something warmer than the storage rooms downstairs. She took the chance of calling Mairin's name in each room. The child might not answer, but if she had been taken against her will and could still cry out, surely she would do so when she recognized Rose's voice.

Driven by deepening suspicion, Rose also searched the rooms claimed by the New-Owenites. It was possible, after all, that the seven of them were working together. The jumble of conflicting information they tossed at Rose could be a clever ploy to keep her confused while they carried out their real plan. They could keep Mairin in one of their rooms, or move her from room to room, while all lied about it to Rose.

In her previous search of the South Family Dwelling House, Rose had stopped with Earl's room. This time she sped through examinations of the other two men's rooms. Their contents told her nothing. Then she went on to the next room and realized immediately that it must have been Hugh's. Earl and Celia had said that they'd packed everything and sent it home. They'd told half the truth, anyway. Everything was packed up, but clearly nothing had been sent anywhere.

Time was growing short, but Rose had to check. The crates were probably the same ones the New-Owenites had used to move to North Homage. They had lids but weren't sealed shut. Rose quickly opened several until she came to one that held books and papers. Near the top, she found some notes Hugh had made to himself about the flora and fauna of the area. Hugh, at least, had shown true interest in learning and the natural sciences. Hugh's handwriting was readable, but difficult. She dug further and found a draft of a pamplet about the geology of the area around Bloomington. It was printed, and far from neat. Rose was disappointed. She couldn't be sure, of course, but the writing looked similar to that on the suicide note. *Still,* she thought, *why print a suicide note?* She removed one piece of paper, folded it, and stuffed it in her apron pocket. Without too much concern for neatness, she replaced the rest.

Rose remembered all the cubbyholes in the South Family Dwelling House, or so she thought. She wouldn't put it past Mairin to find some new ones. However, a careful search of the first and second floors revealed nothing except that the New-Owenites seemed to be exploring the building, as well. Furniture was being distributed to the unused rooms, as if North Homage's guests were preparing for guests of their own. They seemed more and more confident that they'd be allowed to stay, even bring in new members, and continue to use the Shakers' resources.

She hurried through the dim kitchen, with a cursory look in the pantry. Despite the nearness of food, the room was too open and too frequently used to provide a safe hiding place. As she headed for the stairs to the storage rooms, she glanced over at the corner where she'd listened through the pipes to the New-Owenites' meeting. The pipes were still there, but not where they should be. The whole system had been disassembled and lay in pieces on the already littered floor. A thick piece of wood leaned against the wall as if someone might be trying to find a way to block off the pipes. It certainly wasn't the brethren—they would have done a quick and efficient job and not left behind a mess. So the New-Owenites had indeed heard Mairin and her that night. They might not realize that one voice had belonged to her, but they surely knew that Mairin would have been the other.

Rose ran down to the storage rooms, so afraid of what she might find that she ignored the warning pains in her left knee. She scoured every nook and cranny, softly calling Mairin's name. She saw and heard nothing except the occasional skittering of a rodent, probably on its way to or from the kitchen. She was panting now, fighting off tears. She told herself to stop and breathe; she had a lot more of the village to search. She would find Mairin. She wouldn't give up until she did.

"You are overwrought, my dear," Agatha said. "Have some of my tea. It's peppermint, quite good. Gertrude always brings me an extra cup these days, in case a visitor drops in during the noon meal. Now, tell me what's been happening."

Rose accepted the tea gratefully and sank into her chair. "You heard that Mairin has disappeared?"

Agatha nodded. "Gertrude told me. I've been praying to Mother Ann to protect the child."

"No one else seems to be taking it seriously," Rose said, "even though she disappeared between the schoolroom and the Schoolhouse storage room hours ago, and it's getting colder outside, and . . ."

Agatha reached out and touched Rose's hand. "A prayer wouldn't hurt you right now, either," she said.

Rose caught her breath and followed Agatha's advice.

"Tell me, then," Agatha said, after a few moments of silence, "where have you looked so far?"

She told Agatha of her frantic search through the South Family Dwelling House, including the information she'd gathered. "It'll take days to search the entire village," Rose said.

"I see we do have a great deal to fear from these people," Agatha said. She began rocking gently, which usually meant she was thinking. Rose felt as grateful as a child who has turned her problem over to the all-knowing grown-ups. At the same time, she worried about Agatha's frail health. Agatha hadn't bothered with her white cap, and her pale scalp showed through the thin white hair pulled back into a knot at the nape of her neck. Her small body seemed thinner and more bent every day. But somehow, her soul kept growing, and Rose wondered how much longer it could be contained within her fading body.

Agatha stopped rocking. "Nora," she said. "I have watched the friendship grow between those two. If Mairin has gone off of her own accord, Nora is the only one who will know where she is likely to hide."

Rose felt a surge of energy. "Of course! I've been so convinced that the burden was entirely on me that I forgot about Nora. Thank you, my friend. I'll go find her right away. Shall I take your tray back to the kitchen? Gertrude must be exhausted, what with the extra mouths to feed and delivering meals."

"Oh, Gertrude didn't bring my noon meal," Agatha said. "Elsa offered to do so. I was quite pleased that she went out of her way to be of service to a sister."

"Elsa? Elsa brought your meal to you? Has she ever once done that before?"

"Nay, but I've prayed often that she will turn her heart more completely to our faith."

If there was a weakness in Agatha's wisdom, Rose realized, it was that she insisted on hoping that people would change for the better, even while she acknowledged all evidence to the contrary. Rose had long ago given up on Elsa, and she had seen no reason to change her view. If Elsa had brought Agatha's meal, it was because Elsa had a purpose.

"Agatha, those drawings of Mairin's—the ones I asked you to look at and keep for me—where did you put them?"

Impossible as it seemed, Agatha's face paled even more. "Oh dear," she said. "You don't mean . . . I'd left them on the desk, over there," she said. "I can't really see that far, you'd better check."

It took only a glance. "The drawings aren't there," Rose said, with as much gentleness as she could muster. Agatha couldn't afford another stroke. "I'm sure there was just a mix-up," she said lightly. "She probably picked them up by mistake. I'll talk to her. You needn't worry."

"Nay, I sure enough didn't pick up no pictures," Elsa said, when Rose cornered her in the kitchen. "I don't go around stealing things from folks' rooms. I ain't no thief."

"I didn't say you were, Elsa. I just wondered if by any chance you picked them up by mistake. Mistakes happen to all of us."

"I ain't stupid, neither. I know when I'm gettin' accused of stealing, and I don't have to take it. Elder Wilhelm knows I'm a good Shaker, even if nobody else around here does." Still mumbling, Elsa thrust her hands in the hot soapy water and clattered a sinkful of plates as loudly as she could without breaking them.

Rose would get no admissions out of Elsa, that much was clear. She gave up. It didn't matter anyway; she had a fair idea about what had happened. She was certain that Elsa had indeed taken the drawings, and that she had done so at Wilhelm's request. Perhaps he had told her the drawings were gifts belonging to the whole Society, and Rose had no right to exclusive ownership. She wouldn't be surprised if Wilhelm—or more probably Elsa—had searched Rose's room, found nothing, and chosen Agatha as the next likely keeper of the drawings.

Rose paused to sit in the parlor of the Center Family Dwelling House with her head in her hands. Elsa would do all this only at Wilhelm's bidding. She would never have thought of it herself—which meant that Wilhelm now had all six drawings. With or without Mairin, he would go on with the planned evening worship service, hoping to catch the New-Owenites off guard and convert them easily. She could only pray that

Wilhelm or Elsa did not find Mairin before she did, because they would force her to attend the service. And there would be at least one person in attendance who did not want the information in Mairin's drawings to be brought into the light.

TWENTY-THREE

ROSE NEEDED TO KEEP MOVING, SO SHE WALKED TO THE CHILdren's Dwelling House instead of phoning. Normally everyone would be at worship in the Meetinghouse by this time on a Sunday afternoon, and the rare change in schedule had left some folks at loose ends. The adult Believers just went back to work, but the children grew cranky at the suggestion of more lessons. Given the chilly weather, Charlotte had gathered them all inside the Children's Dwelling House and set them to cleaning their rooms more thoroughly than usual. Charlotte herself was sweeping the corners of the gathering room when Rose found her.

"Nora? She should be up in her room, cleaning, but I wouldn't stake my soul on it," Charlotte told her. "She's been out of sorts since Mairin disappeared. I think she's worried to death, so I've been gentle with her. But she does keep disappearing herself. I suspect she's slipping out to look for Mairin on her own, poor child."

"Remind me which room is hers?"

"Top of the stairs and two down to the left," Charlotte said. "Good luck."

Rose was not surprised to find Nora's room only tolerably tidy—and empty. She checked the bathroom and the other girls' rooms, but Nora was nowhere to be found. Just to be sure, Rose climbed the stairs to the little-used third floor, once filled to capacity with orphaned and abandoned children. She found neither Nora nor Mairin in the sad, empty rooms, but there was evidence that someone had used the area recently—a blanket tossed into a corner, bread crumbs on the floor, a soiled white cup.

Rose descended the staircase to the second floor. On impulse, she revisited Nora's room, and there she was, frowning in concentration as she dusted the mushroom-shaped pegs that encircled her room, low enough for a child's reach.

"Nora, where were you just now?"

"Um, just now? Right here," Nora said, with wide-eyed innocence. "Charlotte sent us to clean our rooms."

"I know that, but I checked a few minutes ago, and you most certainly were not here. There's no place for you to disappear from view in here," Rose said, glancing around the plain, sparsely furnished room.

Nora didn't respond, apparently hoping the moment would pass and Rose would lose interest. Rose arched an eyebrow at her. Avoiding the dreaded eyebrow, Nora gazed down at her hands, which were clutching a cleaning rag. Her face lightened.

"I needed a clean rag," she said. "So you must have come by while I was downstairs in the cleaning closet."

There wasn't much Rose could say to that, though she was sure it was an outright lie. Her suspicions were ballooning. Nora was clever and unpredictable, but Rose didn't believe she would lie except for a very good reason. She was fairly certain the reason was Mairin. If she asked Nora directly where Mairin was hiding, Nora would lie again. Clearly, Mairin had sworn her to silence. No matter, Rose felt her heart lift. If Nora was in contact with Mairin, then the child was hiding of her own accord.

"Okay," Rose said. "You'd best get back to it, then. I'll see you at dinner." She hoped she'd hit the right balance of cheerfulness and sternness, so Nora would not suspect that she had figured out the secret. Nora would be far easier to follow if she had no reason to believe anyone might be doing so.

*   *   *

Rose positioned herself just at the edge of the grove of maples behind the old burned-out Water House. She was hidden from view, and she could see both the front and back entrances to the Children's Dwelling House. Short of climbing out a window in broad daylight, those were the only ways Nora could leave the building.

Rose's knee began a dull throb after about an hour of standing behind a thick maple trunk, peeking out toward the village. She was also feeling silly, as if she'd transformed into one of the children herself. But she couldn't afford to give up. The worship service—and night—would be upon them in four or five hours, and Rose had to know where Mairin was.

She shifted her position so she could lean more comfortably against the tree, and as she looked again, she saw Nora's slender figure slither out the back door of the Children's Dwelling House. Nora peered in all directions but didn't seem to perceive Rose among the trees. Nora edged along close to the building until she reached the southeast corner, then she was out of sight.

Ignoring the objections of her knee, Rose bolted toward the fields in back of the Children's Dwelling House. There were no crops to hide her, but it was the best she could do. She ran east and gradually toward the building until she could see around the corner at which Nora had disappeared. She was just in time to see Nora's head dip down, followed by the cellar door of the South Family Dwelling House.

Rose ran toward the dwelling house, not sure what she'd do when she got there. It would be difficult to follow Nora through the storage rooms and the kitchen without being seen, but she might have to. If Mairin really was in the building, she was extraordinarily well hidden, and following Nora might be the only way to find her.

Nora would surely be moving along fast. Rose lifted the cellar door just enough to slide through, even though it meant twisting her knee. She winced both in pain and at the squeak of the door as she moved it, but she didn't have time to go more slowly. Nora was well out of sight, and probably hearing, too.

The dirt floor absorbed the sound of her feet, so Rose hurried through the storage areas, looking quickly into each one as she passed. She could not imagine Mairin hiding in any of the dank, clammy underground rooms, despite the proximity to food. She expected Nora to stop in the kitchen to pick up a snack for Mairin and then head upstairs, so she was caught off guard when she reached the last area and peered into the dimness to see Nora's back. The girl seemed to be deciding between raspberry and peach preserves. There was no sign of Mairin.

Rose flung herself back against the wall outside the storage room and looked around her. She couldn't stay where she was; Nora would see her. Briefly she considered confronting the girl and ordering her to reveal Mairin's whereabouts, but there was a good chance she'd endure punishment before she would break her word to a friend. Besides, knowing Nora, the more dramatic the situation became, the more she'd enjoy her role.

Edging backward so Nora wouldn't sneak out without her knowing, Rose tiptoed into the next storage area behind her. By easing around the edge, she was able to see the opening from which Nora would emerge. With luck, Nora wouldn't doubt she was alone and look in Rose's direction. A delicate plea to Holy Mother Wisdom probably wouldn't hurt, either, so she said a silent prayer.

The angels must have been listening, because Nora left the storage area at a normal pace, her eyes on the jar she'd selected, perhaps still wondering if the other choice might not have been better. She turned toward the stairs to the kitchen without looking up.

Now Rose wasn't sure what to do. She thought she should wait a few minutes because surely Nora would pick up some bread for the preserves, and perhaps some cheese, if she could find some that hadn't hardened to a rock after being left uncovered. Rose moved into the area Nora had just vacated and counted seconds until she'd gotten to three minutes. She couldn't wait much longer, or she might lose Nora altogether.

She left her hiding place and headed for the stairs. Just as she reached the bottom step, she heard a scraping sound near the door. She flew back to the safety of a storage area, on impulse choosing the one across from the preserves. Nora's feet appeared, then her arms, laden with food. Rose flattened herself against the wall of the storage area, her cheek touching the rough planks used to shore up the room. Through the cracks, she could smell earth and mildew and ancient dust. It occurred to her to wonder just when the brethren had last done any maintenance in these rooms.

Rose heard Nora pass the opening, then the earth swallowed her footsteps, and Rose could hear nothing until the cellar door creaked. Hoping it was safe to leave her hiding place, she entered the narrow hallway and headed for the steps leading to the cellar door. A streak of gray light disappeared as the cellar door shut.

Again she counted, this time for a minute, before she pushed up the cellar door a crack, just enough to see that no one was outside. Another couple of inches told her that Nora was long gone. She eased through the opening as quickly as possible and ran from one corner of the building to the other, looking for the small figure. Her heart beat at a panicked pace as she spun around and saw nothing—until she squinted out at the fields where she had stood earlier. There was Nora, running through the crusty soil, heading south of the village.

Confused, Rose stayed where she was. There were no trees in that direction, not that she knew of, and surely Mairin wouldn't be hiding out in the open. As she tried to decide what to do, she saw Nora swerve east, toward the orchard. Of course, the orchard. Instead of running after her, Rose stayed behind the southernmost buildings and headed toward the orchard. She tried to stay in the shadows, since now and then Nora stopped and glanced around.

Nora had planned this carefully, the clever little imp. There was no one about. It was nearing the dinner hour, and Wilhelm had suggested that everyone return to their retiring rooms to change into their Sabbathday best. The worship service would be held immediately following the evening meal.

As Rose watched from the southeast corner of the Meetinghouse, Nora entered the orchard from the south end. Even without leaves on the trees, the area was too dense for Rose to see where the girl had gone. She was about to go searching when Nora surprised her by emerging from the north edge of the orchard. She stopped and looked around. She'd piled the food in her apron. Clutching her booty tightly against her stomach, she bolted north, toward the barn.

The barn made perfect sense. It was the village's newest structure, rebuilt after the old one had burned down. At Wilhelm's insistence, they'd built it larger than necessary, in preparation for the new members the elder was certain would arrive soon. There were unused corners and haylofts that might seem safe and warm to a frightened child. She could easily stay out of sight of the brethren as they went about their chores.

In no hurry now, Rose walked toward the barn, keeping Nora in view, just in case. But this time there were no surprises. Nora disappeared through a small side door of the barn. Rose followed, less concerned now about being seen. She knew Mairin was in the barn. Finding out where was only a matter of time.

The task turned out to be simple. Rose entered to the familiar and not unpleasant smells of hay and manure. She took a moment to adjust her eyes to the dim light and her ears, to filter out the sounds of grunts and lows and pacing hooves. Within moments, she heard the giggling of young girls, coming from somewhere above her. And nearby.

She followed the sounds to a ladder leading to a hayloft. She hoisted her long skirts over her arm and climbed the ladder to find Nora and Mairin sitting on a blanket, sharing brown bread, cheese, and preserves, which they scooped out of the jar with their fingers.

"I see you won't be needing supper tonight," Rose said.

The girls jumped and clutched each other. They looked far from relieved when they saw it was only Rose. Mairin loosened her hold on Nora and straightened her frail shoulders.

"It's my fault, not Nora's," she said. "Nora just didn't want me to go without food. I told her it was okay, I'd done it lots of times before, but she's too nice."

"And too enticed by a good adventure," Rose murmured. Louder, she said, "We three are going to have a little chat." She settled cross-legged on the blanket facing them.

"Don't blame Mairin," Nora said. "She just got really scared and had to hide."

"What scared you, Mairin?"

Mairin picked at the fuzzy wool of the blanket.

"Did it have to do with the service scheduled for this evening?"

The girl's eyes flicked toward her, then back to the blanket.

"And did it also have to do with what you saw in the orchard and with whatever frightened you in the woods outside the Schoolhouse the other day?"

Mairin flashed a coppery glare at Nora, who edged away. "You said for me not to tell Charlotte," Nora said. "You never said I couldn't tell Rose."

"I *meant* not to tell *anyone*."

"Nora was worried about you," Rose said. "She did the right thing. She followed her conscience—and her heart. She's your friend. And so am I, if you will let me be. You don't have to do this on your own. We can protect you."

Mairin hugged herself and for once didn't dam her tears. It was a start. Rose slid over to her and put an arm around her shoulders. "Now, tell me," Rose said, as the crying subsided.

"I can't," Mairin said, hanging her head. "I want to, really and truly, but I can't."

"You want to . . . Mairin, has someone threatened you?"

Mairin's mouth dropped open.

"That's it, isn't it? You saw someone hurt Hugh, didn't you? And that person has threatened to harm you if you tell. It's okay, Mairin, don't you see? You didn't tell me, I guessed, and furthermore, I can protect you. The whole village will protect you. Just tell me who threatened you."

Mairin shook her head.

"If you don't tell, I will," Nora said. "I've got to follow my conscience, Rose said so."

"You don't even know."

"I do so. I know some stuff you haven't told Rose, and maybe she can guess the rest, like she did before."

Mairin lunged at Nora and pinned her to the ground before Rose could stop her. "Don't, don't, *don't.*"

Mairin might be used to climbing trees, but she was still suffering the effects of malnutrition, while Nora was bigger and well fed. With a grunt, Nora twisted away from Mairin's grip and grabbed the smaller girl's wrists to keep her from trying again. Rose clamped a hand on Mairin's shoulder, and the fight went out of her.

"I'm going to tell," Nora said. "See, she only told me because I found out she was going to hide, and I wanted to come, too, and Mairin wanted to scare me away. She said he'd hurt me if she told—me and you and Agatha."

"Who threatened her?"

Nora's self-satisfied expression faded. "I don't know. She wouldn't tell me that."

Rose sighed. If adults were as stubborn about keeping their promises as these children, the world would be a better place—and even more frustrating.

"So *you* are protecting *us*. Tell me, Mairin, why did you choose now to go into hiding? Was it your doll?"

Mairin wrapped her arms around her knees and rocked herself.

"Your doll that Agatha gave you?" Nora asked. "What happened to it?"

Mairin rocked harder. "Somebody hurt it," she said, barely above a whisper.

Immediately, Rose understood. Mairin had not hanged the doll; it had been left as a warning to Mairin of what would happen if she talked. Rose lightly touched Mairin's shoulder. "Are you frightened about this evening's service?"

Mairin nodded. "I'm afraid someone will trick me into telling. Then I won't be able to protect you anymore."

"I see. So the man who threatened you will be at the service tonight, and you are terrified that if you say the wrong thing, he will hurt Nora, and Agatha, and me."

"He will kill you. He said so."

Rose rested her chin on her fists and thought. At least she now knew that Hugh had been killed and that a man was involved, someone who would be at the service. Maybe she could figure it out from there. Most important right now was to keep Mairin safe. Rose was certain that the real target of the threat was Mairin, not her friends. The child was in danger of being eliminated whether or not she told her secrets. Perhaps it was best for now to let her stay scared and hidden, at least until after the service. It wouldn't hurt to keep Nora out of view, as well.

"All right, you two. I want you to stay here, out of sight, until I come back to get you. And keep very quiet. No giggling. Is that clear?"

The girls nodded.

"I'll explain to Charlotte, so no one notices that you're gone, too, Nora. It's close to time for evening meal, so the sun will set in a little while. It'll be dark in here. Sleep, if you can, but don't leave. Promise?"

"Promise," both girls said together. Mairin's features brightened with relief, Nora's with excitement.

TWENTY-FOUR

THERE WAS LITTLE ROSE COULD DO BEFORE THE SERVICE, SO she decided to attend the evening meal. At least then she could keep an eye on everyone. She changed quickly into her beige wool Sabbathday dress, newly mended and laundered for winter use. She looked forward to having a new one, woven from Isabel's true butternut-dyed yarn. As an afterthought, she slid her list of questions about Hugh's death in the pocket of her dress. On her way out, she made a quick call to the Sheriff's Office and left a message for Grady to drive out to North Homage that evening, if he could. She wouldn't be surprised if it was never delivered.

She joined the sisters in prayer outside the dining room. As she prepared to lead them in, Josie arrived, red-faced and puffing. She stood just inside the door, catching her breath. Concerned, Rose sent the others in single-filed silence into the dining room without her.

"Is someone ill?"

"Goodness," Josie said, shaking her head. "I shouldn't run so, not at my age. I'll be the one ill. Nay, I hurried because it's Andrew, calling from Bloomington, Indiana. Says he must speak with you at once. You'd best do some running yourself."

The Infirmary was a short distance from the Center Family Dwelling House, but Rose's knee kept her from sprinting. It was several minutes before she grabbed up the receiver Josie had left hanging.

"Rose? Good. I don't have long. I'm on my way soon to have dinner with one more man who might have some useful information about our visitors, but I wanted to catch you first. Is all well?"

"So far, but Wilhelm is determined to hold a joint service this evening with the New-Owenites."

"Well, it could be quite a spectacle. I've learned a lot about these New-Owenites. A few leaders stayed behind to, um, take care of matters, while Gilbert and his group paved the way, shall we say."

Rose pulled over a ladder-back chair. "There are more of them, aren't there, waiting to move to North Homage?"

" 'More' is a modest word for the number of folks waiting to pack their bags. Gilbert, it seems, made a study of Robert Owen's methods, hoping both to emulate his successes and avoid his mistakes. Robert had gathered new members by going around the country on a speaking tour and making all sorts of promises he couldn't keep about the land and the work that would be available to people who moved to New Harmony. They didn't have to contribute anything, just show up. It was a disaster. So Gilbert decided all he needed to do was find a town that was already organized, had farming and businesses already going, just a need for more people."

"How *many* people?" Rose asked, holding her breath.

"About one hundred and fifty . . . so far. More are arriving every day, camping out in fields owned by a fellow who wants to come along."

"Dear God. How can Gilbert believe such a plan would work?"

"Gilbert didn't study hard enough. He didn't understand that by promising utopia and asking nothing immediate in return, he'd entice all sorts of folks with no skills and no ideals, just as Robert did. Gilbert told them he'd have a complete village for them, with money to take care of them and free education for their children. He mentioned nothing about Shakers already living there, or about faith or vows of nonviolence and celibacy. The leaders I spoke with are at their wits' end and about ready to send them all ahead to North Homage."

"What? Can you stop them?"

"Apparently Gilbert sent word yesterday that it shouldn't be long now. I've tried to let them know that Gilbert's promises can't possibly be kept, but so far no one seems to be listening. It'll take something dramatic, I'm afraid."

"That's what I'm afraid of, too," Rose said. "Did you find out anything about Hugh?"

"Quite a lot. I got to talking with a young man named Tommy who has been with the New-Owenites from the beginning. He's frustrated enough to leave, so he was eager to unburden himself." Andrew chuckled. "It seems most folks thought of Hugh as an easy touch, generous to a fault. Anybody with a sob story could get money out of him. However, Tommy said there'd been some complaints about Hugh making promises and not keeping them. Seems to run in the family."

Rose kept her appreciative laughter short, aware that they had little time. "Could gambling debts have been a factor?" she asked.

"Tommy said he'd heard second- and third-hand rumors about gambling debts, but he himself didn't know anything definite. He said Earl and Gilbert might have gotten wind of a gambling problem, because both of them had been at odds with Hugh in the days before they all left. Everyone suspected Earl was half in love with Celia; at least, he was always being nice to her, and she was never nice to anyone. At any rate, Tommy knew there wasn't much of a marriage between Celia and Hugh."

"Was Hugh cruel to Celia?"

"According to Tommy, it was the other way around."

The line crackled, and Andrew's voice disappeared for a few moments. Rose waited, unwilling to break the connection herself. She fiddled with the lid of an apothecary jar Josie had left on her desk. In the silence, the tinkle of glass against glass made her aware of her isolation. Her thoughts wandered nervously to the evening service. No one would be there to support her, and she had no time to convince Wilhelm he could not control the outcome.

"Are you still there, Rose? Good, because there's more. Before they left, Gilbert and Hugh had been arguing. Tommy said he heard part of one argument, and it seemed to be about money for the community and whether the project lived up to its ideals. There was something about 'the ends justifying the means,' but Tommy wasn't clear about that. So that's about all I've found out for now. I'm late, I'd best get going."

"Wait, Andrew. One more question. Did anyone see Hugh mistreating Mairin?"

"Nay, no one did. It's interesting—again the story seems to be twisted around. Tommy, and several others remarked that they suspected Celia of neglecting and mistreating Mairin. Hugh seemed to be rather fond of her, in his ineffectual way. He talked about changing his will to provide for her."

"Truly? I wonder how Celia reacted to that!"

"Not well, is what I was told. They were heard to argue about it. Rose, I really must go now. If I find out anything else that might help, I'll call; otherwise, I'm heading home on the morning train. I wish I could be there tonight. Take care." The receiver clicked, and Rose felt a wave of loneliness.

"I wish you could be here, too," she said softly.

Rose glanced at the small clock on Josie's desk. Nearly seven. The evening meal would be ending, and very soon everyone would gather across the street in the Meetinghouse, the Shakers' place of worship. There might be time to snatch some bread from the kitchen first, but Rose wasn't hungry. Instead, she took her list of questions from her pocket and unfolded it. Many of the questions had now been answered, but she still didn't know with certainty why Hugh had died.

She found a pen in Josie's desk drawer. Next to each of her questions, she wrote down what she now knew. When she'd finished, the pattern of lies was clear. Hugh's alleged cruelty was a sham. If Celia had complained that he was a tyrant to her, she was lying. But why? If she wanted to be thought innocent of murdering her husband, surely she would have been wiser to claim that she loved him. She certainly loved his money and had every intention of inheriting all of it. If she was involved, she had an accomplice; no matter how unpleasant her temperament, she didn't possess the strength to hang a man.

Gilbert, as far as she remembered, had not called Hugh cruel. But by all accounts he wanted Hugh's money, one way or another. If Hugh had started to withdraw his backing, either because of gambling debts or disapproval of Gilbert's methods, Gilbert might have thought he'd have an easier time if Celia inherited. Gilbert was pedantic and single-minded in pursuit of his utopian dream—was he also ruthless enough to kill for it?

Earl was solicitous of Celia and criticized Hugh. Was he in love with Celia—or perhaps only with her money? Like Celia, Earl had expensive tastes. His devotion to New-Owenite principles could easily be deception, to move him into the inner circle.

As for Hugh's purported gambling debts, Andrew had found no proof of them. Yet during her painful stay in the South Family Dwelling House kitchen, Rose had heard the New-Owenites express concern about the debts—and about who might come to collect them. Any or all of the visitors might have been tempted to fake Hugh's suicide, rather than let him waste his inheritance.

Finally, Rose had to consider the brethren, Matthew and Archibald. Archibald surely was a follower. If he were involved in Hugh's death, it would probably be under someone else's influence. Matthew's, perhaps? He was infatuated with Celia and inclined to simmering resentment. Might he have convinced himself—or had help doing so—that he could have Celia simply by eliminating her husband?

Rose wished she could make her mind work faster, but it stalled. She knew one thing for certain—Mairin was in mortal danger. She had seen the killing, and the killer knew it. She was safe for now, but he wouldn't let her live indefinitely. Her habit of drawing pictures was altogether too threatening.

Shadows crossed the west window, and she looked up to see figures moving, alone and in groups, toward the Meetinghouse. She had no more time. All she could do was stay alert, hope for the best, and beg Holy Mother Wisdom to send her angels to watch over the girls and keep them from wandering into danger.

TWENTY-FIVE

ROSE'S FOREBODING DEEPENED AS SHE OPENED THE WOMEN'S door to the Meetinghouse. Her first impression was that she'd stumbled on a three-ring circus, like the one she'd sneaked a peek at as a child, when Agatha had taken her along on a trip to Languor. Wilhelm stood, a grim statue, in the center of the high-ceilinged meeting room. On one side, the sisters sat in an attempt at prayerful silence, while their eyes darted around the room. On Wilhelm's other side, several of the chairs were empty, and the remaining brethren scowled at the pine floor as if its smooth surface offended them.

Behind the brethren's seats, a group of men huddled in a circle, whispering to one another. Rose recognized four of them, including Matthew and Archibald, in their dark blue Sabbathday surcoats. The other two men were New-Owenites, dressed in their usual baggy brown trousers and shirts. Hands waved and heads nodded, as if they were negotiating a plan.

The third ring clustered at the far end of the room, across from where Wilhelm stood. The group included Gilbert, Earl, Celia, and the other New-Owenite women. Unlike the others, Celia's outfit was both elegant and odd. She was covered in black, from her ebony hair to her shiny dancing slippers. A black lace shawl barely disguised the sleek fit of her satin gown. She gazed around the room as if scouting out dance partners.

Rose wished she'd eaten something. This promised to be an

exhausting evening. Thank goodness they had decided not to open the service to the public—and that Mairin was safely hidden away. She chose a seat on the end of the back bench on the sisters' side, so she could observe everyone. Frustration was gnawing at her; she longed to do something active to control the mounting tensions, but she could think of nothing. With her eyes open, she prayed inwardly for guidance and inspiration.

Wilhelm straightened, closed his eyes, and raised his arms to call for quiet. The seated Believers were already silent, and they remained so. The other two groups ignored him. Wilhelm, in turn, ignored their rudeness and motioned to three sisters and two brethren to stand at his side and sing a welcoming hymn. The noise level increased, and Rose was able to recognize only a few words. There'd be no dancing if this kept up.

Wilhelm nodded to the confused singers to begin another hymn. Despite the chill outside, the large room had begun to feel stuffy, as if the world had crowded inside with them. Wilhelm's powerful baritone strengthened the singing, while Matthew's group seemed to be whipping themselves into an angry lather. The New-Owenites laughed and chattered as if they were at a ball, giddy with champagne.

Rose shrank in her seat to escape the cacophony. She wondered if the Meetinghouse walls were thick enough to withstand the insult. Spending the evening hiding in a hayloft was beginning to sound appealing. She considered slipping out and leaving everyone else to fight it out—but nay, she couldn't leave the other sisters. She could sense their confusion and fear. None of this was their doing, and they needed her presence, even if she could not provide protection.

A deep roar rose above the din. "Silence! Silence, now!" The shout erupted from Wilhelm like the blast of a train whistle. It startled everyone speechless just long enough for Wilhelm to claim the room's attention. He wasted no time, and for once Rose was grateful.

"We all agreed to gather together in this place of worship.

Believers," he said, with a stern look at Matthew's group, "this is not a town square, it is a sacred place for thee. Mother Ann is with us here, and be assured that her heart is breaking to see us behave like squabbling children."

Matthew stared at the floor with a sullen frown, but he remained quiet. Archibald and the other brethren looked abashed. The two New-Owenite men with them, though they said nothing, watched Gilbert across the room, awaiting instruction.

Gilbert watched Wilhelm. "I have a suggestion," Gilbert said, in a conversational tone. "It's obvious that we all have important issues to discuss. Let's take turns, shall we? That's fair."

"This is a place of worship," Wilhelm repeated. His voice rumbled like thunder building in the electric air.

"For you," Gilbert said. "Not for us. And you might find that the place has become less than sacred for some of your own folks. However, we do acknowledge that this is your building, and we've never really stopped to observe your . . . ritual. So I suggest that you folks take the first turn. Show us why this worship business holds such power for you." The New-Owenites pulled an empty bench away from the wall and sat down, polite interest on their faces. Celia whispered something in Earl's ear, and they both smiled.

Rose felt as if her heart were pumping lead. The worship service was turning into a debate by performance. She couldn't believe such a scene would unfold in their Meetinghouse. Surely Wilhelm now recognized the foolishness of his plans. The angels must indeed be crying their eyes out.

If Wilhelm understood his error, he showed no sign of it. With a forceful nod, he indicated to the anxious Believers that it was time for dancing worship. The Shakers pushed their benches back to open the floor for dancing. Rose made the choice to stand with her sisters. They formed a line facing the small number of brethren across the center of the room.

But before the chorus could sing a note, a querulous male voice shouted, "Nay!" The command had come from the group standing in back of the brethren's seats. Scraping sounds followed, and Matthew's head appeared above the brethren. He'd climbed on a bench, shocking enough in itself, but then he deepened his impropriety by stripping off his surcoat and flinging it on the floor. The Believers fumbled back to their benches and huddled close together.

"This time we aren't waiting," Matthew said. "You all have kept us quiet long enough, and now we're going to have our say." Murmurs of support came from the men around him.

"By all means," Gilbert said, before Wilhelm could bellow an order for silence, "speak your piece. Wilhelm and I are patient enough to wait." He smiled across at Wilhelm, who said nothing. *How could he?* Rose thought. *He has been outmaneuvered.* She had no doubt that Gilbert had always intended for Matthew's complaints to come first.

"You all think you've got a heaven on earth here," Matthew said, "but this ain't heaven for us." The others agreed with growing assertiveness. "You think it's heaven to work all day and into the night, without pay, without even a nickel saved up? This village is dying. In a year or two, this'll be a ghost town, and we'll all be out on the streets with nothing—no jobs, no money, no family to take care of us."

Wilhelm's ruddy features were contorting in fury. "Foolish sinner," he shouted, "Mother Ann will always—"

"Nay, Wilhelm, you listen to me! Mother Ann is watching us die, and she isn't lifting a finger to help. And you know why? Because Mother Ann is *dead,* that's why. Dead and buried and rotted away long ago."

The sisters around Rose gasped and whispered to one another. Matthew turned on them.

"You're shocked, are you? Well, maybe you should have thought of this yourselves. Most of you are old. What's going to happen to you when North Homage collapses? You pinned all your hopes on your Mother Ann, and now you don't have husbands or children or grandchildren. You're like our sheep; you went along with the Ministry telling you how to live, it never entered your minds you should have had a say in how they got to be the Ministry."

Using a gesture copied from Wilhelm's more fervent homilies, Matthew thrust his arm straight up, his index finger pointing to the heavens. "There ain't no Holy Mother Wisdom up there, smiling down on you. You're on your own. We all are. All we got is our brains and our strength. As I see it, we got one chance to come out of this alive. We join whatever strength we have left with these folks here." He pointed toward Gilbert, who listened with a benign air. "We don't have to become just like them. We own the buildings and the business and the know-how, and they got the people. If we put our heads together, we can make it through this Depression, and come out the other end in one piece. That's all I got to say."

He jumped off the bench to applause from his own comrades and the New-Owenites led by Gilbert.

Wilhelm's stone-faced silence disturbed Rose more than an eruption of fury would have. She knew that look. He wasn't worried. He had a plan.

He nodded toward the five-voice chorus, and they took their places again. With reluctance, Rose again led the sisters to form a row facing the brethren. At Wilhelm's cue, the singers began a shaky a cappella tune that Rose had never heard before. Apparently, neither had anyone else, because the worshipers stood still. Even the singers wavered, and Wilhelm joined in to bring them back to the pitch.

The lyrics spoke of the beauty of the heavens and described the flowers and foods and sheer joy that Believers would encounter, once they had completed their life of chastity and hard work. The sweet, simple tune intrigued Rose—for about ten seconds, until she tumbled to what was happening. At that moment, the tune began again, made stronger yet by the addition of a rich contralto at the other end of the sisters' row. Sister Elsa Pike. Of course. Wilhelm had Elsa's unquenchable devotion. She had surely taken Mairin's drawings for Wilhelm, and so of course she had helped him plan this service. And it would no doubt be quite a service.

As the chorus began the tune a third time, Elsa led the dancing. Elsa Pike, a plump, flat-featured hill-country woman, was transformed in worship to a graceful and competent dancer. She performed controlled, choreographed movements matched to the song lyrics. She bowed from the waist to show her humility, made sweeping and cleansing movements to represent her willingness to work. She held her hands aloft to receive the bounteous celestial foods and, finally, began to twirl in grateful ecstasy.

The other sisters were familiar with most of the gestures and learned them quickly. Soon they were dancing in flowing unison. Wilhelm joined the brethren and demonstrated a version of the dance that mimed sawing and building and other work normally done by the men.

Rose hung back. The dance was lovely and stirred her heart, but she had learned from experience. When Elsa led the dancing, it soon became the frenzied, trancelike worship that Believers had practiced in their early years, and again during Mother Ann's Work. Rose believed in the dancing, but not in Elsa's practice of it.

Many of the other observers seemed intrigued by the spectacle. Matthew watched sullenly, but his brethren followers swayed as if they longed to join in. Gilbert's group was less than mesmerized, though they had stopped whispering among themselves. From her smirk, Celia must be assessing the dancers' grace and beauty, and judging herself superior. Gilbert's thin, scholarly features showed detached interest. Earl looked wary.

At the moment, no one paid much attention to Rose, though she knew she was visible to everyone. She returned to her back-row bench and began adjusting her shoe, as if it pinched. Something was going to happen, and it would be soon. Rose fought off a sense of helplessness. There was no time. She couldn't imagine what she alone could do when the three-way struggle intensified, but she had to think of something.

Gilbert's group was now to her right and in front of her, so she could watch them more openly. They'd begun to fidget.

Celia's shoulders drooped with boredom, and Earl took her hand. And Gilbert . . . Rose scanned the New-Owenites twice and couldn't find Gilbert's bony profile. She counted them. One was missing. They were close to the men's entrance. Gilbert must have slipped out while Rose fussed with her shoe.

A sound like a dog barking came from the dancers. It had begun. Elsa hopped in a circle, her arms rigid at her side. The other sisters—and the brethren, too—joined in, keeping their distance from each other, of course. Then Elsa flung out her arms and began to twirl, followed by the others, creating a kaleidoscope of butternut and dark blue swirls. Elsa twirled dangerously close to Wilhelm, and the New-Owenites were no longer bored. Rose's limbs felt tight, bunched up for action. She still had no idea what that action might be, but her gaze darted from group to group, alert to danger.

As Rose expected, Elsa stopped twirling and went rigid with a suddenness that almost threw her off balance. Except for her quick-step recovery, she gave every appearance of being in a deep trance. The other Believers stopped their dancing and formed a broken circle around her, sisters on one side, brethren on the other.

A few moments passed, and Rose became suspicious. She expected Elsa to begin speaking in tongues and perhaps convey messages from Mother Ann, but the silence continued. Elsa seemed to be waiting—for what, Rose understood as soon as she saw Wilhelm step inside the circle. He held large sheets of paper that could only be Mairin's drawings. He handed them out to three sisters and three brethren, murmuring instructions. The Believers turned their drawings outward, all facing Elsa.

Rose checked the New-Owenites' reactions. Clearly, they had not expected this. Celia and Earl leaned close and whispered to one another. The other New-Owenites closed ranks with them, and hands jerked in agitated gestures.

Matthew and his group also huddled together and appeared to be arguing. Wilhelm ignored them all. He stepped outside the circle surrounding Elsa and signaled to the chorus to begin another unfamiliar song. Rose couldn't hear the lyrics, but the tune was unusual. Most Shaker songs had a sweet simplicity and could be sung by most anyone. This one extended beyond the range of most Believers, and, to Rose's astonishment, included some harmony. She wondered if this had been Elsa's idea, and if it was meant to give her a special place as the chosen instrument who brought truly new music to the Believers.

Elsa opened her eyes and stretched out her arms, palms upward. She began a slow circle, round and round, giving her a few seconds' view of each picture, as if she were studying a mural. The plan was now clear. Elsa would slip into a trance and become an instrument for—whom? Probably for Holy Mother Wisdom, since she was thought to be the giver of gift drawings. Then what? Rose could guess. Elsa was to bring forth a message from Holy Mother which instructed the New-Owenites to open their hearts to the Society of Believers in Christ's Second Appearing. They would be urged to give up their carnal ways and accept the guidance of Mother Ann—and undoubtedly of Elder Wilhelm.

Of all Wilhelm's schemes to reinvigorate the Shakers, this was surely his most foolish—and his most desperate. He must be worried. He was not alone. Matthew and his followers watched, their hands tightened into fists, ready to fight.

At the New-Owenite end of the room, Celia bolted upright. She began to moan and sway, while her companions fell back to let her be seen.

"Who are you?" Celia wailed. "Make yourself known to me. Why have you called me?" Her body grew still, and her head jerked backward as if she'd been hit. She fell back, and Earl caught her, in a movement too seamless to be spontaneous. He lowered her limp body onto a chair and stepped aside.

Celia's body stiffened as if a jolt of electricity shot through her. She raised her hands toward the ceiling, and her lace shawl slipped off to reveal slender, bare arms. Slowly, she stood, arching her body in a graceful movement that seemed almost to lift her off the ground. She had the attention of the room. Most Believers' faces showed fascination as well as discomfort. Matthew's expression was closer to worship.

"I have returned to help you, my faithful followers," Celia said. Her voice came out in a lower register, with a distinctly British accent.

"You are Robert Owen, aren't you, sir?" Earl said. "You can see we are in turmoil. Tell us what we must do."

Rose edged back to the wall, unwilling to be a part of the charade. Across the room from her, close to the ceiling, was the observation window, where elders and eldresses sometimes used to watch worship services, especially when the public attended. The small room had not been used since Agatha, frail and ill, had stepped down as eldress. Rose preferred to be an active part of the worship. Now she had a strong desire to be closeted away, watching from behind glass. To reach the door leading upstairs, she would have to sneak around half the perimeter of the room, behind the Shakers and behind Matthew's group, but it was worth a try. Near the observation room was a small office with a phone, should she need to make another effort—no matter how fruitless—to convince the Sheriff to come.

With everyone's attention on the show, reaching the door proved easy. Matthew and his followers were especially oblivious to anything but Celia. Rose was through the door, up the stairs, and into the dark observation room before Celia had finished entrancing the audience with her lithe movements. As Rose pulled a chair up to the window, Celia began again her rendition of Robert Owen. It was loud enough for Rose to hear. The acting was quite good, Rose had to admit, but Celia had miscalculated the accent. Robert Owen had been Welsh, and Celia's tones were pure, public-school English. Rose had heard both accents during her time as the Society's trustee, in her dealings with businessmen from the world.

"First, you must hear the truth," Celia/Robert announced. "I, Robert Owen, am the only one in this room who knows the truth, because I have seen it for myself. I am a shade from the spirit world. Yes, there is a spirit world, where all of you will go someday. But there is no God, and there is no heaven. I know it is hard for the Shakers among you to hear this, but it is best to hear it now. Stop living a lie!" By now, Celia/Robert was shouting over the agitated voices filling the air.

"Enough of this blasphemy!" Elder Wilhelm's voice boomed across the room. "We know the truth already. Do not allow these godless liars to mislead you, brethren. It is a trick—and a test of our faith. Mother Ann will never—"

"She is here!" Celia's voice deepened with power. "Mother Ann is standing here beside me."

The room grew quiet. Even Wilhelm was stunned into silence.

"Mother Ann is a shade, like me. She has been trying for countless decades to reveal the truth to you. She loves you, and she grieves when she sees how you've lost your way."

Across the room from Celia's drama, Wilhelm conferred with a group of nearby Believers, including the chorus and Elsa. They leaned toward him to hear what must be whispered commands, then they spread apart. The chorus took its place again, and the sisters and brethren passed a message down their rows, which began to straighten. Wilhelm stood with the chorus.

"Listen. Listen to Mother Ann. Listen to me!" Celia's voice rose to a higher pitch, but maintained its English accent. This time Celia had done more study—or perhaps she just knew how to imitate a Cockney accent, but not a Welsh one. In a compelling, uneducated voice, "Mother Ann" said, "My beloved children. So often I've sent you word of your misunderstandings. I've tried to show you the right way. I can't rest until I have corrected the false beliefs that have been forced upon you in my name. I've sent messages through a child—"

The chorus began a boisterous march, bellowing so loudly that voices cracked. After a few fumbled steps, the Believers clapped, stomped their feet, and marched in time with the music. Celia was startled enough to interrupt her rendition of Mother Ann and scowl at the dancers. Earl stepped forward to whisper in her ear, then pulled a bench away from the wall. Celia climbed on top of the bench, forgoing grace for speed, and faced the Believers, who were coming to the end of their dance. Earl stayed just behind her, well placed to catch her should Mother Ann nudge her off balance.

Celia inhaled deeply and shuddered. But before she could speak, the chorus began singing again.

"This is your loving Mother Ann." Projecting over the ruckus gave her voice a harsh edge. "Listen! You have been duped. Fight these evil leaders of yours. Hear the truth from me!"

Wilhelm and the chorus joined in with the dancers' foot-stomping and clapping. Rose's eyes darted back and forth between the enemies, judging whether it would be wise to leave and call the police, with the hope that she might get Grady. She gave up the idea as Matthew's group came out of its stupor and filtered among the dancers. At first, Rose thought they planned to join the brethren in the march.

They slipped through the line of brethren and approached the sisters. Matthew reached one of the younger sisters and reached out a hand for her. She took it. She slid into the circle of Matthew's arm, and the two began dancing to their own rhythm. One of the New-Owenite men claimed the hand of another young sister and danced away with her. As the couples swirled around the meeting room floor, Rose caught sight of the women's faces. They were Lottie and Frieda, the young sisters Celia had lectured on the Shakers' unfairness to women.

The remaining Believers bumped into one another as they witnessed the sin unfolding before them. Celia, having parted ways with Mother Ann, watched with a smirk on her face. Earl helped her down off the bench and swept her into a dance.

The brethren's door to the Meetinghouse opened. Gilbert entered. Rose felt her heart pound in her head. She'd forgotten about Gilbert, had forgotten to worry about what he might be up to. Now it was clear. Behind him, dragging away from his firm grasp, was Mairin. He had found her, and he intended to use her to turn the battle in his favor. Using his free hand,

Gilbert grabbed Mairin's arm and pushed her in front of him. Before she regained her balance, he picked her up and held her around her waist, flopping against his hip. She struggled, but Gilbert had a wiry strength that easily overpowered her.

So far, Rose was the only one who'd noticed Gilbert and Mairin. Three couples still danced around the floor, and the Shakers were trying to reestablish their dance lines, while a couple of New-Owenite men grabbed at some protesting sisters. Wilhelm threatened the men with eternal damnation in between shouting choruses of a march the singers were belting out with increasingly hoarse voices. For the first time in her memory, Rose cheered Elsa as she executed a deft twirl away from the grasp of a New-Owenite man.

Gilbert marched Mairin into the center of the room, between the sisters and the brethren. He plunked her down on the floor in front of her drawings, which had been dropped in the confusion. A New-Owenite woman ran forward and arranged the drawings in a circle around Gilbert and Mairin. Taking the girl by the shoulders, Gilbert turned her in a circle around the drawings. He whispered something to her, and she shook her head.

A primal rage surged through Rose's body. She felt compassion for the sisters, but they could take care of themselves. But not Mairin . . . Mairin had no one but herself—and Rose. But what could Rose do, besides confronting Gilbert and stealing Mairin away, which might not work?

Gilbert nudged Mairin toward her own drawings, keeping a tight grip on her small shoulder. Mairin turned slowly until she came to the drawing of the lovely, bejeweled bird with the emerald eyes. She stopped and stared at the image, and Rose made her decision. There was no time for a futile call to the Sheriff's Office. She ran down the stairs and through the door to the meeting room, no longer caring if anyone saw her. She entered a spellbound room. Even the dancing couples had stopped to watch Gilbert and the little girl. Rose walked openly toward the center of the room.

"Tell them, child," Gilbert said. "Tell them all what you have seen, and what it really means."

Rose's senses were alert. Rescuing Mairin was her object, and she had to know her enemy—all of them. Matthew's group was silent, waiting, while the Believers twittered in confusion. Celia watched, like a rapt play-goer. Next to her, Earl stood motionless and expressionless.

Mairin reached down and picked up the bird drawing. She held it to her chest as she moved to the drawing of the snake climbing up the tree.

"Tell them," Gilbert said, with impatience. "Tell them how rotten their tree of life is. Tell them that you are the child sent by Mother Ann, that their only hope for survival is in giving up their foolish beliefs and joining with us to form a new world."

Rose stopped in her tracks, her thoughts tangled in confusion. Gilbert believed what he was saying. He truly believed that the Shakers could be saved only by becoming New-Owenites. He was ruthless, but not a liar. He believed that Mairin was an instrument of Mother Ann and probably Robert Owen, too.

All at once, several puzzle pieces snapped into place. Everything made sense—Mairin's fear, the contradictory information about Hugh, even the divergent opinions about Celia. Her mind flashed quickly through the time since she'd returned from the east. She knew she was right. All the confusion had come from one source. One person had insisted that Hugh was a monster and Celia an innocent victim. One man had nurtured the rumor that Hugh was being hunted down by gangsters because of his gambling debts, even though there'd been no sign of dangerous visitors since the New-Owenites arrived: Earl Weston.

The suicide note was a puzzle. Earl Weston had fed Rose the information that Hugh had sometimes printed, instead of using script. Printing is easier to forge. He must have planted it in Hugh's room, so Gilbert would find it as he gathered Hugh's notes. If the note was ever exposed as a forgery, Gilbert would be the first suspect. But why didn't Sheriff Brock sense a hoax?

All eyes except Rose's were on Gilbert and Mairin, in the center of the room. Rose watched Earl as he edged toward the sisters' entrance. She guessed that he was planning to slip out the door and make his escape. She made an instant decision. The inner doorway she'd just come through also led to a back door. If she could get to the sisters' entrance as Earl emerged, maybe she could stop him. She considered letting him escape and sending Sheriff Brock after him, but she doubted the Sheriff's diligence, and Mairin would never be safe as long as Earl roamed the countryside.

She ducked through the door, grabbed her skirts, and ran outside onto the dew-soaked grass. The darkness would be useful, she thought. Perhaps she could surprise Earl as he came out the door, catch him off guard. She had no idea what she would do then. Violence was abhorrent to her, but she trusted Holy Mother Wisdom to grant her an inspiration when the time came.

There was no one in sight when Rose reached the sisters' entrance. The door remained closed. Rose took the risk of moving to a window and peeking inside, hoping the darkness would keep her invisible to the inhabitants. She could see the area in front of the sisters' entrance. Earl was still backing toward it.

She hadn't expected him to move so slowly. He was several yards shy of the exit. She just had time to slip through the door and trap him inside the Meetinghouse, where the others could help restrain him.

Rose entered the sisters' door and closed it behind her just as Earl turned to make his escape.

"What the hell . . ." Earl said, as he saw Rose. "Get out of my way."

"I won't," Rose said. "You've killed another human being and threatened a child. I can't let you go free." Her voice shook. She was well aware of his superior size and strength.

"Look, just get out of the way." Earl took a step toward her. "I don't want to hurt you."

"Your real concern is escaping unseen," Rose said. "If you harm me, the others will come after you immediately; you won't have time to get away."

Earl reached in his trousers picket and withdrew a small

object. With a practiced flip, he opened it into a knife. Rose drew in her breath to shout for help.

"I'd keep very quiet, if I were you," Earl said. Beads of sweat dotted his forehead, and his face had turned an alarming red. "These are your choices. Let me go and give me time to get out of here, and you'll never hear from me again. If you send anyone after me, I'll kill them, if I have to—do you want to be responsible for more killing? I don't think so. Or you could scream, and I'd have to hurt you, and then, so help me, I'd hurt that little girl you're so fond of." Rose heard the desperation in his hoarse voice. He was likely to do anything.

"Earl?" Celia was walking toward them. "Earl, what's going on?"

Earl started at the sound of her voice. Rose jumped sideways to escape the knife point aimed toward her stomach. She opened her mouth to scream and warn the others, but Earl was quicker. He lunged at her, grabbed her around the waist and held her in front of him. Rose felt the sharp tip of his pocket knife pricking the skin covering her right kidney.

Celia screamed and screamed again, as she backed away. The cacophony in the large room hushed to silence, and all eyes turned toward Earl and Rose.

"What's all this about?" Gilbert looked more puzzled than frightened.

"You shouldn't have brought the girl here," Earl said. "You should have let her stay lost. Send her over here to me."

"Now, Earl, we've gone over and over this. The girl's the only one who can convey the real meaning of these drawings. It's the only way we can really show the Shakers the truth about—"

"Gil, I don't deny that your foggy grasp on reality has been useful to me more than once, just as your cousin's was, but right now, don't try to think. Just push the girl over here, and we'll leave, and the rest of you can go on with your lives."

"Nay, you must not!" Rose cried out.

"Earl?" Celia had regained her composure, now that Matthew stood beside her. "I don't understand. I thought . . . well,

I thought we were going to get married and let Gilbert take care of the village. We were going to build a mansion, that's what you said after Hugh died. You promised." Her bright red lips formed a pout that might have been appealing had her voice been less shrill.

Earl's gaze skimmed Celia's body with a mixture of irritation and regret. "That was the plan," he said. "More or less. It isn't the first plan I've had to change at a moment's notice."

"You killed Hugh!" Celia's eyes widened until the whites showed all around the intense blue irises. "You killed Hugh so you could marry me and get Hugh's money, didn't you?"

Matthew pulled Celia back behind him.

"Very brave," Earl said, with a laugh. "I wish you well with her. I don't think I could have stood it, even for the money."

"Why don't you get out of here," Rose said. "You can take one of our horses, or our car, whatever you want. We'll let you go, I promise you," she said. "Just leave Mairin with us."

"I can't," Earl said. "She's got to go, and so do you." He pressed the blade harder until Rose felt it break through the thin wool of her dress and touch her skin.

"You can't get away," Rose said. "It's time to give up."

"I have no choice. Don't you see?" Earl had begun to plead.

"You do have choices." Rose forced herself to relax in his grip. "If you kill me and Mairin, it will be cold-blooded. I don't think you ever wanted to kill anyone, did you? Not Mairin, surely, or you would have done so the day you threatened her in the woods outside the school yard. My guess is you didn't want to kill Hugh, either."

Earl shuddered and almost withdrew his knife, but he recovered before Rose could pull away. "Of course I didn't want to kill anybody. I'm not a murderer, I'm really not. I just didn't have a choice. Hugh didn't give me a choice. He was going to turn me in, ruin my life. I'd have gone to prison anyway, if I'd let him live."

"Hugh knew something about you, didn't he? Something he threatened to reveal? Did it have to do with gambling debts?" Rose guessed.

"Earl!" Gilbert said. "What's she saying? Hugh never used to gamble; are you the one who led him into it?"

Earl made a sound that was somewhere between a snort and a sob. "Hugh? Gamble? Hugh the saint? No, all he ever did was give his money away to the needy. Well, I was needy, too, and the only way I could get any money was to win it. I was good at it, too, until my luck ran out. Hugh was so kind to others, but when I asked him for a loan, he just lectured me on how well off I was, compared to the truly poor. I was thousands of dollars in the hole. I was getting threats. So I offered to hand out his checks for him—he always preferred making the promises, anyway."

He scowled at Gilbert. "Hugh was a lot like you in that."

"You forged the suicide note and left it for Gilbert to find, didn't you?" Rose asked. "Was that so he would be a suspect, in case the sheriff suspected a forgery?" She twisted to watch his face.

Earl didn't answer, and she knew she'd hit upon the truth.

"Why didn't the sheriff suspect?" Rose asked.

Earl's eyes flashed as if a circuit in his brain had blown. "If it hadn't been for you . . ." He jabbed the blade a fraction harder until it broke her skin.

Rose gasped in pain but held still.

"No, he'll kill you! He said so!" Mairin broke away from Gilbert and threw herself toward Earl's feet. She grabbed his ankles and tried to pull him off balance, but she was far too tiny. He staggered and Rose squirmed out of his grasp. Earl regained his balance, then reached down and grabbed Mairin by her thick, fuzzy hair and yanked her off the ground. She screamed in pain. A roar of fury surged through Rose's body, and she threw herself at Earl like a crazed lioness. She felt a searing pain in her upper arm, yet her rage was stronger. She hung onto Earl, leaning her weight against him until he started to fall sideways. She heard a child's scream and then a gunshot, and blacked out with a prayer for forgiveness on her lips.

TWENTY-SIX

"THIS TIME IT'S YOUR TURN TO REST IN THE INFIRMARY," Andrew said, as Rose drifted to consciousness. Mairin sat on the edge of her bed.

"Why does my shoulder hurt so much?"

"Because you were stabbed, remember? You—Shaker eldress, bound by a vow of nonviolence, flung yourself at an armed man, in defense of a sweet little girl. Is any of this sounding familiar?"

Rose groaned. "I'll have to confess for the rest of my life for this."

Andrew laughed. "Agatha declared that you've been punished enough," he said. "One confession will do the trick."

Rose pushed herself up on her good elbow. "Mairin, were you hurt at all?"

Mairin offered a larger-than-normal smile and shook her head.

"Mairin is staying in the Children's Dwelling House," Andrew said. "Given her treatment at the hands of the New-Owenites, it looks like we can keep her with us."

"Thank God." Rose fell back on her pillow with a grimace of pain.

"Indeed."

"And the New-Owenites themselves?"

"That's another story. Did you realize that Earl Weston was killed? Nay, you didn't kill him," Andrew said, at Rose's ex-

219

pression of horror. "You were stabbed in the shoulder, and the pain and loss of blood were too much for you. You blacked out just as Deputy O'Neal burst through the women's entrance to the Meetinghouse. He thought Earl had killed you, and he shot by instinct. He killed Earl with one bullet."

Mairin seemed unmoved by Andrew's description.

"How long have I been here?"

"Just over a day," Andrew said. "Josie gave you a sedative we've been working on in the Medicinal Herb Shop, and it worked better than we'd predicted. Just as well, though. Josie said you missed quite a lot of pain, including the stitching up. I was glad for that. And now you need to rest."

"Not until I have answers to all my questions," Rose said. With the arm that wasn't taped up at her shoulder, she reached over and took Mairin's hand. "You were hiding in the barn and you saw what happened to Hugh, didn't you? All of it?"

"Yes."

"Can you tell me?"

"I was up high, and Hugh came in first," Mairin said, without emotion. "He looked really scared, and he pushed a big box over and stood on it and reached up with his arm. I didn't know what he was doing. He couldn't reach that high. Then he got a long rope and laid it out like a snake, and then Earl came."

"Did they fight?"

"The way they always did, with yelling. I didn't understand all of it. It was something about money. Hugh was really mad at Earl and said he had to go tell the police what he'd done, and Earl said he wouldn't, and then Hugh pointed to the rope and said . . ." Mairin frowned. "It was something like 'take the way like gentlemen.' "

"Take the gentleman's way out?" Rose guessed.

"That's it. Then he started to leave, and . . ." A hint of fear cracked Mairin's impassive mask.

"It'll help to talk about it."

"Earl picked up the rope and came up behind Hugh and threw the rope around his neck and squeezed really hard. Hugh was the only one who was nice to me. I'm glad Earl got killed."

Rose squeezed the girl's hand and said nothing about the sin of violence. If anyone had earned a moment of anger, it was Mairin. And feeling anger was better than not feeling anything at all.

"Did you see Earl take Hugh out of the barn?" she asked.

"Yes. I didn't understand what he was doing. He looked at a window, and then he took the rope and just threw Hugh over his shoulder and left really fast. So I got down and followed him. That's when he went to the orchard, and I climbed a tree to see what he was doing."

Rose nodded. "He was worried about daylight, and the brethren arriving for their early chores. So he moved to the abandoned part of the orchard. And I'll bet the rope was too long, and he had to cut it, right?"

"He used a penknife, a really dull one. My penknife is sharper than that," Mairin said, with scorn.

Rose rested her head against the lavender-scented pillow. Earl's penknife had been sharp enough to do damage. "Andrew," she asked, "how did Grady know to come to North Homage?"

Andrew laughed. "He said he hardly had a choice. He'd had a call from me, from the train station, telling him I'd had dinner with Hugh's lawyer, who suspected Hugh was being swindled by Earl. Then Nora called him. When Gilbert came to get Mairin—he'd watched you go in there, by the way— he couldn't manage two girls, and he didn't really take Nora seriously. He should have. And finally, Grady had confronted Sheriff Brock about his failure to pursue Hugh's death as murder. Brock will be resigning."

"What?"

"It's true. Brock *had* suspected, after he thought about it awhile, and he tried to call Gilbert, who'd gone out of town. He got Earl. And Earl dropped a number of hints that, if the sheriff would forget his suspicions, then he—Earl—would personally see to it that we Shakers disappeared, and our land

and businesses would become available for purchase at a very reasonable price. But Languor is stuck with us. Gilbert has admitted defeat, and his group is packing up to leave. We'll be auctioning off quite a lot of furniture to help bring our finances back to order."

"Have they gone yet?" Rose sat up, suddenly alert.

"Nay, not yet."

"Then would you do something for me? Would you find out what Gilbert kept locked in his wall cabinet? If he is chastened enough, perhaps he will even tell you."

"Oh, I know what's in there," Mairin said. "Hugh told me once. He said Gilbert made drawings, like me, but he always kept them locked up because he didn't want anyone to mess with them—you know, add things or anything."

"Gilbert made drawings of his dreams?"

"Well, sort of. Hugh said he was always dreaming about towns, perfect towns, and he had lots of drawings of them that he carried with him everywhere he went."

"So that was all," Rose said. "His precious plans for the future of North Homage."

"Never to be realized, thank goodness," Andrew said. "Now, Rose, will you rest?"

Rose was asleep before the smile had left her lips.

With a public auction scheduled for the next day, and the threat of snow rolling in from Cincinnati, Rose and Andrew decided the time was right to fulfill one of Rose's dreams. Because of the New-Owenites, North Homage now had rooms full of restored Shaker furniture. Though Rose accepted the need to auction off much of it to restore their financial stability, she wanted to share some of it—along with the salvageable food from the South Family Dwelling House kitchen—with the poor families living in the barren outskirts of Languor.

Early Christmas, they'd all been calling it. Nora was thrilled beyond words, and even Mairin sparkled, though she had little concept of Christmas. However, she did understand that her life had taken a happy turn, for the first time. With luck and care, perhaps she was still young enough to learn to hope.

Archibald had volunteered to help them. After Matthew announced he was leaving the Society, Archibald had asked for forgiveness and received it. He'd already begun his special lessons, along with Mairin.

Rose took Mairin with her to the South Family Dwelling House. "Now *this* is a Shaker kitchen," Rose said with satisfaction. The sisters had spent days picking up and scrubbing down until the kitchen was spotless. They hadn't known what to do with the bits of cheese and half-eaten hunks of bread, so, not wanting to waste anything, they'd just wrapped everything up and stored it in the pantry.

Rose carried a large basket, filled with wooden boxes, round and oval, that she'd collected from other rooms in the dwelling house. She opened the boxes and laid them along the work-table.

"Help me pack these, will you? My shoulder still hurts." Rose and Mairin put all the left-over food in the boxes, then fit the boxes back in the basket. Mairin did an admirable job of controlling her still-troublesome hunger. It was easier, now that she was well fed.

Andrew and Archibald had already left with the horse-drawn cart, filled with a selection of ladder-back chairs, candle stands, and anything else useful that Rose could rescue as the brethren prepared for the public auction. Mairin and Rose stashed their basket of food in the back of the Chrysler, where Nora was waiting, and the trio headed for the outskirts of Languor. After a few miles, they caught up to the wagon and followed slowly behind.

"You're very quiet today, Mairin," Rose said. "Is anything troubling you?"

Mairin started by shaking her head, then changed her mind. "It's just . . . lots of times people don't like me and call me names. Will these people, the ones we're going to visit?"

"I'll get really mad if they do!" Nora said from the back.

She quieted down as Rose turned briefly and raised an eyebrow at her.

"Mairin, sometimes people laugh at me because I'm a Shaker and I dress differently."

"Does it make you mad?"

"I'm afraid it does. But then I remember that sometimes people come along who don't care that I'm different from them, and they like me anyway."

"Like me."

"Like you."

Mairin nodded solemnly and gazed out the window for several minutes.

"Rose?"

"Hm?" With a silent prayer for guidance, Rose prepared herself for the next difficult question.

"I miss my doll. Can I have her back?"

"Of course!"

Mairin is becoming the child she was meant to be, Rose thought, as she sent a prayer of thanks to Mother Ann, Holy Mother Wisdom, and anyone else who might have been listening all along.

We hope you have enjoyed this Avon Twilight mystery. Mysteries fascinate and intrigue with the worlds they create. And what better way to capture your interest than this glimpse into the world of a select group of Avon Twilight authors.

Tamar Myers reveals the deadly side of the antique business. The bed-and-breakfast industry becomes lethal in the hands of Mary Daheim. A walk along San Antonio's famed River Walk with Carolyn Hart reveals a fascinating and mysterious place. Nevada Barr encounters danger on Ellis Island. Deborah Woodworth's Sister Rose Callahan discovers something sinister is afoot in her Kentucky Shaker village. Jill Churchill steps back in time to the 1930's along the Hudson River and creates a weekend of intrigue. And Anne George's Southern Sisters find that making money is a motive for murder.

So turn the page for a sneak peek into worlds filled with mystery and murder. And if you like what you read, head to your nearest bookstore. It's the only way to figure out whodunit . . .

December

Abigail Timberlake, the heroine of Tamar Myers' delightful Den of Antiquity series, is smart, quirky, and strong-minded. She has to be—running your own antique business is a struggle, even on the cultured streets of Charlotte, North Carolina, and her mean-spirited divorce lawyer of an ex-husband's caused her a lot of trouble over the years. She also has a "delicate" relationship with her proper Southern mama.

The difficulties in Abby's personal life are nothing, though, to the trouble that erupts when she buys a "faux" Van Gogh at auction...

ESTATE OF MIND

by Tamar Myers

YOU ALREADY KNOW THAT MY NAME IS ABIGAIL TIMBERLAKE, but you might not know that I was married to a beast of a man for just over twenty years. Buford Timberlake—or Timbersnake, as I call him—is one of Charlotte, North Carolina's most prominent divorce lawyers. Therefore, he knew exactly what he was doing when he traded me in for his secretary. Of course, Tweetie Bird is half my age—although parts of her are even much younger than that. The woman is 20 percent silicone, for crying out loud, although admittedly it balances

227

rather nicely with the 20 percent that was sucked away from her hips.

In retrospect, however, there are worse things than having your husband dump you for a man-made woman. It hurt like the dickens at the time, but it would have hurt even more had he traded me in for a brainier model. I can buy most of what Tweetie has (her height excepted), but she will forever be afraid to flush the toilet lest she drown the Ty-D-Bol man.

And as for Buford, he got what he deserved. Our daughter, Susan, was nineteen at the time and in college, but our son, Charlie, was seventeen, and a high school junior. In the penultimate miscarriage of justice, Buford got custody of Charlie, our house, and even the dog Scruffles. I must point out that Buford got custody of our friends as well. Sure, they didn't legally belong to him, but where would you rather stake your loyalty? To a good old boy with more connections than the White House switchboard, or to a housewife whose biggest accomplishment, besides giving birth, was a pie crust that didn't shatter when you touched it with your fork? But like I said, Buford got what he deserved and today—it actually pains me to say this—neither of our children will speak to their father.

Now I own a four-bedroom, three-bath home not far from my shop. My antique shop is the Den of Antiquity. I paid for this house, mind you—not one farthing came from Buford. At any rate, I share this peaceful, if somewhat lonely, abode with a very hairy male who is young enough to be my son.

When I got home from the auction, I was in need of a little comfort, so I fixed myself a cup of tea with milk and sugar—never mind that it was summer—and curled up on the white cotton couch in the den. My other hand held a copy of Anne Grant's *Smoke Screen*, a mystery novel set in Charlotte and surrounding environs. I hadn't finished more than a page of this exciting read when my roommate rudely pushed it aside and climbed into my lap.

"Dmitri," I said, stroking his large orange head, "that 'Starry

Night' painting is so ugly, if Van Gogh saw it, he'd cut off his other ear."

Some folks think that just because I'm in business for myself, I can set my own hours. That's true as long as I keep my shop open forty hours a week during prime business hours and spend another eight or ten hours attending sales. Not to mention the hours spent cleaning and organizing any subsequent purchases. I know what they mean, though. If I'm late to the shop, I may lose a valued customer, but I won't lose my job—at least not in one fell swoop.

I didn't think I'd ever get to sleep Wednesday night, and I didn't. It was well into the wee hours of Thursday morning when I stopped counting green thistles and drifted off. When my alarm beeped, I managed to turn it off in my sleep. Either that or in my excitement, I had forgotten to set it. At any rate, the telephone woke me up at 9:30, a half hour later than the time I usually open my shop.

"*Muoyo webe*," Mama said cheerily.

"What?" I pushed Dmitri off my chest and sat up.

"Life to you, Abby. That's how they say 'good morning' in Tshiluba."

I glanced at the clock. "Oh, shoot! Mama, I've got to run."

"I know, dear. I tried the shop first and got the machine. Abby, you really should consider getting a professional to record your message. Someone who sounds . . . well, more cultured."

"Like Rob?" I remembered the painting. "Mama, sorry, but I really can't talk now."

"Fine," Mama said, her cheeriness deserting her. "I guess, like they say, bad news can wait."

I sighed. Mama baits her hooks with an expertise to be envied by the best fly fishermen.

"Sock it to me, Mama. But make it quick."

"Are you sitting down, Abby?"

"Mama, I'm still in bed!"

"Abby, I'm afraid I have some horrible news to tell you about one of your former boyfriends."

"Greg?" I managed to gasp after a few seconds. "Did something happen to Greg?"

"No, dear, it's Gilbert Sweeny. He's dead."

I wanted to reach through the phone line and shake Mama until her pearls rattled. "Gilbert Sweeny was never my boyfriend!"

January

From nationally bestselling author Mary Daheim, who creates a world inside a Seattle bed-and-breakfast that is impossible to resist, comes Creeps Suzette, *the newest addition to this delightful series...*

Judith McMonigle Flynn, the consummate hostess of Hillside Manor, fairly flies out the door in the dead of winter when her cousin Renie requests her company. As long as Judith's ornery mother, her ferocious feline, and her newly retired husband aren't joining them, Judith couldn't care less where they're going. That is until they arrive at the spooky vine-covered mansion, Creepers, in which an elderly woman lives in fear that someone is trying to kill her. And it's up to the cousins to determine which dark, drafty corner houses a cold-blooded killer before a permanent hush falls over them all...

CREEPS SUZETTE

by Mary Daheim

"As you wish, ma'am," said Kenyon, and creaked out of the parlor.

"Food," Renie sighed. "I'm glad I'm back."

"With a vengeance," Judith murmured. "You know," she went on, "when I saw those stuffed animal heads in the game room, I had to wonder if Kenneth wasn't reacting to them.

231

His grandfather or great-grandfather must have hunted. Maybe he grew up feeling sorry for the lions and tigers and bears, oh, my!"

"I could eat a bear," Renie said.

Climbing the tower staircase, the cousins could feel the wind. "Not well-insulated in this part of the house," Judith noted as they entered Kenneth's room.

"It's a tower," Renie said. "What would you expect?"

Judith really hadn't expected to see Roscoe the raccoon, but there he was, standing on his hind legs in a commodious cage. The bandit eyes gazed soulfully at the cousins.

"Hey," Renie said, kneeling down, "from the looks of that food dish, you've eaten more than we have this evening. You'll have to wait for dessert."

Judith, meanwhile, was studying the small fireplace, peeking into drawers, looking under the bed. "Nothing," she said, opening the door to the nursery. "Just the kind of things you'd expect Kenneth to keep on hand for his frequent visits to Creepers."

Renie said good-bye to Roscoe and followed Judith into the nursery. "How long," Renie mused, "do you suppose it's been since any kids played in here?"

Judith calculated. "Fifteen years, maybe more?"

"Do you think they're keeping it for grandchildren?" Renie asked in a wistful tone.

Judith gave her cousin a sympathetic glance. So far, none of the three grown Jones offspring had acquired mates or produced children. "That's possible," Judith said. "You shouldn't give up hope, especially these days when kids marry so late."

Renie didn't respond. Instead, she contemplated the train set. "This is the same vintage as the one I had. It's a Marx, like mine. I don't think they make them any more."

"Some of these dolls are much older," Judith said. "They're porcelain and bisque. These toys run the gamut. "From hand-carved wooden soldiers to plastic Barbies. And look at this dollhouse. The furniture is all the same style as many of the pieces in this house."

"Hey," Renie said, joining Judith at the shelf where the dollhouse was displayed, "this looks like a cutaway replica of Creepers itself. There's even a tower room on this one side and it's . . ." Renie blanched and let out a little gasp.

"What's wrong, coz? Are you okay?" Judith asked in alarm.

A gust of wind blew the door to the nursery shut, making both cousins jump. "Yeah, right, I'm just fine," Renie said in a startled voice. "But look at this. How creepy can Creepers get?"

Judith followed Renie's finger. In the top floor of the half-version of the tower was a bed, a chair, a table, and a tiny doll in a long dark dress. The doll was lying facedown on the floor in what looked like a pool of blood.

The lights in the nursery went out.

February

Carolyn Hart is the multiple Agatha, Anthony, and Macavity Award-winning author of the "Death on Demand" series as well as the highly praised Henrie O series. In Death on the River Walk, *sixtysomething retired journalist Henrietta O'Dwyer Collins must turn her carefully honed sleuthing skills to a truly perplexing crime that's taken place at the luxurious gift shop Tesoros on the fabled River Walk of San Antonio, Texas. See why the* Los Angeles Times *said, "If I were teaching a course on how to write a mystery, I would make Carolyn Hart required reading ... Superb."*

DEATH ON THE RIVER WALK

by Carolyn Hart

SIRENS SQUALLED. WHEN THE POLICE ARRIVED, THIS AREA would be closed to all of us. Us. Funny. Was I aligning myself with the Garza clan? Not exactly, though I was charmed by Maria Elena, and I liked—or wanted to like—her grandson Rick. But I wasn't kidding myself that the death of the blond man wouldn't cause trouble for Iris. Whatever she'd found in the wardrobe, it had to be connected to this murder. And I wanted a look inside Tesoros before Rick had a chance to grab Iris's backpack should it be there. That was why I'd told Rick to make the call to the police from La Mariposa.

The central light was on. That was the golden pool that

spread through the open door. The small recessed spots above the limestone display islands were dark, so the rest of the store was dim and shadowy.

I followed alongside the path revealed by Manuel's mop. It was beginning to dry at the farther reach, but there was still enough moisture to tell the story I was sure the police would understand. The body had been moved along this path, leaving a trail of bloodstains. That's what Manuel had mopped up.

The sirens were louder, nearer.

The trail ended in the middle of the store near an island with a charming display of pottery banks—a lion, a bull, a big-cheeked balding man, a donkey, a rounded head with bright red cheeks. Arranged in a semicircle, each was equidistant from its neighbor. One was missing.

I used my pocket flashlight, snaked the beam high and low. I didn't find the missing bank. Or Iris's backpack.

The sirens choked in mid-wail.

I hurried, moving back and forth across the store, swinging the beam of my flashlight. No pottery bank, no backpack. Nothing else appeared out of order or disturbed in any way. The only oddity was the rapidly drying area of freshly mopped floor, a three-foot swath leading from the paperweight-display island to the front door.

I reached the front entrance and stepped outside. In trying to stay clear of the mopped area, I almost stumbled into the pail and mop. I leaned down, wrinkled my nose against the sour smell of ammonia, and pointed the flashlight beam into the faintly discolored water, no longer foamy with suds. The water's brownish tinge didn't obscure the round pink snout of a pottery pig bank.

Swift, heavy footsteps sounded on the steps leading down from La Mariposa. I moved quickly to stand by the bench. Iris looked with wide and frightened eyes at the policemen following Rick and his Uncle Frank into the brightness spilling out from Tesoros. I supposed Rick had wakened his uncle to tell him of the murder.

Iris reached out, grabbed my hand. Rick stopped a few feet

from the body, pointed at it, then at the open door. Frank
Garza peered around the shoulder of a short policeman with
sandy hair and thick glasses. Rick was pale and strained. He
spoke in short, jerky sentences to a burly policeman with ink-
black hair, an expressionless face, and one capable hand resting on the butt of his pistol. Frank patted his hair, disarranged
from sleep, stuffed his misbuttoned shirt into his trousers.

When Rick stopped, the policeman turned and looked toward the bench. Iris's fingers tightened on mine, but I knew
the policeman wasn't looking at us. He was looking at Manuel,
sitting quietly with his usual excellent posture, back straight,
feet apart, hands loose in his lap.

Manuel slowly realized that everyone was looking at him.
He blinked, looked at us eagerly, slowly lifted his hands, and
began to clap.

Nevada Barr's brilliant series featuring Park Ranger Anna Pigeon takes this remarkable heroine to the scene of heinous crimes at the feet of a national shrine—the Statue of Liberty. While bunking with friends on Liberty Island, Anna finds solitude in the majestically decayed remains of hospitals, medical wards, and staff quarters of Ellis Island. When a tumble through a crumbling staircase temporarily halts her ramblings, Anna is willing to write off the episode as an accident. But then a young girl falls—or is pushed—to her death while exploring the Statue of Liberty, and it's up to Anna to uncover the deadly secrets of Lady Liberty's treasured island.

LIBERTY FALLING

by Nevada Barr

HELD ALOFT BY THE FINGERS OF HER RIGHT HAND, ANNA DANgled over the ruined stairwell. Between dust and night there was no way of knowing what lay beneath. Soon either her fingers would uncurl from the rail or the rail would pull out from the wall. Faint protests of aging screws in softening plaster foretold the collapse. No superhuman feats of strength struck Anna as doable. What fragment of energy remained in her arm was fast burning away on the pain. With a kick and a twist, she managed to grab hold of the rail with her other hand as well. Much of the pressure was taken off her shoulder,

237

but she was left face to the wall. There was the vague possibility that she could scoot one hand width at a time up the railing, then swing her legs onto what might or might not be stable footing at the top of the stairs. Two shuffles nixed that plan. Old stairwells didn't fall away all in a heap like guillotined heads. Between her and the upper floor were the ragged remains, shards of wood and rusted metal. In the black dark she envisioned the route upward with the same jaundice a hay bale might view a pitchfork.

What the hell, she thought. *How far can it be?* And she let go.

With no visual reference, the fall, though in reality not more than five or six feet, jarred every bone in her body. Unaided by eyes and brain, her legs had no way of compensating. Knees buckled on impact and her chin smacked into them as her forehead met some immovable object. The good news was, the whole thing was over in the blink of a blind eye and she didn't think she'd sustained any lasting damage.

Wisdom dictated she lie still, take stock of her body and surroundings, but this decaying dark was so filthy she couldn't bear the thought of it. Stink rose from the litter: pigeon shit, damp and rot. Though she'd seen none, it was easy to imagine spiders of evil temperament and immoderate size. Easing up on feet and hands, she picked her way over rubble she could not see, heading for the faint smudge of gray that would lead her to the out-of-doors.

Free of the damage she'd wreaked, Anna quickly found her way out of the tangle of inner passages and escaped Island III through the back door of the ward. The sun had set. The world was bathed in gentle peach-colored light. A breeze, damp but cooling with the coming night, blew off the water. Sucking it in, she coughed another colony of spores from her lungs. With safety, the delayed reaction hit. Wobbly, she sat down on the steps and put her head between her knees.

Because she'd been messing around where she probably shouldn't have been in the first place, she'd been instrumental in the destruction of an irreplaceable historic structure. Sitting on the stoop, smeared with dirt and reeking of bygone pigeons, she contemplated whether to report the disaster or just slink away and let the monument's curators write it off to natural causes. She was within a heartbeat of deciding to do the honorable thing when the decision was taken from her.

The sound of boots on hard-packed earth followed by a voice saying: "Patsy thought it might be you," brought her head up. A lovely young man, resplendent in the uniform of the Park Police, was walking down the row of buildings toward her.

"Why?" Anna asked stupidly.

"One of the boat captains radioed that somebody was over here." The policeman sat down next to her. He was no more than twenty-two or -three, fit and handsome and oozing boyish charm. "Have you been crawling around or what?"

Anna took a look at herself. Her khaki shorts were streaked with black, her red tank top untucked and smeared with vile-smelling mixtures. A gash ran along her thigh from the hem of her shorts to her kneecap. It was bleeding, but not profusely. Given the amount of rust and offal in this adventure, she would have to clean it thoroughly and it wouldn't hurt to check when she'd last had a tetanus shot.

"Sort of," she said, and told him about the stairs. "Should we check it out? Surely we'll have to make a report. You'll have to write a report," she amended. "I'm just a hapless tourist."

The policeman looked over his shoulder. The doorway behind them was cloaked in early night. "Maybe in the morning," he said, and Anna could have sworn he was afraid. There was something in this strong man's voice that told her, were it a hundred years earlier, he would have made a sign against the evil eye.

April

Sister Rose Callahan, eldress of the Depression-era community of Believers at the Kentucky Shaker village of North Homage, knows that evil does not merely exist in the Bible. Sometimes it comes very close to home indeed.

"A complete and very charming portrait
of a world, its ways, and the beliefs of its people,
and an excellent mystery to draw you along."
        Anne Perry

In the next pages, Sister Rose confronts danger in the form of an old Utopian cult seeking new members among the peaceful Shakers.

A SIMPLE SHAKER MURDER

by Deborah Woodworth

AT FIRST, ROSE SAW NOTHING ALARMING, ONLY ROWS OF strictly pruned apple trees, now barren of fruit and most of their leaves. The group ran through the apple trees and into the more neglected east side of the orchard, where the remains of touchier fruit trees lived out their years with little human attention. The pounding feet ahead of her stopped, and panting bodies piled behind one another, still trying to keep some semblance of separation between the brethren and the sisters.

The now-silent onlookers stared at an aged plum tree. From

a sturdy branch hung the limp figure of a man, his feet dangling above the ground. His eyes were closed and his head slumped forward, almost hiding the rope that gouged into his neck. The man wore loose clothes that were neither Shaker nor of the world, and Rose sensed he was gone even before Josie reached for his wrist and shook her head.

Two brethren moved forward to cut the man down.

"Nay, don't, not yet," Rose said, hurrying forward.

Josie's eyebrows shot up. "Surely you don't think this is anything but the tragedy of a man choosing to end his own life?" She nodded past the man's torso to a delicate chair laying on its side in the grass. It was a Shaker design, not meant for such rough treatment. Dirt scuffed the woven red-and-white tape of the seat. Scratches marred the smooth slats that formed its ladder back.

"What's going on here? Has Mother Ann appeared and declared today a holiday from labor?" The powerful voice snapped startled heads backward, to where Elder Wilhelm emerged from the trees, stern jaw set for disapproval.

No one answered. Everyone watched Wilhelm's ruddy face blanch as he came in view of the dead man.

"Dear God," he whispered. "Is he . . . ?"

"Yea," said Josie.

"Then cut him down instantly," Wilhelm said. His voice had regained its authority, but he ran a shaking hand through his thick white hair.

Eyes turned to Rose. "I believe we should leave him for now, Wilhelm," she said. A flush spread across Wilhelm's cheeks, and Rose knew she was in for a public tongue thrashing, so she explained quickly. "Though all the signs point to suicide, still it is a sudden and brutal death, and I believe we should alert the Sheriff. He'll want things left just as we found them."

"Sheriff Brock . . ." Wilhelm said with a snort of derision. "He will relish the opportunity to find us culpable."

"Please, for the sake of pity, cut him down." A man stepped forward, hat in hand in the presence of death. His thinning blond hair lifted in the wind. His peculiar loose work clothes seemed too generous for his slight body. "I'm Gilbert Owen Griffiths," he said, nodding to Rose. "And this is my compatriot, Earl Weston," he added, indicating a broad-shouldered, dark-haired young man. "I am privileged to be guiding a little group of folks who are hoping to rekindle the flame of the great social reformer, Robert Owen. That poor unfortunate man," he said, with a glance at the dead man, "was Hugh— Hugh Griffiths—and he was one of us. We don't mind having the Sheriff come take a look, but we are all like a family, and it is far too painful for us to leave poor Hugh hanging."

"It's an outrage, leaving him there like that," Earl said. "What if Celia should come along?"

"Celia is poor Hugh's wife," Gilbert explained. "I'll have to break the news to her soon. I beg of you, cut him down and cover him before she shows up."

Wilhelm assented with a curt nod. "I will inform the Sheriff," he said as several brethren cut the man down and lay him on the ground. The morbid fascination had worn off, and most of the crowd was backing away.

There was nothing to do but wait. Rose gathered up the sisters and New-Owenite women who had not already made their escape. Leaving Andrew to watch over the ghastly scene until the Sheriff arrived, she sent the women on ahead to breakfast, for which she herself had no appetite. The men followed behind.

On impulse Rose glanced back to see Andrew's tall figure hunched against a tree near the body. He watched the crowd's departure with a forlorn expression. As she raised her arm to send him an encouraging wave, a move distracted her. She squinted through the tangle of unpruned branches behind Andrew to locate the source. *Probably just a squirrel*, she thought, but her eyes kept searching nonetheless. There it was again—a flash of brown almost indistinguishable from tree bark. Several rows of trees back from where Andrew stood, something was moving among the branches of an old pear tree—something much bigger than a squirrel.

May

Once upon a time Lily and Robert were the pampered offspring of a rich New York family. But the crash of '29 left them virtually penniless until a distant relative offered them a Grace and Favor house on the Hudson.

The catch is they must live at this house for ten years and not return to their beloved Manhattan. In the Still of the Night Lily and Robert invite paying guests from the city to stay with them for a cultural weekend. But then something goes wildly askew.

IN THE STILL OF THE NIGHT

by Jill Churchill

I REALIZED THAT MRS. ETHRIDGE WASN'T AT BREAKFAST AND she hasn't come to lunch either. I kept an eye out for her so I could nip in and tidy her room while she was out and about and she hasn't been."

"She's not in the dining room?" Lily said. "No, I guess not. There were two empty chairs."

"She might be sick, miss."

"Have you knocked on her door?"

"A couple times, miss."

"I'll go see what's become of her," Lily said.

Robert, who had been ringing up the operator, hung up the

phone. "I think it would be better for me to check on her."

"But Robert . . ." Lily saw his serious expression and paused. "Very well. But I'll come with you."

They went up to the second floor and Robert tapped lightly on the door. "Mrs. Ethridge? Are you all right?" When there was no response, he tapped more firmly and repeated himself loudly.

They stood there, brother and sister, remembering another incident last fall, and staring at each other. "I'll look. You stay out here," Robert said.

He opened the door and almost immediately closed it in Lily's face. She heard the snick of the inside lock. There was complete silence for a long moment, then Robert unlocked and reopened the door. "Lily, she's dead."

Lily gasped. "Are you sure?"

"Quite sure."

"Oh, why did she have to die *here*?" Lily said, then caught herself. "What a selfish thing to say. I'm sorry."

"No need to be. I thought the same thing. It's not as if she's a good friend, or even someone we willingly invited."

"What do we do now?"

"You go back to the dining room and act like nothing's wrong while I call the police and the coroner."

"The police? Why the police?"

"I think you have to call them for an unexplained death. Besides, if we don't, what do we *do* with her? Somebody has to take her away to be buried."

June

*Patricia Anne is a sedate suburban housewife living in Bir-
mingham, Alabama, but thanks to her outrageous sister, Mary
Alice, she's always in the thick of some controversy, often with
murderous overtones. In* Murder Shoots the Bull, *Anne
George's seventh novel in the Southern Sisters series, the sisters
are involved in an investment club with next door neighbor
Mitzi. But no sooner have they started the club than strange
things start happening to the members . . .*

MURDER SHOOTS THE BULL

by Anne George

I FIXED COFFEE, MICROWAVED SOME OATMEAL, AND HANDED
Fred a can of Healthy Request chicken noodle soup for his
lunch as he went out the door. Wifely duties done, I settled
down with my second cup of coffee and the *Birmingham
News.*

I usually glance over the front page, read "People are Talking" on the second, and then turn to the Metro section. Which
is what I did this morning. I was reading about a local judge
who claimed he couldn't help it if he kept dozing off in court
because of narcolepsy when Mitzi, my next door neighbor,
knocked on the back door.

"Have you seen it?" She pointed to the paper in my hand
when I opened the door.

"Seen what?" I was so startled at her appearance, it took

me a moment to answer. Mitzi looked rough. She had on a pink chenille bathrobe which had seen better days and she was barefooted. No comb had touched her hair. It was totally un-Mitzi-like. I might run across the yards looking like this, but not Mitzi. She's the neatest person in the world.

"About the death."

"What death?" I don't know why I asked. I knew, of course. I moved aside and she came into the kitchen.

"Sophie Sawyer's poisoning."

Mitzi walked to the kitchen table and sat down as if her legs wouldn't hold her up anymore.

"Sophie Sawyer was poisoned?"

"Arthur said you were there yesterday."

"I was." I sat down across from Mitzi, my heart thumping faster. "She was poisoned?"

"Second page. Crime reports." Mitzi propped her elbows on the table, leaned forward and put a hand over each ear as if she didn't want to hear my reaction.

I turned to the second page. The first crime report, one short paragraph, had the words—SUSPECTED POISONING DEATH—as its heading. Sophie Vaughn Sawyer, 64, had been pronounced dead the day before after being rushed to University Hospital from a nearby restaurant. Preliminary autopsy reports indicated that she was the victim of poisoning. Police were investigating.

Goosebumps skittered up my arms and across my shoulders. Sophie Sawyer murdered? Someone had killed the lovely woman I had seen at lunch the day before? I read the paragraph again. Since it was so brief, the news of the death must have barely made the paper's deadline.

"God, Mitzi, I can't believe this. It's awful. Who was she? One of Arthur's clients?"

Mitzi's head bent to the table. Her hands slid around and clasped behind her neck.

"His first wife."

"His what?" Surely I hadn't heard right. Her voice was muffled against the table.

But she looked up and repeated, "His first wife."

THERE'S NO MYSTERY TO THIS TERRIFIC WEBSITE REBATE OFFER!

IN THE STILL OF THE NIGHT

(A Grace and Favor Mystery)

JILL CHURCHILL

Winner of the Agatha and Macavity Mystery Awards

Despite losing the family fortune in the crash of 1929, Lily Brewster and her brother Robert can still live the high life thanks to their Great Uncle Horatio, who left them Grace and Favor Cottage. Though his will stipulated they have to earn their keep, it won't be too hard thanks to Lily's brilliant scheme: lure their society friends to the cottage for a paying weekend with the promise of big-name celebrity guests.

Despite their best laid plans, the bash turns out to be low on luminaries and high on hostility, with a group of disgruntled guests trading barbs instead of bon mots. And before Lily and Robert know it, their glamorous affair has become a whodunit with one guest dead, one missing, and the hosts on the trail of a murderer who's ready to strike again. . . .

Buy and enjoy IN THE STILL OF THE NIGHT, save the sales receipt, and then go to www.avonbooks.com/twilight and click on the rebate coupon button for instructions on how to receive a rebate check for $2.00. You'll be glad you did!

*Offer valid only for residents of the United States and Canada

Expires 9/7/00

Avon Books is an *Imprint* of HarperCollins*Publishers* www.harpercollins.com